Brandon Tietz

Otherworld Publications, LLC
Louisville, Kentucky

Otherworld Publications, LLC
4949 Old Brownsboro Rd. Suite 113
Louisville, Kentucky 40222
www.otherworldpublications.com

Cover design by Jen Trenchard and Copyright © 2011 Jen Trenchard

Interior design and typesetting by Lynn Calvert
Interior design Copyright © 2011 Otherworld Publications, LLC

Printed in the United States of America

Paperback
ISBN13: 978-0-9826494-7-3

Hard Cover
ISBN13: 978-0-9826494-8-0

2nd Edition

To Richard Thomas: For opening the door.

And to Ray Leatherwood: For no particular reason.

"A man who kills on his own is a murderer. A man who kills at his government's request is a national hero." -Ramman Kenoun

"As for an authentic villain, the real thing, the absolute, the artist, one rarely meets him even once in a lifetime. The ordinary bad hat is always in part a decent fellow." -Sidonie Gabrielle Colette

The guys who showed me how it's done: Chuck Palahniuk, Bret Easton Ellis, Jeffrey Eugenides, Irvine Welsh, Alan Moore, and Brian Michael Bendis.

Special thanks to: The Chuck Palahniuk Writers' Workshop and all the good people that keep it going.

Acknowledgements: Derek Beals, Dr. Croutons, Monica Drake, Aran Eversman, Pete Goutis, Gordon Highland, Paris Hilton, Mirka Hodurova, Sarah Hull, Derek Hynes, Jonathan Kabol, Tyler Knight, Nik Korpon, Joe McGinniss Jr., Dustin McKamie, Wendy O'Brien, Emily Piper, Caleb J. Ross, Michael Sonbert, Richard Thomas, Jen Trenchard, Mark Vanderpool, Samantha Verde, Dennis Widmyer, my friends, my family.

SESSION 01
FLIGHT

In the end, you learn the difference between an origin and a coming of age can be as simple as an airplane crash. Just your typical, everyday mile-high disaster. This model in particular—the one that I'm on, is a Boeing 747-400. It holds 416 passengers, has a wingspan of 64.9 meters, and is notorious for storing in-flight meals five degrees below the recommended temperature. These are the types of things you know when you're a commercial airline pilot, an engineer, or me. If you want to break something correctly, it's best to know everything you can about it. Potential food poisoning or diarrhea by way of an undercooked Salisbury steak ranks right up there with understanding how the landing gear and turbines work. Study your statistics and diagrams. Never overlook the little things.

From seat 5G of the first class section, it's a parade of coach passengers trudging along on the blue and cream carpet, admiring the oversized slate gray leather seats, these "thrones of the skies," as they're sometimes called. They revere the padded armrests and expansive legroom, the bottles of French champagne already being poured. Ornate tins of caviar and cashmere blankets patterned in tasteful pilot wings. For all of about ten seconds, these people get a sample of the good life. Just a taste. Airlines do this to encourage people to upgrade their tickets. It's their way of saying, "This is what you're missing."

For at least the first hour of the flight, all the coach passengers are haunted by this same luxurious imagery. Anyone in marketing or sales knows this just as well as I do. In a few hours though, prestige will be the least of their concerns.

Flight 8160 is scheduled to cross an ocean today, but it'll

1

never make it.

Holding over 57,000 gallons of fuel, this aircraft has a maximum range of approximately 7,200 miles. That means, theoretically, we could fly from New York to France on a half tank of gas. A rigged fuel gauge and an absent pump technician is all it would take to get the job done, but that's being optimistic.

If you're me, then you already know the captain has two successful emergency water landings on his record. Another three on land. Your weekend would be split between a cramped life raft and a rescue freighter. Then a police station.

When a $266,000,000 aircraft drops out of the sky, everyone gets questioned, including first class. Even Mr. Hero Pilot would get a turn in the interrogation room, so it's important to get this right the first time.

No survivors.

No questions.

Overhead, the red and off-white "fasten seatbelt" sign illuminates, accompanied by the formal announcement to raise all tray tables and turn off our cell phones and any electronics. Forget what you've heard about these items causing any sort of damage to the plane or its instruments. That's a rumor. You could start a telemarketing firm in here and all the pilots would notice is some light radio static.

Being able to discern a scare tactic from a threat is important when you're 40,000 feet above the ground. If you're a terrorist, a hostage, or me, then you already know this.

Meanwhile, on ground-level, the spray-tanned stewardesses pitch us the safety spiel from their respective aisles, hand-gesturing along with the FAA-standardized commentary as the plane distances itself from the terminal. We're given the "how to" walkthrough of operating a seatbelt and the correct way to apply an oxygen mask, a systematic tutorial on seat cushion floatation devices.

The speakers say things like "don't panic" and "calm, orderly fashion."

They pair the words "in the event of" with some sort of disaster.

Emergency exits are pointed out. Nobody looks.

We're all barely listening.

Even on the brink of a catastrophic affair, these people are more concerned with reading USA Today *or their in-flight magazine. Playing travel-sized board games. When you're surrounded by this much ignorance, you can pretty much get away with murder.*

Or in this case, over four hundred of them.

We can relax for now.

Calculate cruise speed in relation to the rate of ascent, and we've got at least four hours to reflect on our lives. That's plenty when you think about how it's all going to flash before your eyes anyway. One last montage of spouses and children, your immediate unconditionally loving family. Pet dogs and cats.

If you were about to bite the big one in the dead center of the Atlantic Ocean, more than likely, that's what you'd get.

But not me.

Just like anyone who's been tampered with and brainwashed, I'll end up seeing the person that got me into recreational terrorism in the first place. She's the one that taught me everything I know, including how to take down this airplane.

About a year ago, she was my therapist.

Her name is Dr. Paradies.

SESSION 02
WOUNDS

Each traipse into my shrink's office of #2 Pershing Square is usually met with the same two questions.

Did I do this to myself?

Or was it someone else?

I'll walk in and she'll see the zigzagging shoestring stitches tying some part of my face back together, the brow-line or the cheekbone or chin. She'll notice a series of cuts. Of bruises. A loose tooth or a future scar. Every session it's something different, but the inquiry never changes.

"Is that wound self-inflicted?" Dr. Paradies asks, indicating it with pen and legal pad at the ready, her knuckles white in anticipation with those blush red fingers. She waits for that avalanche of bullshit to cascade out of my mouth while I pose in the frame of her office door, conjuring a defense mechanism.

"Oh, this?" I casually motion to the left side of my face, indicating the injury. Technically, it's a black eye but it stopped being that color a couple days ago. It's finally reached that medical disinfectant shade of yellow with a trim of opaque purple on the outer rim. A "sight for sore eyes," as they say. It literally looks worse than it feels, but I could say that about all my injuries, past and present alike.

Let's get back to the question, though. The issue at hand.

"My eye...fell down some stairs?" I potentially smile at Paradies.

"You're evading again," the doc says, scribbling on her legal pad. She's always scribbling and speaking in terms. I'm almost used to it by now: her "doctor's speak."

Examples of this would be:

You're never making light of a situation; you're "evading."

You're never placing blame on someone; you're

"projecting."

You're not a numb-nutted freak; you're "somatically deficient."

I finally come clean and tell her someone clocked me a few nights ago at a bar, and FYI: This isn't the first time I've had this sort of encounter for those of you just tuning in.

"Did you provoke him to do it?" Dr. Paradies asks.

"*Her*," I correct, rousing a glare of cross-examination (of disgust possibly) as the doc checks out my eye again. Closer this time. "And, yes," I admit, "I provoked it."

"Have a seat," she advises after a few scribbles, mildly sighing.

One of the things I don't like about this office is the doc's $6,000 imported chaise lounge, which almost makes it *my* chaise lounge since I'm the one sitting on it all the time. Doctors have this tendency to spend most of their office budget on high-end patient furniture, almost seeing it as an investment. The active theory here is that the more comfortable the patient is, the easier the information will flow, but comfy things sort of work the opposite with me. Honestly, I wouldn't mind standing, but Paradies seems to think that would be "anti-productive."

That's more doctor's speak in case you didn't catch it.

"By the way, how's the Colace working out?" she asks, ready to scribble.

One of the major "perks" of my affliction is I have no idea when I'm supposed to go to the bathroom. That stinging burn of having to piss or the bruising pressure of a major dump brewing—I don't feel those things, so sometimes I have accidents. The doc's first suggestion was for me to start wearing an adult diaper. I told her to go fuck herself and to think of a better idea. That's when the Colace came in. It was Plan B for my bathroom scenario. Typically, it's used on people who can't go or won't go. Not with me. I just don't know when I'm supposed to.

Everyday at 1:00 P.M. I take it.

At 1:30 P.M. I sit down and start pushing.

By 2:00, I'm done. That's the schedule.

Keep in mind that this wasn't my idea. Dr. Paradies

says that we need to control my condition—not the other way around, so now there's a timetable for everything: with pissing, with eating, with shitting. Everything. This is why she gets paid the big bucks; because she's done something I never thought possible—potty training the same person twice.

The Colace is working out fine. "Just fine," I tell her.

"It must be," she says. "Looks like you've dropped some of the weight," pointing with her pen at my midsection, my shrinking love handles and man boobs.

Paradies is referring to the residuals of my eating binges from when I first developed this little curse. Much in the same way bathroom time eludes me, I also don't know when to eat, or more importantly, when to stop eating.

I never get hungry.

I never get full.

It's really the taste that I'm addicted to. And I stress the word "addicted."

Up until Dr. Paradies came along with her food schedule and portion control I was averaging ten meals a day, and one of those was usually cheesecake. Not a slice, mind you. The whole thing. All 3,800 ass-fattening calories of it.

When my jeans started to not fit quite right, I knew there was a problem. It took me a week of fasting and colonics just to get back into a 34. If you're taking notes, that's another place the Colace comes in handy.

Dr. Paradies still is.

She's always doing this.

"Stick out your tongue," she orders.

I do it and she makes a face. Takes more notes. Last time I checked, the tip of it was mashed and purple. A blister cluster. She's probably notarizing this right now, that I've got this nasty little habit of chewing it, almost on a par with a canker sore. It hurts like hell and it's irritated, but for the life of you, you just can't seem to stop rubbing your teeth against it.

Just to check.

Just to see.

When that familiar taste of copper hits, I know it's time to stop.

"If you keep doing that it's going to get infected," she warns. "I want you to start chewing more gum and I'll prescribe you an antibiotic," she says with more scribbling. "And try not to smoke so damn much."

The good news is that if the antibiotic stings, it's not gonna hurt. Same goes for lighter burns, razor cuts, and facial abrasions. Anything painful. This is something Dr. Paradies has been trying to get me to do: seeing the bright side of things.

"I take it you're still using your proof object?" she asks, the scribbling silent for now. "Your arm is bandaged," she points out.

Anytime you see someone who is handicapped, whether they're blind, deaf, or crippled, there's always this little part of you that has doubt. Most people, normal people, need to see hard evidence to remove that last shred of disbelief. They have to know you're the real deal before they start dispensing pity. Before they decide to care.

The blind have their seeing-eye dogs and walking sticks.

The deaf have their sign language and speech impediments.

I have my little sewing needle.

That's what Dr. Paradies means when she says, "proof object," because anytime I tell someone about my condition they never believe me. Ever. No one wants to believe they're meeting a guy who can't feel anything.

The science on that is the body sends my brain a message that I'm feeling pain or that I'm not hungry anymore or whatever the sensory-related respondent is, but the message my brain is supposed to send back informing me of these events never makes it. It's a one-way street, but that's way too complicated for most people (or too complicated for me), hence, the proof object: my little sewing needle. It's the simple answer to that unspoken mistrust.

How it goes:

I tell them my condition.

They say they don't believe me.

I unflinchingly stab myself in the arm.

In the event that they still don't believe me after that, I offer them the needle and tell them to have a go at it. Most don't take me up on this offer.

"Yes," I admit to her. "I'm still using it."

"You've got remember that you have nothing to prove," Dr. Paradies says, the scribbling on full throttle again. "Even if you can't *physically* feel it, you're still hurting yourself. The sooner you realize that, the better."

And I'm thinking, *Oh, that's deep, man.*

I say nothing. I'm working on keeping my snide comments to myself.

"We need to get you in touch with the inner-you," she says, not writing, but looking at me instead. As if she really cares. I let out a long foreboding sigh, adjusting my body on the blue suede cloud that is the chaise lounge, thinking about how this is going to be yet another long mind-numbing session at #2 Pershing Square. My visits here usually are.

But let's go back to my "pre-condition" stage for a bit.

About one month ago. In the "before" period.

SESSION 03
HUSH

June 17th.

A Saturday.

I toss my Ferrari key to a Mexican or Puerto Rican (is there really a difference?) valet while the three girls behind me stumble along the cement walkway in designer heels. To Hush. They're giggling and coked out of their minds, trying to catch up as I sift through the queue of people. Toward the black velvet rope and I meet eyes with Derrick or Brad or Oliver (whatever the doorman's name is), who shoots me the look of recognition. Of acknowledgment. Barely nodding. It's a little past 11:00 P.M. and I'm always flanked. Untouchable but completely available. Free. It's a Barbie conference in front of the black velvet rope, and the girls play the part so well that sometimes I fool myself into believing they'll anatomically follow in suit; a crackless ass. Blank crotch and stolid breasts. Standard shades of tan. Of hair and make-up. And their eyes never blink. Ever. They bat. Because a woman can be an object if that's her objective. She can be a product, and I spot a couple of blondes not-so-tastefully begging to get in. Leaning and squeezing and flirting, and when the doorman unhinges the rope for me and my group, I whisper to the nearest one that they can join my table for drinks. They (of course) accept (because they'd be dumb not to), and I slide the doorman a crisp fifty for no good reason, being led inside now by a hostess whom I've fucked a couple times on speed-laced X and French champagne two and five weeks ago after a couple rare nights of nonsuccess with other patrons, but I look her over and recall it unflinchingly. Feeling nothing except indifference. Mild callousness. And then the lights hit. Of magenta. Of teal and yellow and orange and jade that flash and wave over the wood

9

and steel, and I put on black Versace sunglasses because my pupils are the size of dinner plates as side effect and growing. Because I'm making an impression walking in here with five Barbie clones in designer clothing by Burberry and Guess and D&G. But mostly because I can. And the girls are still giggling and chatting when we're seated in our tan suede leather sectional, talking about my car with the air-conditioned seats. About how un-stepped on my coke is. About nothing. Still playing the part, moving their shoulders, their hips, to the music. I blow out the pearl votive candles arranged on the table. It's 11:27 and the Asian girl across the table from me has bronze skin and bleached blonde hair. A glossy little advertisement of a mouth. I think she works at BeBe. Bottle service is delivered to our table consisting of two bottles of vodka (one Belvedere, one Grey Goose), a bucket of ice, black plastic stirring devices, glasses, mixers (cranberry and orange juice, tonic water), eight Red Bulls, a bottle of Voss water, and I have only a vague idea of how much it costs but that doesn't matter. The DJ gives me a nod from the steel and glass booth across the room and my hands are shaking a little. The blonde to my left asks me what I do and I tell her I'm a doctor. A surgeon. She touches my leg and I don't get excited, then says something about wishing she had bigger boobs. Fuller lips. Club lights pulse from above. I look away. There are three blondes planted on the suede couch across the way giving me the eye. I wave them over and they pop up a little too eagerly for my tastes. We have just reached full table capacity. They introduce themselves as Hannah, Nikki, and Fallon, but all I hear is whore, whore, and coke-whore since I already know their reputation and I'm, metaphorically-speaking, all-knowing and all-powerful here. At Hush. I ask for three more glasses even though they already have drinks. I consciously act a gentleman, noticing the queue at the bar is three-deep when I sneak a glance. The dance floor has already spilled over to the seating areas and it's not even midnight yet. Everybody is shoulder-to-shoulder. Wall-to-wall. I light a cigarette (a Parliament) and blow smoke in one of the girls' faces (maybe on purpose). It doesn't bother her so I put it out after a couple drags and my mouth tastes like ashy garbage now. I make myself a drink with no mixer and lots of ice. Take four large swallows. It's gone. Then a manicured hand belonging to a future rape victim lands softly on my shoulder and I flinch. She wants to know if I have any X so I give her a Flunitrazepan (a roofie) and she goes away. Satisfied. Her legs: hard and tan. They remind me of polished wood. Like oak layered on bone. I set my cell phone to go off in 15 minutes and she's wearing a red low-cut dress, taking the pill with a swallow of cranberry juice. The DJ bends over but I can't tell if it's to mix songs or to do a line. A moment passes and the song remains unchanged, some rap anthem that's popular this week. I take a Xanax and feel a foot in my crotch. There are three girls sitting across from me so I apply an ice cube to the foot to identify which one it is. The blonde in the black Gucci top flinches then smiles, but this is nothing to me. She's nothing. The manager of the club comes up to me and shakes my hand, and just like the hostess and all those gatekeepers that seem so much the same, I don't remember his name, either, but he informs me that the four gentlemen across the way would like to invite me over for a drink. I glance over and it's four guys in lame suits but with no women. Lawyers, I'm thinking, and now I know it's not necessarily me they want to meet, but rather, the girls I'm with, which is a fairly logical play on their part. The Hush trickle down effect. Club Reaganomics. I tell the manager to let them know I politely decline, and send them a bottle of Cristal to keep them at bay. At Hush, or at any other club for that matter, this is informally known as a "restraining order." Another blonde at the far end of the table is wearing a black top with a silver A|X set tastefully on her right breast. I think about chopping her skull in half with an ax and wait for the Xanax to kick in. The blonde Asian girl that might or might not work at BeBe says something in gook-speak and I tell her to never do that again even though I liked it. She smiles unhappily. I make another vodka straight and wait for my Xanax. The lawyers get their bottle of Cristal and give me a wave. An appreciative set of smiles and nods. I return the gesture and take two large swallows of vodka, looking away. The song changes. Some remix of some popular song that's being played too much.

11

I'm not sure what it is. My cell phone buzzes in my pocket and I turn to look at the girl in the red dress I roofied earlier. She looks sleepy and less tan. Less Barbie. More human. Weaker and vulnerable, and therefore, accessible to me and my immediate needs. The group eyes me when I move to stand, and I announce my quick return, though I have no idea how long this departure will last, escorting the red dress to the men's restroom. Downstairs. She's wobbly and out of it but still able to walk. Her hands clutch weakly to my shoulders. To my waist. Inside are two well-dressed Middle Eastern guys who don't seem to think a woman inside the men's restroom is out of the ordinary. One of them apologizes for not calling me back and I tell him it's okay even though I don't know what he's talking about. They're both doing coke off the onyx marble countertop and I'm waiting for my Xanax to kick in. Inside the stall, I sit the girl on the toilet and unfasten my pants. I don't put on a condom. I have one, but I don't put it on, and her legs are smooth and polished. Like wood. Expensive wood you see in IKEA catalogues, brochures, and high-end store windows. I slide her dress from under her ass and prop her legs on my shoulders, noticing vanilla-scented shave lotion mixed with Clinique or the new Versace. She's wearing the kind of thong that could fit between teeth. I move the crotch of her underwear to one side. She smells expensive, so when I start fucking her…it feels a little bit like shoplifting. It's a little dry but adequate. The Middle Eastern guys are snorting outside the stall and listening. Chortling. I fuck her for about ten minutes, five or six fragmented songs, but can't come. Can't stay hard because my Xanax is kicking in. Relaxing me. Every part of me, and when I leave her on the toilet with those hard legs and soft center exposed, I don't wonder why the Middle Eastern guys eye what's in the stall inquisitively. Hungrily, even. I don't question it. Everything makes sense when you don't care, and after exiting the restroom and sifting through the crowd, I return to the table and find to my displeasure that the lawyers have taken the liberty of seating themselves. Chatting up my dates and drinking out of my bottles. One of them is in my spot, and when I point that fact out to him, he apologizes and promptly stands, mentioning something about him hoping I don't mind that they joined my table. I tell him aside from the fact that it's incredibly rude, no, I don't mind at all. He forces a chuckle, but I really don't care because my cock is wet and this Xanax feels good. One of the blondes at the table asks me where I went all doe-eyed and slutty. Desperate. So I tell her what I did (what I almost did) and she laughs her little head off, assuming it's a joke or chic. I lean in close enough to taste her and ask if she'd like to be next. She smiles mischievously and tells me you can't rape the willing. Touché. I lie and tell her I'm taking her home with me tonight while dawning a rare smile. The DJ mixes tracks. I've heard these all before. Have had these conversations many times. The lawyer that was in my seat asks me if he can do anything to return the favor. For the Cristal you sent, he specifies, so I ask him if he's got any coke even though I have some of my own. He does. I've also got some X if you want some, he tells me. I take one from him and examine it to make sure it's not a roofie. It isn't. I swallow it down with the vodka that's left in my glass, and I don't detest this guy as much. The girl I told I was going to take home is wearing a sleek silver top with a black skirt and stiletto heels. She smells expensive and wants to know when we're taking off. The two of us. To my place. I run my hand between her legs and she doesn't stop me. There's no hesitation or regard for what surrounds us: the crowd and the noise, the shapeless mass that comprises Hush where people are bought and sold as an act of privilege. Her face relaxes when I ease my fingers inside her. Sampling her. Teasing. They emerge wet and oily, and taste like pocket change when I suck the ends. I tell her soon. She sits and the lawyer I'm standing with elevates his eyebrows impressed, something I enjoy more than what he's reacting to. He asks me what I do for a living and I tell him I'm a broker. A stockbroker, to be exact. We're lawyers, he tells me while motioning to his three counterparts. I try to pretend I didn't already know that and tell him some coke sounds good right about now. He nods, empties his flute of Cristal, and I begin sifting through the crowd for a third time. The girls at my table are all looking at me, even the ones talking to lawyers. It's all about me and it's well past midnight. When we enter the bathroom there's a line. Not for the urinals, because those are completely vacant. The line is for the stall. There are three well-dressed guys standing outside of it, each looking eager yet uncomfortable. I look at the space at the bottom of the stall and see legs that remind of smooth polished wood, and then another set in between those. A black thong sits on the floor surrounded by DNA droplets and condom wrappers. Three Trojans. A Durex. One Lifestyles (ribbed). Heavy breathing heaves from within. The lawyer chuckles and I do the same so he doesn't think I'm a fag. He takes out the bag and starts racking up lines on the counter with an AmEx card. Big ones. I roll up a hundred and take the first one. Sniff. He asks me how it is and I tell him it's good even though my stuff is definitely better. Less cut. The guy inside the stall comes which evokes a mild jealousy. I take another line and try not to feel stretched from all this shit I'm doing. The next guy enters the stall and I'm not sure what happens next. Not sure I want to. I do another line. My Cartier tells me it's 12:47 at night when the sound of another condom unwrapping crinkles in acoustic. I think about fucking the Asian girl tonight. I'm about sixty-seven percent sure she works a BeBe. Not that it matters. I do another rail. Another well-dressed guy comes into the restroom and asks us if we're in line for the fuck-doll. He actually says this. Fuck-doll. I shake my head. The lawyer chuckles, asks me about the girl. The fuck-doll. Wasn't she sitting at your table earlier? I shrug and do another line, tell him I'm no one's keeper. Gotta look out for #1, he agrees. I'm so fucking bored. Or far too acclimated. This is my sixth or seventh line. I do a gummer to get the nasty taste out of my mouth. It sort of works and I think my Xanax has been subdued. After the lawyer re-bags his shit, we both go back out to the table for a drink. He flags the waitress down and gets us a couple Heinekens. One of his buddies suggestively thumbs his nose at him and he smirks in return. The track playing is something by some group, but I can't remember if it's the one song or the other one. Regardless, it's very deep couch and appropriate for the make-out session that's happening between the two girls at the table. It makes sense. The three lawyers are all seated and watching as the rest of the girls look on in either boredom or jealousy. A tingle ripples through my neck. The ecstasy, I think, is coming. Our Heinekens are brought to us. Lawyer drops a $50 on the waitress. We clink necks and swig hard. Tastes good. The expensive smelling blonde that I gave the run-through to earlier gives me her best I-wanna-fuck-you-now look. I turn my gaze to the two blondes making out instead. Kinda hot, the lawyer says. I nod in agreement since being bi is in this summer and take another drink. They stop kissing and both look at me. At *me*. They are looking at me in hopes that I enjoyed the show, and I walk over and squat between the two of them, take another swig. They're both blonde, both wearing black skirts. One of them a mini-mini. I can see between her legs and she knows it. She wants me to see it. It's waxed and egg-smooth. My middle finger enters and she grinds her pelvis into it. I take it out and put it in the other girl's mouth. She sucks. I resume standing position and take another drink. The one not wearing the mini-mini grazes my cock with her hand. Then squeezes, and it's not hard because this is nothing to me. They're nothing to me. Completely expendable. Disposable. In a place like this, like Hush, that's all you'll find, but this is my life right now. Right then. An act. A magazine. An advertisement. These are girls who fuck for tables. For coke and drinks and three hours of glamour. Girls who publicly degrade themselves for pills. For a shot at a lawyer or doctor or whatever my profession is that night, because at Hush you're not your name or your dreams. You're an income bracket and self-promoting socialite. We're all pretending to be more than what we are. Something we're not even close to. It's the trend, and every night I'm doing this. Living this persona: an existence based on surfaces. On face value. I am the result of unregulated freedom and privilege. To get to where I am, you don't own the club. You own the owner. You own the staff. You come to the place where people come to look important, and then you do it better than them. And tomorrow that changes forever.

Tomorrow I'll be out of touch.

SESSION 04
DIAGNOSIS

I think it was around the third session when Dr. Paradies dropped her first diagnosis on me. Maybe the fourth. Not sure. We were still in the "precursory stage," as she put it. This basically meant sorting through the past in an attempt to solve the present. She knew the problem, now she was trying to figure out how I'd acquired it, giving me her diagnosis.

Her "professional opinion," in doctor's speak.

"This is all in your head," she tells me, but not for the first or last time.

"Izit?" I ask, speaking with a slight lisp because I've been using my tongue as a pack of Trident: one of my nervous habits.

Equates to: self-mutilation.

Paradies hands me a sugar-free mint and explains that the big numb was psychologically induced, a mental block like in some cases of sexual impotency or test anxiety.

Present the mind with a scenario that it can't handle: a pistol leveled with your temple or a particularly scary clown. Traditionally, that "fight-or-flight" instinct is supposed to kick in, and you either escape somehow or defend yourself. In the event of a dangerous situation, depending on the person, your response could range anywhere from adrenaline rush to anxiety attack. The brain is like a fingerprint in that way: no two are alike.

"Sometimes though, the mind comes up with unorthodox solutions," Paradies says.

In other words, my problem wasn't just from all the drugs I was doing, a direct counter to my own diagnosis that I had simply "done some bad shit."

Paradies ventures, "This condition of yours is the reaction to a lifestyle of depravity, intense stress...not to mention the worst case of self-medicating I've ever encountered," and I think I'm making a face now. Either defensive or antagonized. Vexed. Because what she's telling me is that this is more my fault then my body's.

It was the driver's mistake, not the car, so this news doesn't exactly please me. I'm officially fully responsible and speechless. The doc asks, "Did you really think there weren't going to be any consequences?" *tap-tap-tapping* her pen against the mini legal pad, almost sounding relinquished.

The question might've been rhetorical, and my mouth tastes like mint blood now. Refreshing copper. My antibiotic is elsewhere and I wish I was, too. Anywhere but here.

"This whole problem started because you think you can find happiness in a pill or living this little magazine life that you live, and ironically, you don't even know what happiness is," she lectures while staring me down.

I clench my fist and get more pissed off when I can't feel my fingers scrape the inside of my palm. Anger unrequited.

"What's really driving you is this approval that you seek from your peers," she continues. "You're so hyper-aware of what's happening around you and what people think that your own person has become neglected in the process."

My teeth stomp the mint and it shatters.

I hold out my hand and she gives me another one.

"This problem can't be fixed with more pills...*or* surgery, so if that's what you're thinking then you can get that out of your head right now, kiddo."

My lower lip curls in between my teeth and splits when she tells me this. I know this because I can taste it. I taste it vividly.

"Money can't fix this, I'm afraid. You brought this upon yourself and only you can fix it," she explains, the scribbling resuming.

I realize I'm crying when the ceiling starts to blur.

Already, I'm convinced that I'm dying because the cure depends upon me.

"I'll help you as much as I can," Paradies tells me when I remain mute. "I promise you that."

A tear landslides off the side of my face and slaps the chaise lounge. Hopelessness sounds like water hitting high-end furniture.

"Look at me," Paradies says.

I do but can only see a watery rendition, not who I know is there. It's easier if I don't see.

"I'm going to help you," she assures me, clicking her pen. "This is just like a puzzle...and we're going to solve it together."

I turn my face upwards, trying to find patterns in the ceiling as Paradies mentions taking a break from talking about the condition itself.

"Good idea," I mumble.

"Now," she segues, a renewed exuberance in her voice, "let's talk about women."

Yeah...it's definitely easier if I don't see.

SESSION 05
PLAYBOY

After Hush:

Cram the blonde Asian girl that might or might not work at BeBe into the Ferrari along with two other up-and-coming socialites (also tan and blonde and employed at some shitty day job like The Gap or Yankee Candle Company, but "weekend goddesses," just the same). I ask Lexi to grab my coke out of the glove box, sternly adding, "And *don't* do any—just hand it to me." She does, reminding me that her name is Stacy, but too messed up on shots (and maybe a tab of X) to care.

At the stoplight of 47th and Ward Parkway: take two bumps off the corner of my AmEx card…light a Parliament…light a joint that smells a little off, and pass it to the backseat.

Pull into the McDonald's on Broadway for fries (to soak up some of the liquor) and pay with a hundred dollar bill that still has coke on it from the bathroom. Leave without getting my change. Eat about six fries, but they're from an old batch, so I chuck them out the window and slam a 5-Hour Energy drink at the next stoplight. Grab a couple random pills from my jacket pocket that taste like Viagra and an orange Tic Tac, but it's too dark and I'm not looking, so that could be wrong.

By the time we get to the gated communities of Mission Hills, my skull is hot and float-y from possibly lacing that joint with something (like H or speed, perhaps), but the girls are giggling and drinking a strawberry Fanta they found in the backseat that tastes *"reeeeeeeeealllllllly good right now,"* according to the one directly behind me. Trisha or Lindsay, I think her name is. They all look and sound so much the same.

In the driveway I take: a Viagra…a Vivaren…two Adderall, with the last of the Fanta, and then park behind my mom's black

Lexus SUV. The girls just assume that it's my "other car" and pay it no mind as they struggle out of the vehicle, remarking on how nice the house is in the way only drunk gold diggers in their early twenties can: enviously.

My parents—or at the very least, my mom, is probably off in Lunesta land, so the giggle fit isn't too much of a concern as we enter through the front doors. Besides the fact that those pills make you sleep whether you want to or not, our bedrooms are at opposite corners, separated by at least a few thousand square feet. And, of course, like most career-driven couples that are in the highest tax bracket, there came that point where the parenting became more about keeping me funded instead of keeping me company. My freedom is mostly based on their preference to remain ignorant, which is a demographical commonality, I've noticed.

This is usually referred to as: "The tragedy of high society," but I don't mind. Neither do my dates. My escorts. Whatever you want to call them.

We're old enough to know how this works.

Mature enough to know it's just a one-night deal.

It's just your everyday post-Hush/pre-hangover sex session, a moment of bliss right before we wake up confused and awkward. Unsure how to depart. Put yourself in this situation enough and you know exactly what to do and when to do it. You're prepared.

As a playboy, you'll need a few standard things:

-money (so much you don't need to keep track of it)

-expensive car (Ferrari, Mercedes, Porsche, etc.)

-designer clothing, accessories, phone, etc.

-privilege: which in this case, would be defined as the ability to access a gourmet restaurant on a Friday or Saturday night without a reservation and/or a chic club or ultra longue, and the purchasing of copious amounts of alcohol (also known as: bottle service) without regard for how much it is or who it's being consumed by.

However, this only comprises the public face of your operation. Domestic life should be greater than or equal to your social prestige.

In this case, it's a 1,400 square foot space, studio-style bedroom with a six-person Jacuzzi stationed on top of heated tiles, high-pressure tanning bed, 55-inch 3-D HDTV, motion-based gaming systems by Sony and Nintendo, a California King-sized bed shrink-wrapped in Egyptian import sheets, full double-tiered wet bar, a medicine cabinet filled with uppers, downers, enhancers, supplements, vitamins, arousers, roofies, slimmers, pain relievers, numb-ers, and hallucinogens. Candles and romantic music can only get you so far. When you really break it down, attraction is nothing more than a chemical response in your body. Lust locked in a tablet.

And by this point, I'm pure want (uncertain of exactitudes, but something unwholesome and hedonistic, I think), popping: Vicodin…(blue dolphin) ecstasy…another Viagra, and my person—all of me, feels physically conflicted and stretched. Full of phantom needs and mixed reactions, such as how my mouth craves cold water, then room-temperature 7-Up, as my back frosts over hot—so hot that the shirt has to be removed, and the girls sort of coo when this happens, thinking that I'm being provocative with my cold, prickling extremities. The flushed cheeks and burning eyeballs. They're kicking their heels off, letting their warm, moist feet breathe the room in an unguided tour, waiting for my next move.

And I say, "Let's do a bunch of coke off each other in bed," because I'm on so much shit that I've lost the ability to be charming or coy or tactful, but the girls strip down to their underwear without much thought, for reasons that can only be speculated upon. Perhaps it's a misplaced sense of affection, or the (most likely) case of sidelining one's moral code for the sake of barter, but I have this bag of coke and a hard-on that will last all night, so it's hard to give a shit when I'm about to get the thing I'm supposed to want.

When you've been doing this for as long as I have, the motivations stop mattering along with the consequences.

21

SESSION 06
FLAVORS

I'm a restaurant tourist now.

After three weeks and seven sessions with Dr. Paradies, this is what I do.

It's all I have left because nothing else works.

Alcohol is a no go because I can't get drunk. Actually, that's not completely accurate. My judgment and conscience still go out the window, I just can't *feel* drunk, and drinking alcohol for the flavor alone is fairly pointless when there are plenty of other things that taste infinitely better.

Like sorbet.

And cheesecake.

Hot fudge sundaes.

I don't do drugs anymore, either. When you can't get stoned or high or spun, there's just no point. After so many harvests of sensation, that world has been reduced to nothing more than side effects and by-products: the distorted depth perception and increased heart rate, mild hallucinations and tracers. Factor that in along with a condition like mine, and it's a disaster waiting to happen. Murphy's Law of partying.

Example: two weeks ago I smoked $80 worth of pot and nearly choked to death on a peanut butter sandwich when I failed to realize I had a severe case of cottonmouth.

Example (2): chugged a $100 bottle of champagne in the hot tub. The 104-degree temperature combined with a liter of bubbly makes me vomit, however, I don't see this coming until it's already spewing out of me and invading the intake filters.

Eating filet mignon is a little bit less dangerous and cost about the same.

At all these different restaurants they're beginning to learn my name.

Like any dope vendor to a faithful client, they're familiarizing.

These gourmet pimps.

These culinary pushers.

They're my new dealers.

And this is true addiction. Just like coke, food is a greed drug, and because I never know when I'm full, I can go all day and all night long.

It's a 24-hour cookie party.

An all night surf and turf binge.

We've traded speedballs for pork dumplings, prescription pills for steaks on a Solaire grill.

After all, you can't be an addictive personality if you're not addicted to something, and food was next natural option. An easy transition:

Trade the trendy club for the popular restaurant, a champagne buffet for a five star entrée.

One minute I'm doing blow off some girl's chest and the next I'm craving cottage cheese croissants with an apricot glaze. I'm stalking from bakery to bakery at first light trying to get my next fix of chocolate chiffon pie or iced lemon bars with a liberal dusting of powdered sugar. Seriously, if I go too long without getting my daily dose of peppermint meringue or Beurre Blanc over sautéed scallops, I start to get a little bit bitchy and irritable. The drug is different but the behaviors are just the same.

"Generalizing," I believe was the doctor's speak Paradies used, as in: my addiction to drugs and alcohol has *generalized* to food. This is my official contribution to the nation's obesity epidemic. My abdominal sacrifice.

"And it's just as dangerous," she warns me.

Leave it to Dr. Paradies to compare high cholesterol and clogged arteries to a drug overdose. I've packed on a few pounds but it's not anything that will land me in a hospital bed. At least I don't think it will.

And, of course, wanting specifics, Paradies asks, "How many meals a day are you eating now?"

BRANDON TIETZ

When it takes you more than a few seconds to count, you know it's bad, but bad doesn't cover it for me. I'm a junkie. Even now I'm whacked out on two hits of fried ice cream with almond shavings and caramel syrup. Dr. Paradies asking me how many meals I eat a day would be like me trying to remember how many lines I did on a binge. The things you enjoy you don't put into increments.

"Twelve?" I guess, but I'm guessing low.

I guess low the way a man pulled over would when an officer asks how many drinks he's had, and just like that guy, I didn't bother counting because it wasn't in the foreseeable future to be questioned about it.

It comes off a bit funny to me when Paradies asks, "Don't you think that's a *little* excessive?" because it sounds like something a cop or my idiot mother would say. To her credit though, she is sort of an authority figure to me.

Countering, "Hey, I quit all the other shit," trying to downplay it, but Paradies says something in doctor's speak about trading one addiction for another, and I can't argue because not so deep down I know that she's right. I am addicted.

This food tastes good to the average patron, but for me it's orgasmic. An experience. Something spiritual. In my little world of side effects my condition has one, too.

"I think your other senses are becoming hyper-aware," Dr. Paradies mentions.

In English, when I taste something, I *really* taste it.

Imagine the first time you ever experienced your favorite food: how it was so good you had to close your eyes and savor it like a dream, and now imagine the same sensation repeating itself over and over with every bite. That's what it's like for me. Every spoonful of vanilla custard or French onion soup is always the first time I've ever had it, as if my palette has no memory. With every single bite, my tongue is a born again virgin waiting to be pummeled by the next flavor.

"It's quite the phenomena, actually," Paradies comments.

I tell her, "Yeah, I've heard of Daredevil. What other super-powers should I expect to develop?" already thinking about my

24

next score: a Cold Stone or Baskin-Robbins, or maybe that new Italian place on The Plaza.

She says, "You're evading again," which essentially means "you know I'm right."

And as much as I don't want to admit it, the evidence is there. I've traded up table for ten at Hush for a single-seater at Ruth's Chris and Cheesecake Factory and Brio.

PF Chang's.

The Plaza Bistro.

Matsu in Westport.

These are the places where I get my fix now, and it's a cause for concern for some people. When the manager of a restaurant comes up to your table and says, "Sir, don't you think you've had enough?" then you might have yourself a problem, and all problems go in steps.

First, you no longer need a belt.

Next, you need to purchase larger jeans.

And finally, you give up on jeans and switch over to sweats because you need the accommodation of an elastic waistband.

Cheesecake alone adds about an inch or so to my waistline, but well worth the sacrifice in my opinion. It's not like I'm killing brain cells or hurting my lungs. I'm not mainlining poison into my veins. The pounds I can handle.

"As concerned as you are about what other people think about you, I'm surprised that you'd subject yourself to the public scrutiny that has to come with these binges," Paradies questions in the form of a statement; another shrink tactic.

She's right, though. I would never let a restaurant full of strangers witness me gorging myself without at least some false pretense. It's embarrassing, and shame is a bitter flavor, no matter what you're eating it with, so now I have a few standard stories I use. Three, to be exact.

The first one came to me about a week and a half ago at The Bristol when I brought a comp book and pen with me to the restaurant. Paradies suggested that journaling would help me make sense of my condition and my life, so now I carry it everywhere with me. After about the seventh course the manager noticed me writing in between plates and assumed the restaurant was being reviewed. I didn't have the heart to disagree and ended up getting ten percent off my tab.

"I'm so glad you were able to use your journal as a coupon," Paradies frowns, scribbling on her legal pad. She looks as disappointed as ever.

But I chuckle and say, "Nice sarcasm, doc."

The second story came a couple weeks ago when my waiter made some snide comment about me having "quite the appetite," which, of course, drastically affected his tip. I told him I was an actor and had to put on at least forty pounds within the month for the part. It shut him up so I've been using that one ever since, too, more so than the reviewer one because there are less questions involved. The only downside is the staff doesn't kiss your ass as much.

"And the third?" Paradies probes, still noting.

The third is simple. There are no questions, no derogatory stares, and no snotty waiters to deal with. I simply order what I want, have the caterers set up everything in the dining room buffet-style, and feast in the privacy of my own home.

"It's expensive," I admit, "but there really is something quite liberating about eating $90 Maine lobsters in nothing but my underwear."

"You do realize that I recommend discontinuing this behavior effective *immediately*, right?" Paradies presses. "Like, *right now*."

I tell her, "You said the same thing about the drugs, too."

Paradies pinches the bridge of her nose, sighing, "Sometimes I think you like acting stupid for the attention," and the scribbling resumes for another moment, legal pad bowing over her knee.

"Do you *really* want to learn the hard way again?" she asks, and I think about it this time because I really don't want to have to hear her say, "I told you so."

Empathy is tough to come by when you've been forewarned. Ask anyone whose ever failed at suicide or didn't overdose enough and they'll tell you: "Resentment always follows relief."

They'll love you for surviving, but treat you like a jerk for almost killing yourself. Just in case things don't go according to plan, always know what to expect.

"Okay, assuming I don't play ball on this one, what's the worse that could happen?" I pose, relenting slightly.

"Well, a couple things," Dr. Paradies begins to explain. "There's all the physical dangers of high cholesterol, high blood pressure, excessive sugar intake, putting yourself at risk of diabetes and heart disease—etcetera, etcetera," she ticks off on her fingers, and somehow this doesn't scare me, but she's not done yet.

"What's the other?" I ask.

"You'll get fat and no one will love you," she states, and quite bluntly. The kid gloves, as they say, have come off, and the sound of this sinking in, it affecting me, is the sound of silence. No words, no scribbling, just a perception of helplessness enveloping me. She knew *exactly* what she was doing when she said that, and now I'm waiting for her to speak. I'm calling for help without words: a silent S.O.S. that only Paradies can recognize.

"I've got some recommendations, if you'd like to hear them," she states open-ended.

I nod my head and try not to think about comfort food.

Try not to think about the next addiction.

Whatever that may be.

SESSION 07
JUNE 18TH

I wake up in my bed to the sounds of snoring. The Asian girl that (maybe) works at BeBe—Kimberly or Stephanie or whatever, is currently resting upon my arm. She must have been laying on it all night because it's asleep to the point where it's not even tingling anymore. It's numb. Can't even feel it. I slide it out from under her and clumsily sneak out of bed, leaving the two entangled blondes and their Asian counterpart as they are. The clock reads just before 10:00 A.M. so I've only really gotten about six hours of sleep (about four short of the norm), but I don't feel in a state of unrest. Now that I think about it, I don't feel hung over, either. Normally, after the kind of night I've had it feels like I've been hit by a city bus. But not this morning. This morning nothing hurts. There's no headache, no nasal pressure, no sore prostate. Nothing. It's like last night never happened, but I know that's not the case.

I see the three of them asleep with their clothes scattered about the floor, the sun shining with the smell of booze and thinning perfume hanging in the air. Tiny blood droplets linger on the sheets, and given the state of affairs, I can only surmise it was either anally discharged or someone had a minor nosebleed last night from all the coke. It's hard to recall (as usual). Regardless, I make a mental note to take the bedding to the cleaners after I kick the girls out, departing my living space for the kitchen for a drink of a non-alcoholic variety.

Something is off.

Walking feels like a well-rehearsed motion rather than actual movement, almost dream-like. I see myself taking steps, but the hit of my heel to the floor and the rolling of my toes in the pace aren't registering. They seem counterfeit, and I nearly bite it going down the first flight of stairs after misjudging a step. This happens three more times before concluding that I might be a little bit more hung over than I originally thought. Or still wasted. One of the two, but I finally manage to make it to the ground floor unscathed, entering the kitchen and missing the usual chill of stone floors on my bare feet, the whisper of cold from the fridge on my shins. Neither of these events happens, but again, I'm writing it off to a new sort of hangover and continue about my business in the kitchen.

I grab a can of Country Time lemonade from the middle shelf and pop it open. It tastes good—better than normal, actually, but something's strange about it. I take another drink and realize it's not cold, and I'd like to assume that this is because it was recently placed in the fridge, but I can't feel the rim of the can pressing against my lips, either, so I've got to be high still. That's what happens when you mix about twenty different substances. Sometimes…maybe, this happens: a rare reaction or temporary stagnation of the senses. There's no other explanation, and it certainly can't be permanent. So I grab the half-gallon of Tropicana orange juice from the fridge door, not bothering to use a glass out of mild panic, and it's much the same result: tastes better than normal (god, this is *really* good for some reason) but room temperature, and I still can't feel my lips. Or my face. Can't sense my fingers gripping the handle of the jug. And it's weightless. Without texture. So I've got to be high right now and the fridge must be broken, I'm thinking, but that theory immediately slips when I open the freezer. When I see the steam pour; the kind of steam they release upon club crowds. My hand waves through the mist and it's not cold. Nothing is. So I must be coked out of my mind right now, and probably experiencing that thing that happens when you do too much shit and you can't smell for a day or so, but with my skin and muscles. I'm just fucked up right now. Or dreaming, but I'm definitely beginning to unnerve when I pull out one of the ice cube trays and twist it over the counter, dumping it. Pick a cube up, feeling it, or trying to, at least, but nothing. I watch it melt in my palm until the water begins to puddle and overflow onto the floor. Drips slap the stone tiling until I toss the remaining fleck into the sink. Hands frantically begin scouring my arms and chest—scrubbing them, trying to generate some sensation, but still nothing. I slap my hands together in a crude attempt to reactivate them. All numb, and yet somehow I continue to be in disbelief this is happening because I've never even heard of something like this before: not being able to feel, and I refuse to accept it, still checking my appendages and torso and face, all the while telling myself, "It's gonna wear off," and "You're fine...you just did a lot of shit," but not fully able to deceive myself.

In doctor's speak, this is known as "denial."

And denial is always the first step.

But since I don't know that, I keep going. For the rest of the morning and into the afternoon, I've officially waged war upon myself. I'm my own hostage torturing myself for information, my own worst enemy.

Injury #1 - I smack the right side of my face against a stair when I misjudge a step and trip.

Injury #2 – In the same mishap, I stub (and possibly break) one of my toes. It's discolored and doesn't wiggle with the others.

When I finally make it back up to the third floor (my room), I'm yelling at the girls to "get the fuck up" as I begin searching the mini bar for a bag, not so much moving bottles as I am slamming my hands and wrists against them.

Injury #3 – I accidently break a highball glass on the inside of my palm. Blood drips onto the carpet.

And one of the girls groans, "Dude...what the fuck, man?" through a yawn (and probably a bad hangover), so I start chucking beer cans at them, missing horribly on my first few attempts, yelling, "We need to find my shit," as I round the mini bar to the bed, yanking the comforter off and away from their still-nude bodies, instantly rousing them, and one of the blondes yells, "What the fuck is your problem?!" and I almost want to tell them, to explain that I'm in total panic mode but I retain my silence, scouring the bedding with my eyes for leftovers because I'm thinking that it might hold the answer. My skin can't feel anything, but some coke should *definitely* do the trick, and like a ray of hope, I spot a good-sized chunk of it under a breast and leap into it nose-first, snorting greedily.

Injury #4 – My nose starts bleeding from either a) doing a huge bump with a dry sinus or b) because I busted my nose on this girl's ribcage.

Either way, I'm bleeding all over the silk bedding and my shirt, but not really caring about that so much as the fact that nothing is happening. The jolt that is supposed to be occurring isn't, and I'm bleeding from my hand and my nose, and my toe is probably broken. My arms start shoveling name-brand skirts and tops and heels, flinging them onto the bed and I'm yelling, "Get the fuck out," because what I'm planning to do next, I don't want them to see. I'm well past panic mode and heading into delirium, pulling the girls off the bed by their ankles and ushering them out of the house while they say words like "prick" and "asshole" and "ow," slamming the door behind them and pacing back into the kitchen.

I open the knife drawer, the thought, *okay, what's the safest way I can do this,* occurring in irony as I peruse the cutlery, settling on what I think is the sharpest one: a small black-handled Ginsu.

Injuries #5 through 14 – I drag the knife down my left forearm, gently at first, but as the absence of sensation remains a constant, I begin actively pressing harder into myself. Sheets of blood pour out, and it becomes difficult to tell where I haven't cut myself as there's too much overflow and my vision is starting to blur.

Injury #15 – I head-butt a cabinet in anger and split my forehead open. Blood gets into my eyes and I think I'm starting to lose consciousness.

My arm is hemorrhaging and I throw up even though I don't feel sick in the least. Puke mixes with the blood and clots on the stone tiles, and it looks something like a murder scene where the victim and assailant are the same person, but I'm trying to make it to a phone now to call for help. There's a phone on the counter, and I grab it just before squatting and sitting in my own blood pool on the floor, wiping blood from my face with the back of my hand, struggling with each number. I dial her. Even though I don't want to, it's the only number I can remember, and I dial it saying I need her help when she picks up, that I'm bleeding to death and probably in need of an ambulance, but everything is so blurry and far away that I can't even remember me saying, "Please...help me," just before I fall over onto the floor, splattering in my own mess.

It's the first time mom and I have spoken in a while.

SESSION 08
ESCORTS

Before renouncing drugs and drink, and way before discovering the enticing wonders that is restaurant tourism: I'm bandaged.

Stitched and taped. Pseudo-mummified in gauze on my forearms, wrists, and palms. My shoulders and forehead. Smothered blood seeps through the fibers, climbing until it reaches the surface and hardening to maroon blotches that stink like rusted aluminum.

We're only a few days into the condition.

I'm unable to orgasm.

For this second formal act of denial, I will examine what's assumed to be the most sensitive part of my body—or at the very least, the one that gives the most visual reaction to stimulus: my penis. Three Viagra and two prostitutes from an escort service out of Kansas City, MO will aid this experiment. Both blonde and highly attractive, ages: around their mid-twenties. And clean (I'm assured). The way these charges are broken down is like a cell phone bill or flight reservation:

-Roundtrip transport (by limo): $400
-Supplies and wardrobe: $350
-Private residence charge: $200
-Booking charge: $150
-Service charge: $600/hr; this base rate doesn't cover the one-time fees that would be incurred for anal, ass-to-mouth, choking/hitting/binding, or what's referred to as: "non-standard fetishes" like when a client wants to role play as an infant or *Star Wars* character. None of that applies to me since my sexual practices are fairly standard, but then the guy who sets the appointments over the phone asks, "Is there anything wrong with

you?"

And I say, "Like...what?" real coy because "wrong" is a fairly subjective term, even though I'm pretty sure that my affliction counts.

"Wrong, man," he says, but his tone comes off like he's had this conversation way too many times. "Are you a cripple? Are you retarded? Do you got herpes or some weird thing with your dick?"

"No," I answer, but it's meek and hints at my situation.

"Better not messin' around, man. If these chicks show up and you're some kind of fucked up weird guy with one arm or no teeth, you better just say it now," he says. "Unless you want to end up like Stephen Hawking talkin' like a robot and shit, you know what I'm sayin'?"

So I come clean, explaining how I generally "don't feel," but all the guy wants to know is if that's an STD or "some new kind of retarded thing," and then he charges me another $500.

For "special needs," he calls it.

This was the lesser of two evils.

Had I decided to go to Hush, all of these charges and surcharges could have been avoided—or at the very least, informally applied through coke and pills and bottle service, which may be slightly less, but that's not really the issue. These people of nightlife, although seemingly oblivious to "important" issues, notice all things surface, which in this case would be my various bandages and wound dressings. If not immediately, then certainly later when I've removed my clothes, looking like a botched suicide attempt or the recipient of the type of beating that yields a bunch of questions, not to mention a real mood-killer.

For the sake of maintaining my reputation, I've decided to go outside the circle. Socialites and prostitutes are both whores in their own way, but you can't pay a socialite to shut up or leave when you want them to. They can be persuaded but not necessarily ordered. Control comes at a hefty premium.

In doctor's speak, this would later be known as: "domineering."

And: "hiding my personal contrition."

It's not entirely uncommon. When something's embarrassing, people will go to great lengths to hide it. Just ask any politician or Hollywood elite who's been caught in the wrong place at the wrong time.

Lying is the cosmetic foundation of our personality. Lipstick and eye shadow do for the face what deceit and half-truths accomplish for the self. That next press conference or public appearance could very well be your extreme makeover.

I'm so charming and debonair.

I'm so full of shit.

Another reason why escorts were ultimately the best choice: they get to pretend they're interested the same way I'm feigning normality. With enough money, you get to pick and choose your women right down to their level of ignorance.

Not unlike nightlife, we purchase prestige the same way we obtain desire. You're only a VIP as long as you're paying for it. Tonight, I'm paying quite a bit.

The escorts show up over a half hour late, accompanied by the type of guy that couldn't get into Hush, even with the amount of money I'm handing him. He's black and smells like knock-off *Armani Code*, mentioning something about "all these rich ass houses lookin' the same" as he tucks the money into the pocket of a faux leather jacket, a white powder circle lining his nostril. A little more framing his thumbnail. He sniffs and mentions, "You don't *look* retarded," before pimp-limping into the night, trampling through my mom's tulip plot.

And after shutting the front door, I turn to the escorts and attempt a smile (probably not doing it right), offering, "Drinks?" to which they both nod, and I motion to the staircase, letting them lead just in case I trip and bust my face again. Choking the banister with each step. Following.

They're dressed in evening gowns. Big hair. Big expensive breasts. Enhanced lips. Indoor tans. More *Penthouse* than *Playboy*, but not trashy enough to be *Hustler*. A nice compromise considering I don't want to get peed on, and Playmates—although ideal looking, are weak in the sack due to something known as the "you should just be happy you're sleeping with me" complex.

On a night that's mostly based on adjectives, I'm forgoing "classy" and "respectable" for "slutty," "audacious," and "emotionally vacant." My situation demands a "trained" and "professional" concubine. At the bar, I explain, "I'm *extremely* hard to please," as they sip outrageously priced Italian red wine, procured from my father's cellar.

Adding, "If you can get the job done, I'll make it worth your while," putting down another couple grand, wrapped in a flesh-colored rubber band on the frosted glass, and they both glare at me—not in anger or disrespect, but knowing a challenge has just been laid down and tonight's "job" might be fun.

The blonde to my right takes a sip of wine and cocks her head in a way that almost looks practiced, and she asks, "What's the catch?" batting fake eyelashes over colored contact lenses.

And once again, veiling my shame in vagueness, I answer, "The catch is you can't ask questions," pacing around the bar and removing my jacket, then my shirt, exposing all those bandages and strips of gauze. Medical tape and stitches concealed by cotton. And they ask nothing, taking their final slugs of wine before crossing the room. To the bed.

Their inquiries are posed in the form of statements.

Such as: "Tell us how to start."

And: "We can go faster or slower."

The hard-on is visually induced by things that are "wet" and "hot" like saliva and heavy, exaggerated breathing, supported by the audio of whore-speak, dirty talk, and sex language. Things most girls won't speak unless they're out-of-their-mind drunk.

One of them will spit and "glistening" glob of "warm" spit, stroking me off and saying, "Now, I know that feels good, doesn't it, baby?" but the erection is pharmaceutically-induced, and much like my clothes and car and club antics: for the sake of appearances. And I feel nothing.

No temperature.

Or surface consistency.

Nor any degree of pressure.

In a world where vaginas, a mouth, are only as good as their adjectives, my body doesn't recognize any of them.

There is no "wet, creaming" pussy or "tight, perfect" ass. No "alluring" mouth or breasts, but the money has already been paid and my denial is steadfast, so the act of sex is fabricated. In the same way they pretend to be aroused and interested, so will my body, and over the hours an observation is made.

Not immediately.

Four hours later, after we're drenched in sweat to the point where the bedding is soggy and my bandages are like wet toilet paper, post-clawing from a particularly intense orgasm that leaves my back weeping with curled ribbons of skin, I'm breathing giant plumes of sex: the stink of bodies and their liquid by-products, breath and wet human blush—smelling them, and tasting their salty/hairspray air on the back of my tongue. My lungs absorb and spit the sex, never tired. The heart punches and strains, but only in audio, and one of the whores slips, screaming with clenched eyes that she loves me, loves me so much as the sweat of three people invade my wounds and dissolve stitches. Devour antibiotics and eat blood clots. The motions of sex are familiar and accurately recreated, but my exhaustion is nonexistent compared to their gasping mouths and cramping, fatigued muscles. Their ability suck, swallow, or pump has been bankrupted. Spent. Because I am the bedroom infinite, completely beyond any sort of pain or gratification. Internal or external, the numb prevails. Unyielding.

So I need to find someone who can help.

And I need a better test.

SESSION 09
PROOF

"You need to stop sticking yourself with that thing," Paradies lectures. According to her, this is not only a physical danger, but a psychological one, as well.

Doctor's speak for: "addiction."

"You're becoming dependent on it," she says.

And I'm thinking, *God, she's really on a roll today.*

I say, "But I'm down to ten pokes a day. Isn't that good enough?"

You'd think we'd be bickering about cocaine or frozen custard or drinking—something relevant, but no. It's all about the needle: my proof object.

A "conditional vice" the good doctor calls it.

"You're attached," she accuses while scribbling on that legal pad as per usual. "You need to cut the damn thing loose while you still can."

"Cut," in the literal sense meaning that the needle is connected to the belt loop of my jeans via fishing line. I kept poking myself in the finger (on accident) every time I dug it out of my pockets so I came up with this. It was yet another small step toward me controlling the condition and not the other way around. Just like the doctor recommended.

I've been doing a lot of stuff like that lately. In fact, my entire house has practically been baby-proofed so I don't inadvertently hurt myself. Every routine revolves around the numb. No action is too small.

In the bathroom: I'm only allowed to use an electric razor so my face doesn't get cut. There's temperature control on the water valves to keep me from scalding myself. Even the toilet paper is quadruple ply and quilted with aloe so I don't have to worry about wiping too hard.

These are all steps to safety, and safety is control.

And the doctor says, "We've put in a lot of time developing a system to keep you out of harm's way, but if I can't get you to stop stabbing yourself then it's sort of meaningless, isn't it?"

"I'm sorry, I didn't realize my mother was in the room. What was that series of bitching again?" I goad, laying the sarcasm on extra thick.

And right on cue, Paradies comes back with, "You're evading again." Scribbling resumes and she asks, "Seriously, *why* do you need it? What's *so* important about this one particular thing? Tell me."

Because it's the easy way out. Out of all the possible things I could do, this is what works. After you tell someone you can't feel, the first thing they want to see is some unrequited pain. If someone told you they could juggle knives, you'd want to see them do it. You'd want proof. To verify they were the real deal. Just to make sure.

I'm incapable of admitting this, however, explaining, "It's either the needle or I end up talking about it the whole night. I've tried both...the needle is less—"

"—Painful?" she cuts in. "Embarrassing?"

"Less of a hassle."

"Well, in my professional opinion, I think you need to stop being such a sissy about this," Paradies throws out there, nonchalant, and for the briefest of moments, it feels like I've been slapped in the face.

"What did you just say to me?" I ask, but I totally heard it.

"Stop being a sissy," she repeats, just as firm as before.

"Is this some sort of whacked-out doctor's trick or are you like, serious...or something?"

"What I'm telling you is that if you want to stay numb for the rest of your life, keep sticking yourself."

She says, "That thing is the last major roadblock on your path to recovery," motioning to my pocket: what's in my pocket.

It wasn't always the needle though. Finding an appropriate proof object takes a bit of trial and error, and there was quite a bit of that. I've been burned, stabbed, electrocuted, cut, and anything else you can think of.

I've torched myself with lighters, on stovetops, in fireplaces, but the first time I got a whiff of my own skin I had to stop. Multiply the stink of a burning fingernail by ten and you might be close.

"People aren't going to take you seriously if you keep treating this as some sort of parlor trick," Paradies tells me, but this couldn't be further from the truth. Twist a cigarette into your palm or run a razorblade down your arm in front of a perfect stranger—and believe me, people take you seriously.

They think, *God, did he really just do that?* And suddenly we're *both* in denial.

They say, "Dude, you're fuckin' sick."

I'll nod my head slightly and tell them, "You have no idea."

No one does, and that's why it's so easy for me to do this, because everyone has at least one thing they're attached to. It could be an iPhone or a Blackberry. A lucky coin, deck of cards, or a photograph of a distant relative.

It could be business or personal.

Vital or unnecessary.

Real or imaginary.

This item can be anything as long as it's important to you, and that's why no one will understand the needle. It's my explanation. My proof. It's how a check to see if I'm still under the weather, my little thermometer that only has two temperatures: numb and normal.

Sick and well.

And Paradies finally says, "Give it to me," to which I pull the line and sever it with a lighter, handing over yet another sewing device. No resistance. This is just another therapy trophy that will end up in the trash, because in all honesty, I have a ton of these things. I know for a fact that I have more in my desk at home, a few more in my bathroom drawer, so it's not like I *really* care, but it's in this particular session that I believe she's finally caught on with the whole sewing-needles-aren't-expensive thing.

Paradies stops her scribbling and says, "I'm going to make

you a deal," in a cryptic, informal sort of way I haven't seen before. "If you can last two weeks without stabbing yourself I'll have a reward for you," she offers, and it's at this point I'm about to become a smart-ass and mention how big my bank account is, but before I can do that she resumes, clarifying, "This is something you *don't* have, nor can it be bought--and believe me, you *do* need this."

Skeptical, I ask, "Okay, what is it?" rolling my eyes so I don't seem so interested. Like smiling or grinning, it comes off contrived.

"Not telling," she states flatly. "Two weeks. No poking. You can go now," she says, pointing to the door.

Sitting up, I inquire, "What happens if I don't stop? What then?"

"Two weeks," she says. "Quit being a sissy."

"Is it really ethical for a doctor to call her patient a sissy?" I ask.

Paradies responds, "I stopped being your doctor ten seconds ago. You can leave now."

SESSION 10
BATTERY

I walk into the office of Dr. Paradies with panda bear black eyes, a split lip and fractured collarbone. My body is littered in bruises of yellow and purple and (on some occasions) green. I walk—not limp, on sprains and twists, joints and ligaments unsettled that creak with every step. I'm damaged: a cracked ribcage here, a torn ACL there, dried blood chipping and flaking away like leaves in the fall. I saunter through the office a runway model showing off the latest in medical fashions: the Dolce & Gabbana neck brace accented with silver Chanel gauze clips. I sport the DKNY ribcage protector/stabilizer with burn balm gel by Calvin Klein, all the while smiling a mouthful of loose chipped teeth to which Paradies returns her usual frown, and once seated upon the blue chaise lounge, so begins the questions.

Lately, it's always been the same two:

"Did you do this to yourself?"

"Or was it someone else?"

Because what Paradies doesn't know is that I've tried to cut away from the needle, am still trying, actually. Although she'd like to believe otherwise, the truth remains that I'm making an honest, although unorthodox, sort of effort, and every mark on my body represents a part of that. I'm bearing the results of my misguided attempts.

In doctor's speak, she'll call these "reinforcement dividends."

Or: getting your ass kicked for no good reason.

"Get this through you head," Paradies stresses, her scribbling coming to halt for a moment. "You are not invincible nor will you ever be, so just stop it already."

"Seriously, what do I need to do to get you to stop

destroying yourself?"

This is before her two-week offer.

Before I had anything to look forward to.

Dr. Paradies has always been telling me to stop. Through the cocaine and cheesecake binges, the vast assortment of experimental orgies with women and prescription pills and bottles of booze, every desired effect unrequited; the needle was the one thing I could count on: my own sensory addiction and the most efficient way of explaining myself. My condition.

Actions speak louder than words, that old saying.

It's like I said before, you can't be an addictive personality if you're not addicted to something, but the issue with Paradies is that she's taken everything away and given nothing back in return.

Up until recently, my little sewing needle was all I had left, and I've tried to cut away from it but I'm just like any other addict. If I can't get my fix the standard way then I'm going to look for alternatives. I need another route.

When there's no weed left, buy opium.

Can't afford coke? Try crack.

The problem is that I can't get what I want by asking alone. This isn't like ordering a pizza or picking up a pack of smokes at a gas station. I can't order this at a bar. What I want has to be begged for. This is harder than you'd think.

Nine times out of ten, the last words I'll hear before getting clocked in the face are, "You asked for it," because most people, normal people, won't hit you without a little coaxing.

A little encouragement.

Sometimes it takes a lot.

Most of these people can't get over the initial shock of some random dude spitting in their face or putting out a cigarette in their Mojito because no one in their right mind does that. Not unless they're crazy. Or me. And the majority of the time I'm covered in bandages and bruises with some part of my face stitched up, so there's typically an inner-debate about whether or not to beat the shit out of a guy who's obviously already had the shit beaten out of them.

Amazingly, even with spit crawling down their face or urine on their pants, people can still feel pity. Everyone experiences a degree of inner-conflict. Now that I'm in denial, it seems like I've made a career in dragging everyone down with me. And without my proof object, I'm acting like I've never had more to prove in my life.

Paradies asks me about this.

"What are you trying to find out that you don't *already* know?"

In short, "What are you trying to prove?"

There's no right answer, but that isn't to say I haven't been learning. Always remember how misfortune is a lesson in disguise, or in my case, a lecture.

I wake up at KU Med with a mild concussion and cigarette burns on my chest.

I wake up at Johnson County less some teeth with green glass lodged in my forehead from a Heineken bottle.

I keep waking up but nothing ever changes. Nothing new is obtained except more medical jargon and doctor's speak. Hospital terminology.

Contusion, not bruise.

Abrasion, not cut.

Suture, not stitch.

I'm educated in most of the names and locations of the bones in the human body, where my arteries and pressure points are. I learn how to do CPR and the procedure to stop internal bleeding. I'm told everything there is to know about the brain and the spine and the central nervous system, how if I had been hit just a few inches lower I would be waking up paralyzed, if at all.

"If he'd stabbed you *here* instead of *there*," Dr. so-and-so told me, "you would've died instantly."

And: "A couple more minutes and you would've had permanent brain damage, young man."

They bring me back and give me the instant replay. This is just like all those medical dramas you watch on NBC and CBS only the main character isn't likeable and the doctors aren't good looking or dramatic.

Today's lesson at Wyandotte County Hospital is how to fix a punctured lung.

Next week we'll be learning the proper way to repair a scratched cornea.

According to anyone wearing a stethoscope necklace, it's not enough for them to just fix you. They want you to know *how* they did it: the process and how difficult it was, that way when you get the bill they won't receive an angry phone call about why it costs $4,000 to reconstruct a shattered femur. If you're going to fork over a few grand to get the blood out of your lungs, might as well know how they did it.

And Paradies says, "If this is you trying to become a doctor, this is the *worst* way to go about it."

I say, "Did you know that the human skull consists of twenty-eight different bones?"

Adding quickly, "And the tongue isn't actually one muscle. It's a group of sixteen."

Burn your mouth with hot oil at The Melting Pot and you can acquire this little nugget of info just like I did. An accident is all that separates you from an education.

"You're evading again," Paradies groans unimpressed, scribbling away.

The brain continues to send out electric wave signals until approximately thirty-seven hours after death. This is the kind of stuff doctors feel the need to share when you almost bite the big one, and oddly enough, I'm retaining a lot of it.

In addition to me being an unsanctioned restaurant critic, I'm also well on my way to having an unofficial doctorate in general medicine.

"Seriously," I rationalize with Paradies. "A few more bar fights and I might be ready to take the MCATs."

Applied learning: you'll never need to study a near-death experience or almost-drowning the way you do a lecture. You're only one dislocated shoulder away from getting the skinny on the humerus and glenoid. If you know anything about skin grafts, you're either a doctor, a burn victim, or me.

But not everyone is a believer in the system.

"I suppose reading a book like everyone else won't work, huh?" Dr. Paradies counters, adjusting her glasses, and the sarcasm couldn't be anymore obvious. You reap what you sow, I guess.

"C'mon, kiddo, level with me...why?" she asks. "Why are you doing this to yourself? I just want to understand." And like the indignant little shit that I am, I scoff at her. Even though I know that Paradies has only good intentions and my best interests at heart, or at the very least, a professional obligation—I'm compelled to rebel against her, saying that she'll never understand. She'll never fix me. No one can.

I glare at her, saying, "You have no fucking idea what it's like to not feel," but she keeps her cool, and what she says next almost makes me lose it. I nearly fly off the handle, not because I think she's wrong, but because I know she's right and it upsets me that I haven't seen it before. I'm *that* shortsighted and ignorant.

With pity in her voice, she says, "Aidin, you haven't felt a damn thing your entire life," and there's no denying this statement. I can't refute it.

The truth is that I began losing my way a long time ago.

SESSION 11
AIDIN: AGE 6

I miss Mommy and Daddy.

They're both doctors, and Mommy says that when you're a doctor it's your duty to help people get better, so she buys me lots and lots of toys so I won't be so bored. I have all the Ninja Turtles and the Shredder and Rocksteady and Bebop, but I can't have all of them fighting at once because I can only hold two at a time and there are no kids around here. Just big houses. I wish Sandy would play with me. She's my sitter, and she's really pretty like a famous singer but I don't think she likes me very much. I tell her she can be Raphael and Michelangelo (the coolest ones!), but most of the time, she just watches TV and eats my popsicles. Sandy is in high school and always talks about boys wanting her but I don't understand. She says I will when I get older and I feel bad for not being smart enough to talk to Sandy because I don't think she's as smart as she says she is, and I want Mommy to come home because sometimes she'll play Turtles with me before dinner. Even when Sandy does *play with me, she doesn't do the voices like Mommy does.*

Daddy never plays with me, but sometimes he'll come home for lunch and bring me McDonald's. I want to play with the other kids at the Play Place but Sandy says that I have more toys than any kid she knows and that I should be happy with that. I'm not, though. I want my old sitter, Rosie, back because she'd play with me and do the voices and take me places, but Daddy said that she was stealing from us, and Rosie went away. I don't think she stole, though. She was too nice to do that. Now I have Sandy, and the only thing I like about Sandy is that she's pretty and Daddy comes home sometimes in the afternoon with McDonald's to check in on us because I think he knows that Sandy isn't as good as Rosie. My Daddy is really smart, so sometimes he'll take

Sandy into his office to help her with her schoolwork, and I'll eat my McDonald's and watch the shows I want to watch. That's why I think Sandy isn't very smart, because Daddy has to help her so much and he never had to come home to help Rosie with anything ever.

I'm not allowed in Daddy's office. I've seen it a couple times and it's big with lots of books and papers but Daddy says it's no place for kids, so I stay out. I like to sit outside of it, though. At night when Mommy's making dinner I can hear Daddy yelling bad words to people on the phone and telling them to do their job, but not when Sandy's in there. He sounds happy and tells Sandy how much he missed her, but I don't understand because he sees her so much and he never talked like that to Rosie. He was never nice to Rosie like he is to Sandy. I hear him tell her how beautiful he thinks Sandy is through the door and she doesn't say anything back, but I hear both of them making noises like they're hurt.

One time I knocked because I got scared and Daddy came out and yelled at me. He said that I was supposed to be downstairs eating and watching cartoons, and he didn't care when I said I finished already and that I was worried. He grabbed my arm really hard so that I couldn't see Sandy sitting on his desk and told me to shut up and I cried a lot. He told me to calm down but it was hard because I was still scared and didn't know what was going on, and then he asked me if I knew what a secret was. I nodded and told him I did, that all the great super heroes have secrets so the bad guys can't hurt them and Daddy smiled.

He said that him helping Sandy was a secret, and that no one can find out about it or people could hurt him and Sandy, and I asked if we could tell Mommy and he yelled no really loud and hurt my ear, but I didn't cry because heroes are tough. I want to be tough like Raphael and he doesn't cry, so I told Daddy I would be tough and keep his secret so he wouldn't get hurt. I don't care if Sandy gets hurt, but if the bad guys show up to get Daddy that'd mean that Mommy and I could be hurt too, and I don't want that.

Daddy won't tell me what he's teaching Sandy, but I think she's a ninja like Chun-Li in Street Fighter *because she always comes out sweaty and tired, and after Daddy leaves she lays on the couch and goes to sleep and I don't have to watch boring soap operas. They both tell me not to talk about when Daddy comes home to help Sandy with her training. If Mommy asks where the McDonald's came from I tell her that Sandy got it for me and that makes her happy. The best part about Mommy coming home is that's when Sandy leaves and I can play with her.*

She asks me what I want for dinner and I always say pizza because she'll play longer with me if she doesn't have to cook and that's what the Ninja Turtles eat. Mommy isn't as good at playing as Rosie, but she tries hard and does the voices so I like playing with her okay. I ask if I can be a super hero when I grow up and she says that I can be anything I want to be, and even though I don't have powers or weapons I believe her. Mommy is really smart and tells me all the time that I'm going to do lots of great things when I get older. She says I'm an extra special kid with lots to look forward to.

I can't wait to be older.

Maybe when I'm Sandy's age Daddy will begin my secret training so that I can be tough like Raphael.

SESSION 12
GROUPS

"My name is Aidin."

And they all say in big dead unison, "Hi, Aidin."

At the suggestion of Dr. Paradies I'm now attending two groups. The one for my condition is called Making Sense. The other—the one for my self-mutilation (my poking and fighting amongst my many forms of conditional proofs) is called Circle of Healing. I'm fairly certain the thinking here is that by going to these meetings I'll stop feeling sorry for myself and realize that there are those who have it worse off than I do, people who can't cope nor afford the kind of help I'm getting. My pity for them is supposed to outweigh my own self. That's the theory, anyway.

Some of these people are pretty fucked up.

This blind guy Charlie stammers, "My best friend just told me that my girlfriend is ugly...and I'll go ahead and admit it right now, man, I was pretty sure she wasn't all that attractive in the first place," he shrugs. "I used to picture other women when we'd sleep together. The ones I could remember from, y'know...before."

Everybody at Making Sense does this with the before and after. They make their condition the dividing line between the now and then. Past and present. They speak in odd tenses and distant persona, as if their former versions are dead and their current persons are mere replacements. Shells of half-life.

And Charlie says, "Before 'the black' I used to have a thing Kathleen Turner."

"Conditional pet names," Paradies calls them.

Plenty of other group members use those, too, and most of them sound like super heroes that never took off.

So far I've heard "the black," "the blank," "the mute," and "the silence," but a lot of the group members simply title it "the loss." It's stupid and pointless to give a name to something that debilitates you, but I'm no different.

I call mine "the numb."

The big numb.

The woman sitting next to the group moderator interprets everything in sign language as Charlie continues on, stating, "She looks like Whoopi Goldberg...like a white Whoopi Goldberg."

There's no sign language for Whoopi Goldberg.

The interpreter has to spell it out. Twice.

"I can't even touch her anymore," Charlie continues. "All I can think about is that ugly bitch and *Jumping Jack Flash*. I may be blind but I can still see nightmares," he says with a sort of thick desperation that the other blinds seem to empathize with while others smirk not so moved.

Making Sense is kind of a cliquey group.

The deafs generally use nothing but sign language towards each other because they don't want the blinds to know what they're saying, and consequently, most of the blinds cover their mouths when speaking because they know most of the deafs are lip-readers.

Like I said, cliquey, but this isn't any different from high school. We're all in the same class for the same reason, although sub-categorized by our own social stigmas. This isn't *The Breakfast Club* or some bullshit teen flick. We're not all going to get along by the time this is over, but we might reach a common understanding.

And with tears in his eyes, Charlie struggles, "I just feel so—I don't know...*lost*." He rubs his brow and concludes, "It's got me thinking about how some lies worth living."

When you devote your entire livelihood to a person or an ideal, the last thing you want to hear is proof that it doesn't exist. Think about this the next time you're on the way to church and the morning DJ says something about scientists disproving God or the president-elect being a devout atheist. Remember how truth is belief's ugly cousin. Ignorance is bliss, and I'm right in the middle of it all. I'm the freak show within the freak show, the rarity, a never encountered walking impossibility. The great equalizer.

At my first session at Making Sense, I did more than my fair share of talking. I laid it all out there in an unabridged numb, and given my lack of cooperation with Dr. Paradies, I don't think anyone was expecting that, including myself.

Not even two steps through the door, Group Moderator Chris pulled me aside to tell me, "Don't worry about the public speaking portion. Half this group is the in-one-ear-and-out-the-other type, if you know what I mean," he cracked with a small chuckle.

A deaf joke.

I'm seeing this shit more and more all the time.

Example: Sometimes the deafs will stop signing at certain points in their sentences, thus stopping the dialogue of the interpreter and placing emphasis on particular words, such as, "I don't *see*...why it matters if she's attractive or not, Charlie."

And Charlie with the oversized shades and mismatched clothing, he throws it right back saying, "You're absolutely right, Steven. I've *heard*...it's what's inside that counts."

"Good for you, Charlie. I'm glad you're turning a *blind eye*...to this particular issue."

According to Group Moderator Chris, this kind of repartee has been going on for quite some time. Even politicians don't mudsling this well. It's all a competition, and in that regard, Circle of Healing is no different.

You practically need a suicide attempt to get into the room. Just like Making Sense, it's all about who suffers the most. It's all about your pain. The main difference being the role I play.

At Making Sense I'm the great equalizer.

At Circle of Healing I'm an icon.

I walk into the room with my shattered bones and nicked arteries, my multi-colored bruises and cuts glazed in antibiotic. Every stitch and scab and bloodstain is viewed as a medal of honor. Of valor, and they look at me in awe as I pass by, some of them even going as far as bowing their heads in adoration. I'm a general. A god, and like all new religions, theories circulate.

They say, "Maybe you're not disconnected from your pain.

Maybe you're so *apart* of it that you're one in the same."

And, "What if you're enlightened and you just don't know it?"

"What if you were chosen?"

These little Goth kids with their bloody gauze wristbands and anarchy buttons, they're not trying to kill themselves. None of us are. They just want to find out if anyone cares, if love exists, and in their search they became misguided, finding comfort in a less conventional means, something dangerous, but tangible in its necessity. It's sad, but the only time most of these people *really* feel seen is when they're under 24-hour suicide watch. And perhaps there was therapeutic misfire somewhere along the way, an unintended result that neither myself nor Dr. Paradies could foresee, but I think I've become the proverbial center of Circle of Healing: a constant martyr self-tortured for all their sins and misadventures.

I'm an outcast, but I'm also the messiah, and with the state of affairs I could easily see how this could turn "anti-productive" or "unintentionally negative" as the group not only reinforces my destructive behaviors, but idolizes them. There's much envy being shared amongst this assembly, but there's also a general impression that they're on the brink of answering those paramount questions they've been asking their bodies for years with razors and needles. Circle of Healing is looking for a cure, but that remedy might very well mean a sacrifice on my part. I would never reveal this to Dr. Paradies, but as I attend this group more and more it becomes fairly evident that they're not really saving me so much as I'm saving them. I'm their channel to better health and spirit, and as unconventional as it is, you might go as far as calling it heroic.

Much the same can be said about my efforts amongst the debilitated collection that is Making Sense, the sensory deprived attendees that wander pitied and calloused in the cruel real world. This room is about as close to a level playing field as they've ever encountered, and according to Group Moderator Chris, no side is backing down.

"We've been needing some new blood in here, and I think

you're just what the doctor ordered," he told me. "Just what the doctor ordered, my friend," he repeats, smiling big.

Blind people do that: the smiling big thing. I guess because they can't see it they want to make sure that you do. I'm surrounded by Stevie Wonder impersonators.

"Just let it all out and say what's on your mind," Chris advises.

And I do.

I say, "My name is Aidin," with my little nametag sticker that only half the room can read.

They say in big dead unison, "Hi, Aidin."

And just like them I draw the line. June 18th. That was the day it all started. My day of rebirth. New, but not improved by any means. I sell it hard. I have to. The whole point of this is to make your situation sound as bad as humanly possible to make everyone else feel better about themselves. Pity is the gateway to recovery. Once you can say to yourself, "I have it bad, but not nearly as bad as that guy," you can finally find some balance. You can move on.

With me around, everyone seems to be moving on just fine. I'm the anti-miracle of Making Sense. Just what the doctor ordered.

Helen Keller, eat your heart out.

Ray Charles, kiss my ass.

I pour it all out there.

I tell them about my former life, the "before": the club goddesses and the models, night after night of absolute bliss on only the purest of drugs, the highest shelf of booze, and the strongest dosage of pills, and how with this shift into the "after," none of that matters. My life and everything I've ever come to know has become extinct, and the closest I could ever get being back in that place and time are the motions. I can have sex for hour upon hour but never climax. Drugs do nothing. Alcohol does nothing, unless we're talking about poisoning or an overdose, and I tell them about that, too. I tell them everything: about me, my absentee parents, Dr. Paradies, and how none of them like me.

Adding with a sort of desperate snicker, "Fuck, *I* don't even like me that much."

It's when I'm telling them these things about me: how I eat and never get full or get cut but not feel pain—a realization occurs, perhaps because I'm finally being one hundred percent open, but mainly in part to how the group is reacting, as if they pity me so much they can't fathom how I can exist. I'm far from dead, but I'm not really alive, either. I'm a shadow, an outline of myself, but a stabilizer, nonetheless.

Because the entire circle is reacting the same way.

They can finally feel for each other because I can't feel at all.

I have no friends. I have no "meaningful" relationships. I'm alone and unhappy and have nothing to fill the void. My entire life has been taking one pill after another drink after another drug before going to bed with some stranger just to *appear* happy. I've never been happy. I'm scared and fat and have nothing to live for. I get beat up on purpose for the attention. I'm uneducated with nothing to look forward to. Nothing is simple. Everything is a danger to me and there's no help. No one is there to help me. I'm in no one's care. There's no one else like me. It can't be fixed. And somewhere along the line I start to hear what I'm saying. I *really* hear it. I'm finally confessing all the things I don't write in my journal and don't speak in sessions, and a surrender ensues. A collapse, and perhaps it was my pride that wouldn't let me do this before or shame of crumbling before Dr. Paradies, but it's definitely happening now. I'm a big, wet, quaking wreck buried in my own palms.

Half the room can't hear the sobs.

The other half can't see the tears.

But none of that matters because collectively they're feeling what I can't in the heavy dank room that is Making Sense. We're all being saved in one way or another, learning how to reciprocate salvation and share deliverance. Emotions boomerang with their words of whisper, words of care and sympathy like I've never known and believed unwanted.

They say, "You'll never be alone again."

And, "We're here for you."

"Everything's okay."

And I look up and the circle is no longer a circle. It's a mass. The entire room—even the translator and Group Moderator Chris have stood up and moved to me, something I couldn't hear over myself but served as a rescue beacon for the deafs. Arm upon arm are laid and folded over my person, their appendages weaving me in, cocooning me: a care shelter. They're holding me and saying, "We'll help you beat this, Aidin."

"You have friends now."

"You have a family."

And I feel the first thing I've felt in weeks.

I'm not sure what it is but I know it's good.

Session 13
Time

One of the major problems with my denial stage, Paradies tells me, is that it isn't necessarily the physical symptoms I'm having trouble coping with, but rather, all the spare time it's given me in the process. The cuts and bruises I incur from tripping and walking into things I can handle. It's the boredom that's killing me.

I'm about two months into the numb and can't remember the last time I had a drink or popped a pill (besides the Colace, that is). My eating habits have balanced out: a mere three a day, never exceeding 1,500 calories. I'm going to Making Sense and Circle of Healing on a regular basis now, and have finally stopped poking myself and picking fights.

"You're doing well," Paradies compliments in passing, doing that scribbling thing she does.

"Yeah, but I don't feel well," I tell her staring at the ceiling, yet again, from the chaise lounge. "I feel..." I begin, not knowing what word to use because this isn't a physical issue. It's emotional, and therefore, difficult to surmise.

"Frustrated? Restless?" Paradies offers. "Like you don't know what to do with yourself?"

"Yeah," I say, sighing. It doesn't help. There's no release.

Because as long as I've known me I've never been myself. I never had to. Never gave myself the opportunity because I was always on something, and consequently, my history, my life experience in general, is deficient.

I've never had a job or went to college. I've never had a serious relationship with a girl or a best friend. I have no hobbies (Paradies was quite specific about recreational drug use, sex, and clubbing not counting). TV, books, and movies have never really interested me. Nor music. I really don't even have a discernible list of likes and dislikes, now that I think about it. Besides knowing what's good at certain restaurants and drugs, there's not a lot in my knowledge base.

I guess you could say I have no personality, and if you don't have a personality, then you basically don't have a soul. The soul is the opposite of surface. Surface is all I am.

"You want to know what your problem is?" Paradies asks in an obvious rhetorical fashion.

I'm thinking, *What? That I can't feel anything?*

I say, "Sure," still looking for patterns and pictures in the ceiling, constellations waiting to be named.

"Your problem is that you can't kill six hours anymore just by popping a pill or doing whatever it is you kids do these days to get yourselves messed up," Paradies explains, sounding almost maternal but definitely outdated. "You just need to find alternatives to fill up your day." She hands me a sugar-free mint when she notices I'm biting down on my lower lip. I pop it and sigh, thinking about Valium and ecstasy and big cloudy white bars of Xanax.

Concerta 36's.

Tangerine Adderall.

How I miss them so.

"It's a stage of transition," Paradies says, scribbling. Always scribbling with white knuckles. "You've stopped trying to destroy yourself, which, I personally am *very* happy about because it was getting a little annoying."

I shoot her a look but she doesn't see it.

She's buried up to her forehead in legal pad.

"Now all we have to do is find something to fill your time with."

Already of a mind that Paradies controls my life enough as it is, I ask, "You're not gonna make me do volunteer work or some shit like that, are you?"

"No," she snickers. "That'd be like throwing a match in a gasoline factory. No, I was thinking of something a little less stupid."

"Yeah, you're not offending me at all right now," I mutter.

"Pipe down," she says. "You can work the soup kitchens later if you want but right now I have a project for you," she tells me, handing over a stack of papers in a clear plastic binder.

I sit upright on the chaise lounge and leaf through the material a bit. It's basically a big to-do list with a box next to each activity that I can only assume I'm supposed to check once I've done it. Some of these have specific instructions while others are plain and simple.

"So, just go through this and pick out the ones I want?" I casually ask, still perusing the material.

"No," Paradies says. "All of them."

I flip to the end. Look up. "There's like, forty fuckin' pages in this thing."

She smirks nonplussed, "You got anything better to do?"

I ignore the question and ask, "What exactly is the point of this?"

"That, my young patient, is a surprise," she says, checking her watch. "Our time is up for today. Go work on your list."

As I move to stand I remember something. Something important.

"Hey, you know it's been two weeks and I haven't poked myself. Didn't you say I was going to get a reward or something?" I inquire.

"You did," she tells me. "You're holding it."

"This big list of shit to do is my reward?" I ask, irritated.

She smiles. "Item #154, kiddo. You can thank me later."

SESSION 14
STARBUCKS

At Starbucks on the Plaza I order a venti-sized vanilla chai tea with a low fat apple scone and take a seat next to one of the windows, away from the crowds. Believe it or not, this is part of my assignment. It's how the list begins.

Item #1: Find a relaxing public place to go to and read through your list. Order a nonalcoholic, non-caffeinated beverage and something light to eat. This should take you at least an hour.

The entire list reads this way:

Forty pages long.

Seven sections.

34 sub-sections.

366 items.

Everything is broken into parts based on their characteristics. Directions are simple and concise. Nothing is left to question. Not unless it's supposed to be. Every category yields a different set of responses and reactions I'm supposed to give. Whether they're emotional or physical or psychological, my feedback needs to be documented. That's the experiment: live, react, record. It's when I see that this list goes on for months that I realize my walk of life has been numbered and Paradies is leading every step of the way. She wants to know every part of me. What I'm feeling and thinking. What I like. And dislike.

For example:

Music: Listen to each album at least once all the way through. Do not skip any of the songs or stop listening to the album unless it's absolutely necessary. Take note of which songs you liked and why. Describe your feelings in reaction to any songs or lyrics that strike a chord in you (feel free to follow along with the lyrics in the CD's booklet). After you have finished listening to each CD at least once, make a mix CD composed of your favorite songs in the order you would want someone to listen to them in.

After her directions there's a list of about fifty CDs I'm supposed to get, each one being a numbered item, and all of them as vague and unfamiliar to me as the next.

There are three remaining categories of section five: one for movies, a reasonably short one of books and novels, and a third for comic books: *Watchmen, Daredevil, The Maxx,* and *X-Men* just to name a few.

It's all well explained and easy to understand.

Some of the other items, however, are extremely cryptic, like the one that's my "reward" from Dr. Paradies.

Item #154: On August 27th don't leave the house and don't plan anything. Work the items you can from home until contacted.

The 27th is nine days from now. "Sneaky bitch," I whisper to myself, taking a large bite of scone.

I keep reading through, noticing how some of the items are either beyond my control or realm of knowledge.

Item #351: Save someone's life.

Item #306: Teach a child a valuable lesson.

Some of the other items are simple to the point of being childish.

Item #56: Assemble a jigsaw puzzle of at least 500 pieces.

Item #49: Build a log cabin out of Lincoln Logs.

Item #63: Fill out a coloring book.

Item #1 is one of the few items I have to do in a particular order. Some of these items are conditional, like how I can't work on Item #213 until I complete all of section five. Most of these, however, I can do in any order I like just as long as I don't overlap them. That's one of the rules.

Rule #3: Never perform more than one item at a time. For example, you cannot assemble your puzzle while watching one of the listed movies or listening to one of the listed CDs. The reason for this is so you are completely focused on each individual item and free from outside influence. I'd hardly want you to associate heroin usage from a film with Legos or Tinker Toys, so make sure you strictly abide by this policy.

Another rule, #1 to be exact, is that I have to write about every item I complete, whether it's a review or reaction or my feelings. Paradies is big on this. Writing. She gave me that comp book but after a few sessions of her not asking to see it, I stopped using it. I guess that's because it's an active reminder of what's wrong with me. I write funny now because of the condition and trying to touch type is a joke, but that's not so much the issue here. It's what I was trying to write about that was the problem.

Up until recently I've never been very good at expressing myself. Drugs used to help me out with that, but not anymore. I've got Paradies and her list of activities to inspire me.

Item #208: Visit the Kansas City zoo and take pictures of the animals.

Item #299: Watch the pilot episode of a television show.

Item #51: Paint a self-portrait.

It's all so cut and dry. Go here. Do this. Try that.

See this movie. Go to this gallery. Visit this place.

Write it down, write it down, write it down.

Watch and review.

See and react.

Live the list.

Item #361: Be at the corner of Southwest Trafficway and Main on the 10th of September at 10:00 P.M. sharp. Wear a nice suit and make sure you have your credit card with you. Bring a dozen pink roses and don't be late.

There are about twenty other items that read as vague as that, about forty or so more that involve me being at a certain place at a certain time for a specific reason.

I take a bite of scone and arrive at the final item.

Item #366: Reread your list, but this time notate all the items that involve appointments using either a Blackberry or PDA (something that you can carry on you), and set the device to remind you of these events. Never set to vibrate. That should go without saying, but I'm saying it anyway.

I think of a smart-ass remark to that, but like a tick in my brain, I hear Paradies say, "You're evading again."

"Go work on your list now," she'd say.
I take a final drink of chai tea and get to it.

SESSION 15
SECTION 1

At around 10:00 P.M. my dad walks into the house and sees what I'm doing, what I've been doing for the last fourteen hours or so.

"What the hell is this?" he asks, surveying the scene in the living room: miniature houses under construction with tiny satellite space stations overlooking blue and canary condos. Plastic skyscrapers tower above intergalactic fighter vessels and moon cruisers, charged by a 9-volt battery. Everywhere are piles of Lego confetti accompanied by the instructions on how to assemble a car, a yacht, or a castle.

"Well?" my father tries again.

I don't answer. Not immediately, anyway.

What you need to know about my dad is that he's a doctor. Both my parents are, but he's a doctor many times over. That's why all the money. He has one masters in chemical engineering, another in brain surgery (or something like that), and a third I can't remember. Something to do with the spine, I think. Not sure. I'd say he's a good doctor but the one time I went to him (for my condition) he ended up prescribing me some generic painkillers and asking if his tie looked okay.

After taking the prescription from him, I told him his tie sucked and called him an asshole.

The tie did look fine (silk, with a nice subtle stripe pattern of peach and tangerine), but the point here is that my dad is an insensitive prick. He doesn't actively care or spend any time with me, but as long as I have his money to spend, he's under the assumption that I'm happy and healthy.

I, on the other hand, am nothing but a constant source of disappointment to my dad, and he never misses a chance to remind me of that since I have no job and no education above the high school level. To him, I'm a living failure, and the fact that I'm sitting here in the middle of the living room floor surrounded by things designed for the ages 6 through 12 demographic isn't necessarily helping my plight.

He tugs his pants at the knees, taking a seat on the Crate & Barrel caramel leather couch and muses, "I wonder what the Department of Military Science would have to say to me if they knew my 24-year old son was drawing a picture on an Etch a Sketch." He gives a contrived little pause before concluding, "They'd probably burn me at the stake for fathering a retard."

Coldly, I respond, "First of all, this is a Magna Doodle. The Etch a Sketch is over there," I tell him, pointing to a space on the floor at my left. Item #10, if you want to get specific.

"And second of all?" he coaxes when I don't continue.

"And second of all, you're an asshole. Now can you go away? I'm a little busy here," hoping he'll walk off for his nightly date with the medicine cabinet and a glass of scotch. He doesn't.

The leather of the couch crinkles as my dad leans over to take a look at what I'm drawing: magnetic particles composing poorly detailed faces and crude suggestions of expressions. After seeing it, he asks, "Is that a picture of you and your mom?"

"Yeah," I answer. Short.

There's a good ten second pause before he asks, "Well...where am I?" with an expectant shrug in his voice.

I don't answer. It would be too easy to remind him that he's an absentee parent.

"Aidin, why am I not in the Magna-drawing?"

Three careless strokes later and my dad is now in the portrait, but in all honestly, I'll probably erase him later.

"There...happy now? You're in the drawing," but already I'm plotting how to forge him into a bush or a small tree. Maybe a traffic sign.

"But I'm all the way in back," he says, offended, pointing at his tiny extremities and modest frame. "Look at how small you made me. I can't be bigger?"

I shake my head, "No, there's not enough space on this thing and it took me twenty minutes to draw mom's SUV."

"My head's the size of a Grape Nut," he examines critically.

I turn on my recorder and speak into the mic, "Item number nine: Magna Doodle drawing of family complete at 10:07 P.M., August 22nd. It makes proper use of vantage perspective and is an honest portrayal of this patient's emotional disposition regarding his parents."

I turn off the recorder and photograph the picture with my new Nikon camera.

That's another rule. Proof has to be documented of every completed item so Paradies is certain I'm not just checking things off my list to get through it faster. Everything has a result that is recorded in time with my reaction. Emotions are chronicled. Creations are spreading like wildfire. There'd be no way my hand could keep up with my current productivity, hence, the recorder.

I asked Paradies if I could do all the written stuff in audio and she said that would be okay.

"It's a pretty good idea," she complimented. "The tone of your voice will say more than whatever it was you planned on writing. Plus, it'll save me hours in trying to decipher your chicken scratches. No offense," she added.

So I picked up a recorder yesterday at Best Buy in addition to the Blackberry and other stuff I needed to get. I even managed to knock off an item while I was there.

Item #211: Buy your driver a gift. Keep in mind he spends more time waiting on you than driving.

I bought him a Playstation handheld and a few games to play. He looked happy when I gave it to him. Pleasantly surprised. He thanked me, a smile clearly evident in my voice when I said modestly, "No problem," before taking my usual seat behind him in the back.

Meanwhile though, in the here and now, my dad is still giving me shit.

"I can't believe your mother is allowing you to do this in the house," he says, shaking his head. "You *do* realize how silly this is, right? Oh, for fuck's sake, *please* tell me you do."

I dump out the contents of a Lincoln Log set in front of me and don't see pieces. It's not a random assemblage of criss-

crossing wood and plastic roofing. This isn't chaos. I see
potential. A blueprint. The future. Now all I have to do is build it.
"We've already established that you know how to destroy,"
Dr. Paradies had said in our last session. "Now let's see how well
you can create."
This is what my father can't understand, how what's
seemingly insignificant to him can mean the world to me. He
can't comprehend how we all have to start somewhere. Even if
you have every conceivable advantage working in your favor,
some people are late-bloomers—plain and simple.
Remember that when you think about how long it took
Einstein to come up with the Theory of Relativity or Dali's
discovery of Surrealism. Even the Son of God didn't *really* start
impressing people until his thirties, and considering what's
already being circulated about me at Circle of Healing, you might
say I'm ahead of the curve.
My father wouldn't, though.
He's still plenty disappointed.
"This is ridiculous...what you're doing here," he says, his
frustration openly building in his forehead and cheeks. "You see
this, don't you?"
I don't answer. It would just wind up lost on him, no matter
how insightful or enlightening the explanation was. "Habitual
dismissal," it's called in doctor's speak.
"Christ Aidin, you're hopeless."
He nudges my house of cards with a finger and it takes a
part of me with it when it falls. Something I had is gone now, and
I'm not even sure what it was.
"You're lucky I documented that already," I tell him in a
hard glare. "Could you please—for me, just *don't* touch anything
else? You're really fucking me up here."
"Sorry," he relents. "I thought it was glued."
"I'm gonna glue my foot in your ass if you don't stop
messing with me," I warn him, setting another log of the cabin in
its place.
"Well, *that* sounds unpleasant," he chuckles.
"Not for me," I say, still building. I force a grin and tell him,

"I wouldn't feel a thing."

He gives me a look that's either fear or respect. I'm not really sure which since the two look the same to me, but it lasts only a single sweet moment before we both hear it: a loud sharp *ping!* It's so loud my hand startles, knocking down one of the walls of my cabin. Construction has officially been put on hold. Arrested development.

"What's that?" he asks.

Item #14: Bake at least two products using an Easy-Bake Oven.

Embarrassment used to feel like carbonated bubbles surfing vertebrae after somebody flicked the spine—a tingle that fizzes at the base of your neck and skull, but not anymore. Not for me.

In doctor's speak I'm labeled as "emotionally challenged."

"You're about two steps away from Vulcan," Paradies told me.

"I think you're a couple cards short of a full deck, Aidin," my dad says. "Look, I understand that what you're doing is part of you're therapy and all, but the fact remains that your mom is cooped up in an office all day working with head-cases, and I'm working sixteen-hour days in a lab with a guy named Phil who won't shut up about *World of Warcraft*. Aidin, look at me. Put the cupcake down a second and look at me. Okay. I don't even know what *World of Warcraft* is. I haven't had sex in eight months. Maybe you needed to know that. Maybe you didn't, but the point here is I'm stressed out and you're a little bit of a failure to me right now. No offense, but you are. I'm not trying to hurt your feelings or anything but, as a father, I'm having some major regrets about having told your mother I was pro-life when we first met just to get in her pants. Anyway...that's...it's really neither here nor there. You need to get a job, Aidin. Understand? You need to get a job and go to school, because *this*, what you're doing here, it's not working. Phil may be an insufferable bore but his son is a neurosurgeon, so he must be doing something right that I'm not. He *must* be, because somehow Phil's son is pulling in seven figures while you're in here making cupcakes and playing kid's games on your mother's $120 per square foot imported Tahitian carpet. You see how this is a little bit of a problem for me? Well, guess what? Now it's *your* problem! It's your problem now, buddy boy! So here's what's gonna happen...you're going to get a job, you're going to get back in school, and you're going to get rid of these toys tonight. You hear me? *Tonight!* I don't want to hear any lip. I don't want to hear about your condition because *God knows* I've heard enough already. Just do it, okay. Do it and start making something of yourself. Now if you'll excuse me...I'm going upstairs to take a Xanax."

His steps fade as he exits and I remain unaffected.

I'm neither sad nor inspired. I'm not that beautiful little euphemism of emotion that's to be expected of me. The state of obligation to my father—I don't recognize it. Never have.

In doctor's speak it's called "passively defiant."

My father would just say I'm lazy. No quotations. Just lazy.

Not anymore, though. This time it's different. I'm different. Changing right before your very eyes. Now I've got a purpose. Direction. A motive. I know where I'm going and can't wait to get there.

It's all in the list.

"We have to find the inner-you," Paradies told me.

"Your soul is your personality," she said.

And I'm beginning to understand how this list works now because I feel it in every task I complete. Without fail. I feel it. Every word jumble and crossword puzzle is merely a means of deciphering myself. My Popsicle stick condo and Lego high-end loft unit aren't buildings. They're reflections of home. The Mr. Potato head family is my family, and dad is in his Tinker Toy lab. Frowning plastic eyes. My coloring book is my diary. The paint by numbers: my mood ring. An Etch a Sketch self-portrait. I'm so transparent yet part of a grander spectrum.

All alone on a Lite Bright landscape.

One in a million in the Sea Monkey society.

The things I build are actually building me, but this is only Section 1. This is only the beginning. The warm-up.

So far it's all been Play-Doh and jigsaw puzzles.

Train sets and model cars and activity books.

Fun and games is drawing to a close.

"You won't understand it at first," Paradies told me.

I understand it now.

I understand how my parents felt when they first got their doctorates. How a person feels when they score a touchdown or bakes a soufflé that doesn't collapse. The first time you win at computer solitaire. A successful oil change. I get it now.

You taste prosperity. Pride.

It feels good and you crave more.

I'm an addictive personality, though.

Remember that when this is over.

Remember how this wasn't my fault.

SESSION 16
ITEM #96

I tell the girl at the front desk that Dr. Paradies sent me but that isn't stopping her from asking me all sorts of questions, the kind of questions I don't feel like answering.

Jamie. Her nametag says **Jamie Reid** in raised black lettering, and what Jamie wants to know when I last ejaculated.

This is a touchy subject.

No pun intended.

"June 17th," I answer grudgingly. "Listen, don't you have my file here?" I ask, trying to avoid any further interrogation. "I coulda swore my doctor said she was going to send that over. You have it, right?"

"*May-be*...I don't know," she says dismissive. "Now, do you mean June 17th as in three months ago? *That* June 17th?" she asks, holding her pen and clipboard not totally unlike Paradies, except for the eye contact. She's looking right at me.

Her mouth asks questions, but her eyes are calling me a liar. She doesn't need to outright accuse me. It's written all over her face. Scrawled in wrinkles and folds and selective muscular tension—it's all right there plain as day, if you know what to look for.

I've gotten rather good at this.

Go to groups for long enough and you can know what a person's thinking without them needing to say it. The cutters at Circle of Healing are so broken they don't even bother trying to hide what they're feeling. What's within. The blinds and the deafs and the mutes—they're encouraged to drop their guard. We're all wearing our worst poker face. It's an unveiled wedding of connection.

Jamie asks, "And you're *certain* you haven't masturbated? You're sure?"

"I think I would've remembered doing that, Jamie. Seriously, can you just read the file?" I suggest again.

She says, "I don't know what I'm supposed looking for," flipping a couple pages, skimming. "Are you religious or something?"

"What?" My head ticks. "What does that have to do with anything?"

Jamie looks up from the file and ponders aloud, "Well, I just kinda figured since you don't masturbate and all that you might be, y'know...religious. It's totally okay if you are," she empathizes. "'Thou shall not touch thyself' or whatever...I get it."

"No, I'm not religious."

She looks back down at the file, "Well, that's just weird then." A pause. "I'm not religious, either, if that makes you feel any better," she says with a heartening smile. "Do you do drugs?"

"Why? What are you looking for?" I react in a kneejerk fashion, my standard response to any semi-attractive girl looking to score.

"No," she chuckles. "No, no, no. For the questionnaire. Do *you* do drugs?"

"Not any--" I cut myself off. I almost say "not anymore," but I'm trying to get through this as painlessly as possible. Again, no pun intended. If she wants to know what I've done or any mishaps, she can look in the file. It's all right there (I think).

Jamie checks the clipboard.

"Family illnesses?" she asks.

"Doctorates," I joke.

"Huh?"

"Nothing. Never mind," I say. "No family illnesses, as far as I know."

She makes another check on the clipboard and keeps questioning.

Occupation: unemployed
Education: high school
Income: trust fund
Marital status: single

Smoke: sometimes

Drink: not anymore

Check...check...check.

"Um...sexual orientation?" she asks hesitantly, her face wincing.

"Uh—*straight*," I tell her a little too firmly.

"Hey, you never know," she remarks non-apologetically before making another check. After a beat, she says, "Okay, Aidin, why don't you go ahead and walk down the hall to Room 3. There'll be a cup to put the sample in and some material available if you need assistance."

My fingers drum on the clean white counter, "Yeah...see, this is why you need to read the file. I'm going to need more than *just* material if this is going to happen for me."

"Well," Jamie stammers. "There's *plenty* of material in there. I'm sure you're bound to find something you like...and it's not like you're under a time limit. There's no rush or anything, although if it really *has* been three months, I would think you'd be done in no time," she assumes, smiling.

I'd kill for a proof object right about now.

A needle, a lighter, or a blade—anything.

"No," I tell her. "You're not getting it. I-don't-masturbate."

She incorrectly recalls, "Oh...right...you're religious."

"No, I'm not religious. I just don't masturbate. I can't," I tell her. "Now look...Jamie," I level with her, lowering my voice to a serious whisper. "I know there's gotta be a way to get me to come--"

"—Ejaculate!" she corrects, shouting. "We don't use the word 'come' as a clinical term here."

"Fine. *Ejaculate*," I relent, somewhat taken aback by her sensitivity to the issue. "I know there's some way to get me to do that without me...y'know...doing it."

"Sir," she says with one of her hands ticking in a cutting motion, as if she's saying to *stop right there*. "I appreciate the offer—it's sort of flattering, I guess...but even if I *wanted* to have sex with you, I certainly wouldn't do it here. I mean, *God*, how tacky would that be?"

I palm and rub my chin in frustration.

As you might expect, it doesn't help.

"I really don't know how to put this to you. If I go in there I could literally masturbate for five weeks and still not come. Do you understand? I'm not gonna be able to do this on my own. I need help," I admit, swallowing what little pride I had left.

She doesn't bother correcting me for using the word "come." Not this time. Instead, she just sort of glares at me, which is a good thing.

My anti-poker face is saying, "I'm not kidding."

In doctor's speak this is known as "unbridled honesty," otherwise known as "progress," in a grander scheme of things.

After a minute, Jamie says, "Ooooookay...I guess I'll send a doctor in to see you, then."

"Thank you," I say, somewhat exasperated. "Room 3?"

She nods, possibly embarrassed, though I have no idea why. I'm the one who just admitted ejaculatile dysfunction here. Not her.

Walking down the hallway now, it's already slipping my mind. On the left is Room 3, which I walk into, taking a moment to check it out since this is the first time I've ever been to a place like this. It has one of those examination tables just like other doctor's office; only this one isn't shrouded in that crinkly white paper on a spool. That, and it sits lower to the ground and has a TV/VCR combo at the foot of it. The counter, which would normally have a row of jars filled with swabs and cotton balls and tongue depressors, has porn in its place.

Magazines and tapes.

Penthouse and *Cheri*.

Playboy and *Swank*.

The tapes never exceed the year 1997 and most of them are part of a series.

Caught From Behind #31.

American Nymphos #18.

I flip through one of the magazines and the centerfold looks like every other girl I've ever had: blonde and airbrushed and inauthentic. Money is one of her turn-ons. Ripples in her breasts display an obvious boob-job. Her belly chain is crooked. My hand starts to shake and I put the magazine back.

There's no soul in there.

The door opens.

A woman in her early to mid-thirties walks in. She's wearing dark frames that are just a shade deeper than her shoulder-length hair. Her face is smooth with subtle features. The white lab-coat forces red lips to a focal point. I can't take my eyes away from that mouth. She introduces herself as Dr. Trask.

"You must be Aidin," she says.

Teeth are so white they look manufactured.

"Sorry about the confusion up front...my receptionist is a bit wet behind the ears," she smiles, those teeth stark white like business stationary.

"She accused me of being religious," I tell her displeased. "*And* gay."

"Well, *that* is certainly a contradiction in terms," she examines, chuckling slightly. "Like I said...wet behind the ears. Sorry," she apologizes while flipping a few pages of the file she's holding. My file. "So, I understand you're currently experiencing a somatic lapse?"

She's talking about the big numb.

Apparently, this one is just as fluent in doctor's speak as Paradies.

"Yeah," I say.

"And I understand you need some assistance in the donation process?"

I feel like I'm asking to borrow $50 from someone I already owe $1000 to.

"Right," I tell her.

She closes the file and places it on the beige counter.

"Okay, Aidin, go ahead and drop your pants down and place your palms on the counter," she advises, fitting herself with a pair of rubber gloves, snarling and squeaking as they friction against her fingers

"What? Why?!" I ask. Shocked.

"So we can get a sample from you," she casually states.

"Don't worry, you won't feel a thing."

That's what I'm afraid of.

"Hopefully, you don't have to be anywhere soon," she says, greasing up the index and middle fingers of her right hand with some sort of goopy, clear liquid. "Three months worth of supply might take a little while to get out."

"Nope," I say a little uneasy. "This was on my to-do list for today."

The life list of Dr. Paradies, Item #96.

"Very good," she says. There's a moment of awkward silence that I find harshly appropriate. A sort of "calm before the storm." The sound of her fingers penetrating my asshole reminds me of a fork spinning in a casserole.

A rubber goulash in KY Jelly sauce.

This is the main course of our prostate potluck.

I redundantly grimace at my own imagery.

"Relax," she says, her mouth smiling in soothe. "You're doing a good thing here today."

I'm only doing what I'm told.

Nothing more.

SESSION 17
SECTION 5

According to Dr. Paradies, the point of this particular section is to allow me to slip into a state where opinions naturally form on their own, to identify the "what" and the "why" of my personal preferences. It's the beginning of that discernible list of likes and dislikes that I didn't have before.

"Before," in the obtuse.

Before the numb.

Before the list.

Remember that about me, how I speak in two tenses now just like the blinds and deafs and all those razor-toting cutters at Circle of Healing, but never forget how this is as much about you as it is me. Open your minds.

In doctor's speak, it's known as "expansive thinking."

Two tenses.

A here and there.

A then and now.

The person you are at work doesn't necessarily carry over to the person you are at home.

School janitor by day. Your wife's personal Casanova by night.

You could be your boss's bitch and your son's hero.

This very well may be your daily duality, your double life. Everyone is at least two people: Miley Cyrus was Hannah Montana.

Spider-Man is Peter Parker.

Everything travels in pairs. I feel good when listening to certain songs or experiencing certain moments in films, but not the same kind of good as what a ball-draining orgasm or a three-line rack of cocaine feels like. There are things that feel good, and there are things that *make* you feel good, and I need to concentrate on the former. This is my major discovery. This is my denial holding up the white flag.

When I relay this to Dr. Paradies she says, "Congratulations, Aidin, I think you just made me proud of you," and when she tells me this she's smiling and truthful and looking right at me. For a moment the legal pad of notes is laid in her lap and positivity swells in the office.

It's the kind of moment you hope to have with your parents but I'll take what I can get for now. I'll be the good son once I master being the good patient because this process runs in steps. It's methodical. All I have to do is follow the list. Stick to the formula.

"Not once in the history of the planet has a soufflé has ever fallen to gravity," Paradies once said. "It's the chef's own fault if they can't follow directions. Not the food."

These things that I do, these items—they're all ingredients.

Every reaction and response: a soul fraction.

A recipe for a personality.

"Luck is when preparation meets opportunity," Paradies says. "Winning the lottery is never an accident. Ever. You give yourself the opportunity by buying a ticket. You were prepared by having the right numbers. It's just that simple."

Now try to define bad luck. Try to define me.

"When you learn to delineate the simple and uncomplicated...when you begin to understand the everyday things that are happening around you all the time, then and only then can you begin to decipher yourself."

I will be the result of a complex equation.

I'll be the outcome to a sequence of events.

The Mona Lisa is merely the final product of a few thousand simple and precise brushstrokes. The list is 366 items long.

How do you define masterpiece?

How do you define yourself?

"Just make sure you record it," Paradies said. "It's no good to me if you don't record it."

I've got hours of this stuff, hour upon hour upon hour of movie quotes and song lyrics and film reactions, audio playback of excerpts and descriptions by a man not finding his soul, but constructing one.

A montage of identity.

A compilation of self.

Sometimes they're short one-liners.

Other times I go into lengthy review.

Recorded reaction to rap music, sub-section of category 5: *"First, let me say that I've never actually listened to rap music. I've heard it...at the clubs and stuff. Passively, I might add, but after listening to it—analyzing it, even, I've come to terms with the fact that this might be the most disposable "artistic" medium in existence—and I'm using "artistic" pretty fucking loosely. The beats, I noticed, were recycled quite a few times or worse, in my opinion, stolen from another song. Thank you for having me listen to this in chronological order, because I wouldn't have noticed it. Point being is that the music...the part where instruments and artistry really come into play—is non-existent. But worse than that are the lyrics, a repeating cycle of "I drive 'this' kind of car, have 'this' much money, and have 'this' much sex, and smoke 'this' much weed—and I do all this while watching* Scarface,*" and then some sort of gangbanger bullshit is usually peppered in there along with area codes, etc. But how these guys really hook people is with the chorus, and that's usually the words "shake it like," and then that's followed up with the appropriate, seemingly clever, simile. They also frequently mispronounce words for stylistic purposes and use bad grammar...and then I looked into that. Did you know listening to this stuff lowers your IQ? Studies have been done on it. You get dumber while listening to this shit. Thing is...sitting here and listening to this stuff...it's...well, it's empty. There's no soul in there.*

Building a personality is much the same as building a house. You *always* start with the foundation. You build from the ground up. Never stray from your blueprints.

My case is no different.

Crawl before you walk.

"One thing at a time," Paradies said.

Item by item I fly right through it. With every album I listen to and film I watch, they're consistently reminding me how much the other senses have been neglected, my conscious mind, how I've been confining my life experience to the most pitiful and depraved genres.

Sex isn't love.

Drugs aren't happiness.

Ignorance slowly melts away.

I highlight and record all the lines in books that make sense to me, words that strike profoundly or propel me further towards my personal enlightenment.

"You are not how much money you have in the bank."

"No one will ever know anybody."

"Disappear here."

The characters I witness only reaffirm how much I don't want to be like them, how desperately I want to evolve if I can only find the means.

American Psycho – materialism.

Choke – sexual promiscuity.

Trainspotting – addiction.

Every novel is an item, and every item teaches me something I didn't know before, helps me identify my bad habits and dark rituals.

When I record the line "How am I not myself?" or can't shake the lyrics "Just 'cause you feel it doesn't mean it's there" out of my head—I know it's just one more step towards building a brand new me.

For the first time in years, I'm thinking clearly and critically. Opinions are forming. Impressions are being made. Convictions sculpt and harden.

My favorite rock band is Interpol. Radiohead is an extremely close second.

I think they should make *Requiem for a Dream* an integral part of the D.A.R.E. program, and I'm also of the mind that in this case the movie was better than the book.

Listening to the *Airdrawndagger* by Sasha is my audio

Xanax.

Dancer in the Dark taught me the meaning of sacrifice.

Item #222: After you have listened to all the albums in the music sub-section, I want you to compose a mix CD of your favorite songs. Refer to the Rob Fleming character in High Fidelity *(Item #198) if you need suggestions on how to put this together (i.e. - never putting two songs by the same artist back to back, etc.). Your CD should also include music from at least three different genres and duly note why you chose each particular song. Burn the disc in MP3 format and make sure it contains between twelve and sixteen tracks. This needs to be prepared and delivered to me by 4:00 P.M. on the 26th of August. No later.*

My mix CD:

1.) "Reckoner" by Radiohead

2.) "Obstacle One" by Interpol

3.) "Clark Gable" by The Postal Service

4.) "Pulling Our Weight" by The Radio Dept.

5.) "Summer Guest" by The Go Find

6.) "Joga" by Björk

7.) "God Moving Over the Face of Waters" by Moby

8.) "Mr. Tiddles" by Sasha

9.) "Lean On Me" by SFTG & Colein

10.) "Breathe" by télépopmusik

11.) "The Reeling" by Passion Pit

12.) "Electro Shock Faders" by Hooverphonic

13.) "Only This Moment" by Röyksopp

14.) "New Day" by Kate Havnevik

15.) "Swollen" by Bent

16.) "Everyday" by Carly Commando

My thinking here is that Paradies will listen to this to further advance her already in-depth analysis of me, that somehow the lyrics will speak for me in a way that I haven't in our numerous sessions, but I'm incorrect on this.

She won't listen to it, she won't open the case, and she won't even bother reading the track listing that I spent close to a half an hour writing out to make sure it was scribed legibly.

Paradies won't.

Someone else will.

SESSION 18
MORNING

August 27th.

Saturday.

5:47 A.M.

I wake up well over two hours before my alarm is set and decide to take this as an opportunity to knock out as many in-home items as possible before Paradies calls. When that will be, however, remains a mystery to me, as much of the rest of Section 7 does.

Item #312 - Be at The Velvet Dog on September 16th at midnight. Find a seat by the pool table and wait there.

Item #300 - Be at Reverse on the Plaza on September 28th at 7:00 P.M. Wear a black suit.

If an assassin wanted to take me out, all he'd have to do is cap the guy wearing the tux on 37th and Main holding the bouquet of white orchids. I'll be there next Saturday at 10:00 P.M.

Sharp.

With the big numb you have to invest your faith in other things, in other people. This is all one big progressive adaptation. You make do with what you have.

Night-lights are in almost every room of the house so I don't trip over my own two feet trying to make it to a light switch.

I don't put my wallet in my back pocket anymore because retrieving it looks an awful lot like I'm groping myself.

You compensate for what you lost with what you have left.

You anticipate and take precautions.

I carry around a spray vial of Acqua Di Gio because I can't hold in farts.

Every bite of food is chewed at least seventeen times to

ensure I don't accidently choke.

Make a small change to the million little everyday things that you do and it all adds up to one huge pain in the ass. Things that used to be second nature become a challenge.

Playing a video game is impossible when you can't feel the buttons.

The guy who said you never forget how to ride a bike never met me.

I could brag like this all day.

This is only a handful of the anti-glamour that's made me the living legend of Making Sense. I'm the king of inconvenience.

If you're licking an envelope and can't taste the glue, then you're not doing it right.

Your second sip of soup or coffee will let you know if the first one burned your tongue.

Live and learn.

Trial and error.

I take baths instead of showers to make sure I don't slip and land on my head. My Remington electric shaver keeps me from cutting myself. The toothbrush head has to be soft.

A million minor changes.

An army of adaptations.

"Try and see the bright side," Paradies said. "I've got cramps so bad today it feels like a horse kicked me in the stomach."

I say, "Yeah, that wasn't too much information at all."

"What?" she questions. "I'm just saying you're not the only one with problems. Don't be so negative." She scribbles on her legal pad. "Nice erection, by the way."

I look down and I'm sporting so much wood I could floor a basketball court. It's the last part of my body that's still in denial. Still hopelessly ignorant.

I, however, am doing great.

"Your list seems to be coming along quite well," Paradies observes, tallying up all the checked items in her notes. "I really liked the boat you carved and the photographs you took at the zoo."

Items #40 and 278.

"Thanks," I say.

Walk along a beach.

Meditate in a field.

Fly a box kite.

It's all in the list. These are the simple steps we take to form a personality, a soul. This is how we become more human. By 9:00 A.M. I'm back on it.

My father is at his lab.

My mother: her office.

I station myself at my iMac and double-click the first track from the Armin van Buuren album on my iTunes. The volume is set low. It has to be. With a computer I have to use my eyes and ears as much as my hands, maybe more.

If I don't hear the distinctive click of the mouse collapsing upon itself then it might not have happened.

The term "touch-typing" is a cruel joke. I have to look at the keyboard to make sure I'm hitting the right letters. "Sight typing," I call it. It's one of the many terms I've made up for my adaptive actions. I'm not the only one that does this, though. Everyone from Making Sense has their own little set of these.

The mutes and deafs don't speak, they sign.

Most of the blinds refer to their seeing-eye dogs as "guides."

We all have special names for our special habits, but that doesn't make us any more unique than you. Everyone does this.

Junkies don't shoot up; they "push off."

Bulimics never throw up. They "purge."

If you haven't thought of some clever term for your masturbation addiction or prescription pill habit then you better get on that. All the good names are going like hot cakes or flapjacks or short stacks or whatever else you want to call them. They're flying fast.

Prostitutes are known as "working girls."

Hockey groupies are called "puck bunnies."

At Making Sense I'm not numb. I'm out of touch.

This is the profile name I end up using for my MySpace page. Refer to the list if you don't know what I'm talking about.

Item #55: Create a MySpace page for yourself making sure that you include photos and descriptions about yourself and your interests. Blog at least once a week and make sure that you request friends on a regular basis. This would be a good place to start when searching for your Internet dates as per mentioned in Item #273.

This is exactly where conditional clauses come into effect.

I couldn't import photos onto my page until I learned how to use a camera (*Item #9*). I couldn't write about myself until I relearned how to type (*Item #202*). The part of my page about my favorite books and movies and music would've been blank had it not been for Section 5.

I think you get it.

Everything is progressive.

One thing leads to another.

Item #55 falls under the social skill building sub-section of my list.

"Who you are and who you portray yourself to be are rarely the same thing," Paradies said. "When a garbage-man says that he works for the city or a porn star says she's an actress—it's not necessarily a lie but it's not the whole truth, either."

Everyone is at least two people.

This is who I am and this is who you *think* I am.

If you've ever heard a plumber refer to himself as a utilities technician then you already know what I'm talking about.

Even if you only know one lame-ass card trick, technically, you can still call yourself a magician.

In doctor's speak your facade of overachievement is known as "misrepresentation."

Or: "falsification."

"Be who you are," Paradies told me. "If people can't accept that, well then, screw 'em."

I'm about seventy-three percent sure I smiled when she said that. It's nice to have someone in your corner.

"Don't be ashamed of the things that aren't your fault," she

says. "And more importantly, don't hide from them, either."
In doctor's speak this would be known as "anti-productive."
Paradies advises, "Just be honest."
The About Me section of my MySpace page deals heavily
with my condition, the when and the what.
My background image is a close-up shot of a sewing needle.
A gigantic proof object.
My avatar: a black and white profile shot.
I spend hours working on this: Importing photos (at clubs, at
home, in cars: Ferraris, BMWs and Benzes, with girls—Barbies
that I barely remember and will probably never see again), adding
captions where I sometimes make up the names of my dates (my
coke-whores and gold diggers) if memory fails to serve, and it
normally does. I copy and paste HTML codes: paragraphs of
alpha numeric/symbolic jargon somehow forming a photo or a
background image or avatar, an Interpol portrait or a playlist for
my music section. Everything is alphabetized: my movies and TV
shows, my music and books, even my interests. It's when I'm
doing this that I realize the therapeutic side of it, the actual point
of the item itself: that I'm not just building a personality, but
defining it, rather. I'm finally finding out who I am, so much so
that I can relay it to the world without shame or disgrace, free in a
way that I've never been, and so I keep going with Armin
providing the soundtrack: importing, uploading, and coding.
Blogging: about conditional drawbacks and scenic park walks,
the typos and mistakes in my keying drastically falling by the
hour. I see a cute girl in the "Cool New People" section and send
a friend request. I add my favorite bands, my favorite authors. An
e-mail comes in whose subject line reads: Big tit honey strip
pussy white slut muffin wetness. I sigh and report as junk, still
waiting on Paradies. It's almost noon and she still hasn't called.
Or e-mailed. Or text messaged. In movies it goes: *V for
Vendetta...The Virgin Suicides...Wedding Crashers.* "Breathe" by
télépopmusik gets added to my playlist. It goes *Donnie
Darko...Eternal Sunshine of the Spotless Mind...Fight Club,* and
my Blackberry goes off reminding me to drop a Colace.
Status: single

Religion: Agnostic

Children: someday

I finally find a decent Batman image in Photobucket (a Jim Lee) and place it in my "Heroes" section right under Spider-Man, and just over Paradies. I put Dr. Paradies in there sort of as a joke, but mostly not. For the most part I'm grateful. Sitting here, the Colace going to work on me and my insides, I realize it's because of her that I'm still here, still alive and well. It's almost as if she's made a career out of saving me: from drugs and bad habits, my condition, but mostly from myself. She's never failed and always delivered, and around six hours later she comes through yet again.

On Item #154. My reward.

She'll call and give me the "when" and the "where," and it'll be everything she said. Something I need. Something I can't buy. This will be everything I could ever want and it'll be more than perfect, more than I could ever imagine.

I need to tell you something first, though.

Otherwise, you might not get it.

SESSION 19
ITEM #273

Fact: I don't date.

Why? No need.

Dating is for people who have to take a girl out first before they can get laid, and with bottle service at the best table at Hush, I've never had to do that. With a high limit AmEx and a Ferrari you don't ask for dates. You don't bother because these Barbie clones throw themselves at you. They don't make you go through the filtering and refinement process, and that's exactly what dating is.

A try-out.

An interview.

Being attractive and charming only gets you so far. It gets you at a table with her, and from there on out it's what restaurant you go to and the kind of car you drive. You are a pay grade and embossed magnetic plastic.

It's a shocker they don't request references and W-2s, your last three places of employment and medical records.

"I can't believe I have to do this," was my first reaction, rereading Item #273 for about the fifth time on the office chaise lounge, failing to comprehend the point.

"Well, you have to," Paradies said. "This is one of the most important items on the list and I won't have you half-assing it."

Think about all the things that seem redundant and pointless:

Playing poker by yourself.

Writing a postcard you'll never send.

Or doing something that leads to sex that you can't have, and when I say, "have," what I really mean is "feel."

"No, no, no," Paradies says, shaking her head. "You need to understand that this isn't about that. Can't you just trust me?"

I shrug.

"God, Aidin, you're such a Gemini!"

Whatever that means.

This is just another step in my evolution.

We're inching beyond my comfort zone.

"This isn't that hard," she says, making notes. Knuckles white. "Reread the directions. You're making this more difficult than it really is."

Item #273: You will go on a series of dates. This would **not** *include picking up a girl at a bar and getting her drunk enough to want to have sex with you. Dates will be defined by you picking said date up at her home and making sure she returns safely and satisfied with the evening. Your dates shall pay for nothing (even if they offer, you will politely refuse). A date should also consist of dinner and at least one other activity (movie, concert, etc.); however, a good date is one that is well planned. You should have your entire evening mapped out beforehand so as to please your date to the best of your ability; that is to say, if your date were an artist, for example, an art gallery might be a good idea. Be spontaneous, but be prepared. Women are attracted to men that have confidence and control. Keep this in mind when you plan your evenings. You must go on each type of date.*

*someone under 21 but older than 17
*someone at least ten years your senior
*with someone of a different race
*one set up through the Internet
*a fifth date of your choice

Do <u>not</u> *under any circumstance date anyone from Circle of Healing or Making Sense. Groups are for rehabilitation and that alone. You may date whomever you'd like as long as they're not in one of those groups. Report on all dates in detail. I'm looking for physical descriptions, what you did, times, places, topics of conversation, and your feelings as to how it went.*

Paradies smirks, "Trust me, kiddo...you'll see the lesson in this if you let yourself."

The thing I really hate about Paradies is that she's always right. She's a big goddamn know-it-all, which is probably why she costs what she does (not sure what that is exactly since my mom pays that bill, but I'm assuming it's a lot).

The problem with most guys is that when they're asking a girl out on a date they're typically speaking from below the waist, from that second head.

They say: "I'd like to take you out to dinner."

Translates to: "I'll feed you if you fuck me."

I'm not programmed this way.

Not anymore, that is.

There's a big difference between doing something because you want to and doing something because you're supposed to. Girls aren't so apprehensive when they know for a fact you don't want sex. When it's an impossibility. The guard goes down. Honesty can take you a long way, and that's what's so unfortunate about this.

I'm giving these girls so much *less* than what they bargained for. A letdown for the ages.

I meet Holly while I'm on assignment at Guess.

Refer to Item #300 in the "acts of selflessness & generosity" subsection if you don't know what I'm talking about. It mostly consists of picking up tabs and doing small favors for people I don't know and will never see again. Random acts of kindness. Random to them, anyway.

I walk up to the socialite-in-training behind the glass counter, this little tan chick hovering over the watch and bracelet display. Remove my card. She half-smiles and I think I return it.

"Can I help you?" she asks.

"Yeah," I say, placing the card on the counter, the AmEx. "Whoever comes up here next, could you go ahead and pay for whatever they get with this?" I ask, motioning to the plastic.

She gives me a look. Incomprehension.

I tell her, "I'm gonna get a pair of jeans, so I'll sign for it when I find the ones I want."

And still, the same look.

"Oh, and if you could *not* tell whoever it is that I'm the one paying for their stuff, that would be nice, too," I add. "Just say the store is picking up the tab or something, okay?"

Mouth slack, she finally manages, "...uh...okay," accepting the card into her possession as I make my way over to the jeans section, the tired tan labels reading slim fit and boot cut and relaxed waist. A variety of different cuts and contours to ensure that these not only fit, but fit well, and all the while I'm thinking about how this couldn't matter less to a man in my situation. With the big numb some things become simplified. There's no such thing as "too tight in the crotch" or "too loose in the thigh," the lack of choice mesmerizing as I stand at the racks, the tap on my shoulder unnoticed and distant to me in this daydream.

"Hello?"

Turn.

Hay blonde. Maybe 21 or 22. Cute. Total hand-holding snuggle bunny.

"Hi," she says shyly.

I say hi back.

Her lips purse a little. Unpainted.

She asks, "Did you happen to pay for this, by any chance?" holding up her bag in front of her person, thin white handles glued to glossy red paper. The current dilemma is: I'm supposed to remain anonymous but I'm not supposed to lie, either. That's another one of the list rules. Number six, I think.

I glance over at the cashier who's already staring at me, cringing apologetically as I slow pitch my "I thought I told you not to say anything" look.

"Don't worry," the blonde says. "I knew she was full of it when she tried to tell me the store was paying for it. Like a place that charges $200 for jeans would do that," she observes, smiling at the absurdity of the idea. "So...what? Is that your pick-up move or something? You go into a nice store and buy clothes for a girl you've never met?"

I snicker boyishly. "No," I tell her.

"Well...*what* then?"

If I enlighten her about my list we're looking at a ten-minute conversation I'm not sure I want to have, so instead I plainly state, "Practice random acts of kindness."

I don't lie.

I selectively tell the truth.

Lawyers have been using this little trick for years to win big cases and pick up after-hours courtroom groupies, women who don't seem to notice or care about that hunk of platinum on their ring finger, the thing that gets taken on and off so much there's not even a tan line.

Sometimes it's what you *don't* say that matters most, and I'm no exception, the difference being that I have no ill intentions. I'm simply doing what I'm told. Nothing more.

"I'm Holly," she says.

"Aidin."

A pause.

"So...Aidin, are you *sure* that wasn't a pick-up move?"

I shrug. "Only if it worked."

She eyes me. Little green eyes go up and down.

"Yeah," she says, nodding not just in agreement, but in approval. "I think it just did."

We're on for tomorrow night.

For all my misadventures and reputation as a playboy, the truth is I know absolutely nothing about women. That is to say, nothing important.

"You know how to buy them things," Paradies said in one of our recent sessions. "You know how to give them drugs and alcohol, and granted, that may be the kind of thing that they're looking for at that particular moment, but that's not a relationship nor the beginnings of a healthy one."

In doctor's speak, she called it "a deficiency in personal relations."

Club rats and socialites, I know. Give me a sober, normal girl, and I'm completely ignorant, so when I approach one, I'm basically copying the male leads in all the romantic comedies and chick flicks I've seen. The ones on the list.

Such as: *Pretty Woman.*

And: *Jerry Maguire.*

You've heard this stuff a million times but it hits you like a slap in the face when it's transposed into life.

When you tell a woman that your dream is to slip her inside

the comfort a Donna Karen and take her to the opera after a five-course meal at The American Restaurant, they usually shake their head as if to say, "Did I *really* just hear him say that?"

That's what Lisa the 38 year-old paralegal did.

We're all set for the weekend.

The problem I'm running into is that I don't have the same wants as most guys. As all guys, I should say. Not anymore. When a person of my age and orientation takes you out and not only refuses sex, but doesn't have the slightest interest in fooling around, then obviously, something's amiss.

Even the Christians act on their impure thoughts at church camp, so what's my excuse?

I'm not gay. I'm not religious.

This isn't a matter of principle.

I'd like to say, "It's not you, it's me," but how lame would that sound?

It's this roadblock in my intimacy that always has my dates concluding with a bad twist ending. It's like watching *Cruel Intentions* for the first time with someone who's already seen it. One of you cries and the other can't because they knew about the main character's demise from the opening credits.

They cry but I can't.

Each time. Every time.

An example:

Kara is 19. I pick her up at her apartment complex in the extended Lincoln town car bearing flowers. Standard red roses. We have a nice dinner at PF Chang's on the Plaza and then go for a ride in one of the horse-drawn carriages. I drape her with my Claiborne blazer when her body shivers and she curls into me, her face pressed into my chest. We ride along in comfortable silence. The Plaza and traffic lights are bright and busy, but never to the point of distraction. Hoof beats and quiet engines providing a relaxing soundtrack. All things amber under the streetlamps in a way they could never be in daytime. We're too comfortable for my own good.

"I've always wanted to do this," she speaks, lips lavender, but smiling. Happy in a way that isn't drunk or pill-induced, and therefore, unfamiliar to me. I slip the driver a fifty for an extra trip around the Plaza, but it goes by too fast. The experience is simple but hands me this emotion that is new and examined not long enough to know. It's reminiscent of a movie. Remembered in lyrics. I'm not romantic, but I think I'm projecting it, perhaps in a way I've done before, yet the moment is over before I can decipher it. We're back at the car and ready to depart, my date happy and myself in a state of emotional unrest. Kara has champagne in the limo on the way back to her place. I nurse a Perrier mineral water, the both of us holding our respective silence until we pull into her parking lot and step out onto the chipped uneven pavement. Faded yellow lines.

Still draped in my blazer with cheeks rosy and wind-whipped, she asks, "Do you have to go?" A *yes-or-no* question, but the look she gives me removes half the answers.

"No," I say, but already I'm regretting this. I know I'm setting her up for disappointment and myself for a possible embarrassment.

"Will you come in?" she asks, hope actively warming her face, the purple in her lips fading to a deep red. She suggests, "We can watch a movie or...whatever."

The movie I can handle. It's the "whatever" part that concerns me, but I decide to gamble it. Maybe it won't turn out bad this time.

"Okay," I tell her. "Let me send Frank home."

"I'm gonna go inside and change," she tells me. "It's cold tonight."

I nod. She walks in, the gales passing faster now, still unfelt but a siren to seasons changing.

"Do you need me to stick around?" Frank asks when I round to the driver's side window. "I got the new *Madden* if you need me to wait."

"Nah, go ahead and call it a night," I tell him. "I'll call a cab or something if I need to get home."

He says he'll see me tomorrow and disappears into the evening, and the moment those red taillights fade from view I wish I had asked him to stay. Just in case. Just so I don't find myself waiting for Yellow Cab in a strange part of town yet again, but I don't. I pace inside the apartment building and enter her unit, door left ajar.

It's candlelit.

A soft orange glow resonates on Kara's young nude body, turning all her edges vignette. She steps to me, runs a slow finger down my chest to my stomach, and speaks. She speaks to me. Into me. Into my eyes.

"I couldn't find anything to wear."

I play hard to get just like I always do.

"Didn't you want to watch a movie?"

She undoes my top button.

The one on my pants. Not my shirt.

"I don't think I'd have the attention span for that right now," she says, her hand pulling me out. "And I don't think you do, either."

I look down and I'm hard.

My last shred of denial walking tall.

And that's what makes this so difficult.

What the old me wants the new me doesn't understand.

She guides my body to turn and pushes me onto the couch.

It's the same scenario all over again. A dejected déjà vu.

Just like Hush, this is an ever-changing sameness. Each time, every date.

Asian Jen will ask with smoky tears in her eyes, "Is it something I did?" nude and desperate as I walk out of her home, crying on her silk-shrouded bedroom pillows amongst the many stuffed animals decorating her bed. She'll sob herself to sleep on top of Hello Kitty and Pikachu and the like—surrounded but alone.

The message from Chelsea reads:

I really don't know what to think right now. I had a great time with you last night and I thought things were going well but...I don't know. I don't understand what happened when we got to my place. I thought we were clicking.

Maybe I came on too strong??

I'm sorry if I did but it felt right to me. If was aggressive it's

only because I went after what I wanted.
You can't be mad at me for that, right?
If you want to go slow (which obviously you do) then that's
okay. I would really like to see you again :)
This, of course, is both our faults.

When she looked at my profile she saw a Ferrari and name brand clothing and opportunity. She saw husband material. Security and stability. When you go hunting for a boyfriend on the Internet, more often than not, you see what you want to see.

I'm equally to blame because I didn't correct her.

There's a lot that I did wrong.

I shouldn't have assumed that she looked at my page, read about me (about my condition), and figured everything out. I shouldn't have let myself think it would be so cut and dry because everyone I've met and known—they've all had questions. They wanted details and proof, the story about "the before" and after.

Everyone is two people, though.

This is who I am and this is who you *think* I am.

We can talk about movies and music and books and everything else under the sun, or we can talk about my condition, my handicap, and I can spend the entire evening having you feel sorry for me. It's not really a choice, and it's no wonder this will never work, because once you get past dinner and conversation and romance, once the date is over, it shifts right over to intimacy, and I simply can't do it.

A mute can't say "I love you" just like a deaf will never hear it. I'm limited just like them. A kiss could never be faked by me. I'd do it wrong and they'd know. My erections are random and fickle, and whether my inability to stay hard or climax came to light first, either way, they'd know. The closer I get with anyone the higher the risk of exposure, and I'm not ready for that. Feeling vulnerable and helpless is something I've had enough of.

Now you might say that I'm misrepresenting myself.

I'm not lying but I'm selectively telling truth.

This isn't complete honesty.

You might say that.

But remember the rules, the stipulations and definitions. All dates should return home safe and satisfied with the evening. They should be happy, and in that respect I constantly succeed. The item and its directions are followed through to the slightest detail, which is the part that matters to me. To Paradies. It's when the date is over that I realize a simple truth:

These girls are just as much a lost cause to me as I am to them.

This is what needs to be understood when we move on.

I think we need to talk about my reward now.

Let's go back to the 27th.

SESSION 20
AFTERNOON

When I finally get done with my MySpace page it's late afternoon, around five 'o clock, and still no word from Dr. Paradies.

Not a phone call.

A letter.

A smoke signal.

None of those things.

"Impatient" doesn't describe me but it's damn near close. Every e-mail and text message I've gotten today inspires a sort of frantic rush to check it, a vehement craze.

At 2:13 P.M. Text message.

From Kimberly (typical Barbie clone).

It reads: *Haven't seen you at Hush lately...heard you were sick. What's up?*

At 3:01 P.M. An e-mail.

Junk is always a nonsensical string of words. The subject line reads: boobs pink double-penetration preteen angel fuck Latina sausage.

Or they read: Want a bigger penis?

Or: Your penis could be SO much bigger!

Or: Think your girlfriend is cheating on you? Try a bigger penis!!

If a strange woman comes up to you in a club and says, "Russian tranny black toy anal car baster facial cake," then prepare to have your brains fucked out for the low price of $24.95 per month.

If she says, "Skank blondie daughter corn muffin rim job dress," then you got yourself a threesome on your hands.

After a few hundred of these you start to learn the lingo.

Sexual Swahili.

That, and you start to feel horribly insecure about your manhood. Even a guy wielding a foot-long cock that could double as a murder weapon will start to have some self-doubt.

Not me, though.

I'm two-fold annoyed over here.

Every message I get *isn't* from the one person I want it to be from, and for every one I junk and delete, I get two more. Spam multiplying like Gremlins.

Eventually, one comes in that says, "Wanna have sexual intercourse with a beautiful girl?" and I spend the next ten minutes trying to figure out what that could possibly mean without opening it. Just so you know, it was State Farm pitching their new insurance plans.

Just like people, e-mail is always at least two things.

This is who I am and this is who you *think* I am. They'll say anything just to get you to go that extra step of opening them up.

If the subject reads: "I love you," then stay the hell away from it because it's probably a virus.

A Spyware pop-up is a magazine subscription ad.

The game at the top of your browser window that says, "Shoot three bears, and win an X-Box 360!!!" wants your organs.

Beware of the words "FREE!" and "Winner!" and "prequalified" because the next page you'll see wants to know your credit card and social security number.

*Just to verify your age.

*To verify your U.S. citizenship.

Which really means, "So we can find the appropriate sized jar to put your balls in."

Understand duality because it might just save your life.

When you're finally able to translate the phrase "Nipple candy smoking Tequila sex condom" to its actual meaning, then you might stand a chance in this world.

Everything is of at least two minds. Two meanings.

If you learn one thing from the Internet, learn that.

I refresh the window of my MySpace page and I've got a new message and a new friend request, both from some chick named Chelsea located out in Overland Park.

The subject reads: Nice Ferrari:)
Translates to: I'm a shallow whore.
I play it nice for the sake of the list.
See Item #273 for details.
It's six o'clock when I finally get a text from Paradies.
It reads: > *Frank will pick you up in a half an hour. Dress casually but nice, and don't eat anything. Have fun:)*
The T-shirt is faded sky blue with a modern design incorporating birds and swirls and cursive lettering (a design Urban Outfitters probably stole from somewhere), and the jeans are a classic boot cut, by Armani, dark blue with fade print on the upper-thigh. Shoes: Aldo loafers. Black. Leather. This saves me about an hour when you take into account all the tying and retying I do throughout the day. And on the left wrist: an armband. Also black, also leather with button-snap fastening.
I look good, I'd like to think, examining myself in a full-length mirror. Satisfied.
I feel good, too. Not literally, of course, but I'm excited. If I could feel an appetite it probably would've slipped away by now with how anxious I am, waiting for Frank to show up. My guts should feel carbonated and bubbly, but no. Impatience and the inability to sit still or concentrate on anything but this appointment consume me. The reward, something I've come to analyze and speculate upon as the date drew closer, never coming up with any definitive answers.
Frank finally coasts into the circle lot of the house, and when I ask him where we're going he gives me the same guilty "you know I can't tell you that" shrug, waiting until my door closes before pulling out of the drive, suburbia turning into traffic as we hit the interstate. Sun ready to set in the distance.
A movie plays in the car.
Lost in Translation.
I nurse a Perrier and get to the part where Bob and Charlotte speak for the first time in the hotel bar before we stop. We're parked in front of the Hyatt downtown near Crown Center and my Blackberry goes off.
The message from Dr. Paradies reads: *Skies restaurant...you*

have a reservation.

Frank says, "I'll be out here if you need me," retrieving his Playstation handheld from a mesh case, adaptor penetrating cigarette lighter.

I remove myself from the extended Lincoln town car, still holding the Perrier. People in the rounded lot eye me, some of them expecting to see more than just myself filing out, I suppose. Three bellhops. Two doormen. Three young women in dresses (ice pink, powder blue, and black) with three penguin-clad dates, an older couple, a businessman holding a Blackberry not unlike mine. A mother arranging her car to be valet parked with a child patiently waiting beside her.

I follow the businessman in through the revolving door that leads to the lobby. There's an opulent chandelier, three different check-in desks and two gift shops. A near-desolate hotel bar. About eight couches. People walking and moving. Moving with purpose. I find an elevator and board it. There's a silver plaque next to the button I press reading: ***Skies Restaurant***

Elevators used to make me nauseous.

Now I have a hard time telling if they're moving.

It tones when the top floor is reached not a moment too soon. Doors open. I step out, and within ten paces is the maitre de standing at his glazed wooden podium. I give him my name.

"I have a reservation...sorry I'm late," I add, just in case I am.

"No, sir. You're right on time," he smiles. "This way," and we begin walking toward the outer-rim of the restaurant.

Side note: *Skies is one of Kansas City's premier restaurants, best known for its physical rotation and floor-to-ceiling windows. The center of it remains stationary while its outer dining ring revolves, thus, patrons will see the entire surrounding skyline every forty-five minutes.*

My mother took me here for lunch once when I was younger, but I got too nauseous to enjoy the view. This is the first time I've been to Skies since then, and oddly enough, this is first time I've ever been slightly thankful for my condition's presence knowing nausea won't be a factor in what I'm assuming is going to be an important night.

I follow the maitre de slowly. Carefully. His scent, what is very likely the new Kenneth Cole, creates a pleasant wake as my fingertips land and leap from handrail to table edges. Poising. Outside is dark geometry: a skyline of crooked teeth representing the cubicle within the office within the floor within the building. Fluorescent rectangles flag the late-night weekend worker. The go-getters obligated by overtime.

"Here we are," he says, halting.

The maitre de pulls out my chair for me to be seated and politely states, "A waiter will be right with you," quickly departing back to his post.

I seat myself in the chair. Across the table of wood and bleached white cloth is a girl. Kool-Aid red hair. Fair skin. Rosy cheeks. Shiny-flavored lip-gloss. Marshmallow Meltdown, the stick on the table reads. To the right of that is a pink cell phone. Next to that is a purse. A black Coach. Magenta C's on lead background. Very expensive-looking. Hair is sleek and styled. Shards of it hang over Dior sunglasses. She's wearing the kind of sunglasses Paris Hilton made famous: huge pearl frames with deep dark lenses. Her ears are pierced and occupied, but by headphones. Not earrings, though she has the punctures to accommodate them. Earbuds are planted firm, stemming white wires from her ever-nodding head to the iPod in front of her. Also pink. Pink like the phone.

"Just let me finish this song," she says loudly enough to get the surrounding three tables to look over, rousing a stir.

I mouth the word "sorry" to one of them and turn back to her, unable to avert my eyes from the device's screen. The bottom of it, which would be the top from her viewpoint, reads upside-down to me: Aidin's Mix

And before I can process that, she's popping the earphones out.

"I've been listening to this all day," she smiles. "You've got good taste. I love Röyksopp."

And then she extends her hand through the air to greet me.

Dana. She says her name is Dana.

And Dana is my reward.
Item #154

SESSION 21
SKIES

The first thing Dana has me do is light up one of her cigarettes. People like us do this kind of stuff all the time. These favors.

For the convenience.

Just to save time.

"Quick, like a bunny," she whispers sharply, manicured hands motioning in the universal sign language for "hurry."

You can usually tell how long someone has been deaf based on whether or not they can read lips. This sort of thing comes in handy when you have an explosive case of diarrhea in department store with not a moment to spare. You either learn to read lips or risk shitting yourself, waiting for the directions.

The industry term for deafs that still use notepads to communicate are known as "paper trained."

With cigarette in hand, Dana smolders, "The reason a lot of these so-called 'classy' restaurants don't allow smoking is really just a con. One cigarette could make all the difference between ordering dessert or the check."

She takes another drag. Breathes, "You take fifty pieces of Oreo Cookie pie that could've been cigarettes, and this place is raking in an extra $250 a night."

It's known as a "health scam."

It's when you charge more for the wholesome alternative.

Such as: Subway sandwich restaurants.

And: Organic fruits and vegetables.

With smoke dancing from her lips, Dana says, "That cigarette sounds really good when you think about the 500 calories that could be swimming to your ass and thighs."

If you ever want to know what it's like, if you ever want to suddenly lose your ability to speak or hear or communicate, all you have to do is forget to pack your translative Dictionary. Leave behind your guide of commonly used international phrases, your maps and foreign currency tables. Just hit up Mexico or Peru or Iraq and watch how irritated the locals get when you're tapping your crotch because you don't know where a public restroom is. See how long you last when all your directions are given in the metric system and foreign tongues.

And above all else, *wear a fanny pack.*

Foreigners *love* Americans in fanny packs.

"The things that are designed for our protection or well-being," Dana continues. "You can bet your ass somebody's capitalizing somewhere."

If it's safer it's more expensive, but chances are, you never needed it in the first place. Think about this the next time someone tries to set you up with hurricane insurance on your Mid-western farm property.

We're all preparing for a worst-case scenario that never was or will be.

"My mom got pulled over the other day for not wearing her seatbelt," Dana says with a wry sort of grin. "You know the justice system is fucked when they can ticket you for that, but when some asshole passes the AIDS virus or a coward walks by a woman being raped in an alley, life moves on."

The phrase "For your own good" could double as a threat.

"This hurts me more than it hurts you," is another favorite.

"It's illegal to pay for sex in this country, but what do you think the guy over at the next table is working towards?" Dana poses.

And I can't help but look.

The woman in the fancy black dress with the chemical tits spilling out the top drops her fork. She gives her date the "aren't you going to do something?" look but nothing happens. Nothing, because this is real. It's truth. It's this kind of honesty that people beg for but can't handle once they get it. This is the puppy you begged for all year but couldn't wait to get rid of the first time it shit on your carpet or chewed up your Malibu Barbie.

Recall the phrase: "Careful what you wish for."

And: "Don't bite off more than you can chew."

"Ever notice how you need a permit to fish or hunt or carry a gun?" Dana puts out there. "But when someone wants to bring a baby into this world, all they have to do is not pull out."

She says, "Everything is a double-standard."

And she says, "Right and wrong can be the same thing."

The crucifixion of Jesus Christ.

Stem cell research.

That's about as bipartisan as it gets.

And with the cutest little smirk of mischievousness, Dana tells me, "You are going to make a great boyfriend, I think."

The waiter with his blinding white shirt and smile combination, this little tip-hounding ass-kisser, he says, "Miss, I will have to ask you to put that out."

This is a *non*-smoking establishment, he tells us.

Everyone is at least two people.

One minute you're this.

The next minute you're that.

Dana's smoking hand plunges the cigarette into her own flute of wine, the cherry hissing like a pissed off cobra. She daintily mentions to the waiter, "I think we'll try a red next." Her pointer finger ticking in his direction, "And God help you if you bring merlot to this table."

He takes the soiled glass and walks away.

But I'm still thinking, *Boyfriend?*

Where did that come from?

"I know about your list, Aidin," Dana reveals, those big black lenses peeling right through me something alien and fashionable. "It's no big secret," she says. "Dr. P gives all of her patients one."

"When they're ready for it," Dana adds.

Refer to the post-denial stage. That's where I'm at right now.

"I'm kind of a cheater, though," Dana admits. "Technically, I'm supposed to light my own cigarettes," she smiles.

Dana is a blind.

Just an FYI.

When Jackson Pollack first discovered the drip-method of painting, no one cared about the final product. Not really. It was all about process, and even that came about by accident.

"A word from the wise," Dana says. "Don't concentrate on the point. That'll get you nowhere fast." A little sigh. "Instead, try to think of everything as a moment."

Find ways of feeling that don't involve your hands or mouth or penis, she says.

Already, I sort of get this.

Type with your eyes, not with your fingers.

Eat with your ears, not with your mouth.

Feel with that blood-pumping organ known as your heart, but not literally, of course.

In doctor's speak this is called "sensory substitution."

Dana asks, "Could you be a doll and slide that over to me?" when the waiter comes over with the red and begins pouring into a fresh wine flute.

I say, "Four inches in from your right hand."

She smiles and thanks me before taking a sip.

I think I smile, too. The waiter walks off.

Dana says, "Y'know, we should probably go to my room to hang out. They're for sure gonna spit in whatever they serve us."

She laughs when I tell her I didn't feel like eating anyway, a numb joke.

Dana packs up her things. I leave a hundred on the table.

And now the real learning begins.

SESSION 22
ROOM 1224

Think about a store you frequent. The one you go to the most. This could be the place where you pick up your monthly allergy prescription or buy your week's supply of TV dinners, your Red Baron pizzas and Ora Ida potato products.

This is your shopping Mecca.

Maybe it's Walgreen's or CVS or Osco Drug.

It could be Hy-Vee or the Price Chopper on the corner.

You've been to these places countless times. And everything is organized. Catalogued. There's a place for everything and everything is in its place. Stocked and shelved and faced.

"Imagine yourself in a grocery store where the sheepskin condoms are located in the bread aisle," Dana says. "See yourself walking by a stalk of broccoli next to a T-bone steak next to a roll of toilet paper in the school & art supplies sector."

You pick up your one-hour prints in produce.

Customer service is located in the stockroom.

Soups and sodas are in the frozen foods aisle.

"This is sort of what being blind is like," Dana tells me. "Nothing is ever where it's supposed to be and no one is around to help when you need them."

Vanilla pudding is in Asian foods.

The Asian foods are in the bakery.

The bakery is in the parking lot.

"Every day is a sort of scavenger hunt," she says, absently running her fingers through her hair, the ones not holding my hand. "If I don't remember that I put my keys on the dining room table or the last place I set my purse, I'm a little bit fucked."

There's a sale on charcoal in the baby aisle.

A red light special on milk in the salad bar.

Dana digs a card out of her back pocket and produces it for me. "Key," she announces.

I accept it from her and unlock the door.

"You know what I love about hotel rooms?" Dana asks aloud, parading inward. "The consistency."

Floor plan cloning.

Every room has at least a few hundred identical siblings.

Dana saunters about the space, informing as she goes, "Beds to the left. TV on the right."

She makes a left turn in between the beds, using their edges to navigate the corners with her hands.

"Nightstand and lamp between the beds."

She opens the top drawer.

"Bible no one will read," she concludes before sprawling backwards on top of the comforter, closing the drawer with her foot.

She says, "If this blanket is as ugly as it is itchy—boy, we're in some sort of trouble."

That classic foliage pattern of green and brown and red.

Think of a Venus flytrap vomiting after too many tequila shots.

At least the view outside is nice: the stars and lights.

"Do you think you could come sit by me?" Dana openly asks the room. "I kinda feel like I'm talking to myself over here."

I move to the bed as requested.

Sit.

She throws a leg over one of mine.

"That's better," she says.

Blinds are like this. If they can't touch you or hear you, to them, you don't exist. People can disappear into thin air from three feet away. Anyone can be David Copperfield if they shut up for more than a few seconds.

"So you feel *nothing*?" she asks me. "How does that work with pooping?"

I tell her about my schedule, the Colace. Unlike the other girls, I don't have to beat around the bush with Dana. She's already "in the know" as they say.

"I usually take a bath afterwards," she tells me. "Y'know...just to be sure."

And suddenly it dawns on me why Paradies wanted this to happen. This meeting. Dana's problems are my problems, but not exactly the same. Strange places are a threat. We both can't drive. Dr. Paradies is our shared physician, but even though the advice doesn't translate over to the other, perhaps we understand each other through a mutual empathy. Most importantly, Dana talks. She speaks her mind. She has opinions and views, and is the polar opposite of all those Barbies I've met at Hush and places of a similar nature. Dana's a little jumpy with her topics and it can be difficult to keep up with at times, but she's interesting to me. Intriguing. Definitely not what I'm used to. My inverse, since I'm kind of on the quiet side.

I've spent time with blinds before at group but I've never spent *time* with one.

There are two sides to every story, and now I'm seeing how the other half lives.

"Just because I can't see a beautiful day doesn't mean I don't enjoy it," Dana speaks, her bare foot moving up and down my leg. Slow. "I smell the grass...the flowers and trees in the wind. I can feel the warmth of the sun kissing my cheeks. The birds singing...I never noticed those things before," she recalls longingly.

Dana uses "before" the same way I do.

The same way all of Making Sense does.

Such as the quote: "You don't know what you got till it's gone."

And: "Absence makes the heart grow fonder."

Dana sits up and positions herself so her butt is against my thigh with her legs over mine. We're face to face. Lights are low and the room, the world, is quiet. She says, "I know a little bit about you, Aidin."

The reflections of my eyes are wide open in her sunglasses when she tells me, "You're the kind of guy that can just buy any girl he wants and throw her away, aren't you?"

I don't answer.

When you're right you're right.

"And you know what?" she continues. "I used to be the same way."

Only at your worst do you find out who your real friends are.

It's only when you're blind and scared and running through the dark that you see who's willing to walk you through it.

"I don't think you're any stranger to abandonment," she ventures, and even with those huge Dior frames hiding her eyes, I can still see those eyebrows of hers shrugging...relating...empathizing, through the blades of candy red hair.

Whether it's sticking a sewing needle in your arm or not being able to navigate a Burger King by yourself, it's all the same.

"It becomes nearly impossible to trust people, but you're so desperate you'll trust anyone," she says.

And, "Nothing is simple or easy. No one ever *really* understands, no matter how much they see you or how many times you explain it to them."

People like us are meant for each other.

We're two halves of a whole.

"I think I can help you," she tells me, her hand smoothing over my face. I smell perfume emitting from her wrist, the heat of it. Hot skin: chemicals posing as temperatures.

"Just keep your eyes open and watch me lean in."

She says, "And when you kiss me, don't do it with your mouth."

I taste Marshmallow Meltdown and robust saliva, red wine and the distant remnants of thinning smoke.

Less than an inch away from my lips, her mouth speaks, "If you can taste me, you know I'm there. If you can breathe me, you know I'm close."

She gives my jaw a little shake. "Relax and listen."

The room is so mute I can hear everything, little saliva bubbles forming and bursting, her hands scrubbing my beard's shadow on either side of my face. Tongues sliding and scouring.

With enough ingenuity you can recreate anything.

Think about this the next time you lay in a tanning bed or enjoy a painting of a landscape when you could be out in the real world getting the authentic.

"Don't feel," she says. "Think."

Adaptation.

Remember this when you see a vegetarian eating a Boca Burger at a Bar-B-Q so they don't feel left out. Everyone is striving to be an anonymous blender-inner.

"The reason that most people close their eyes when they kiss is because the intimacy becomes too much...they just can't take it," Dana explains.

"You need to learn the difference between fucking and making love," she tells me. "And believe me, babe, despite what you may think, there *is* one."

Then I ask, "What are you getting out of all of this?"

And she gives a guilty little smile, "I heard you can go for hours."

I'm sure I'm giving her a look right now.

Then she adds, "*And* I think I kind of like you."

She kisses me but I keep my eyes open this time. It's easier than I thought it would be to do this, and not because I know she can't see me. That has little or nothing to do with it. There's a hard new reality coming into play:

I trust Dana.

I trust her because she's like me.

She's not like me, but she's vulnerable. Vulnerable like me.

She isn't like the other girls, the ones I'll date. She doesn't just want me.

"I need you," she says, mouth slick and wet. I can see that much with my eyes this open.

She promises to me, "We'll save each other."

And I believe her.

I believe.

SESSION 23
AIDIN: AGE 16

We're the result of our absent fathers and mothers weak in will.

We're oxford-clad teens raising each other poorly, but without the foresight of regret and the experience of consequence.

I'm a freshman now at Penbrooke Academy, the place where most of my "formidable learning for what lies ahead" will take place, so says my father. The first unofficial lesson being that we're all so much the same that we must seek our uniqueness through an exterior means. One of surfaces.

Each of us dawns the blue blazer, red tie, and white oxford combination as described in the school's official dress code. Pants can either be blue or khaki, but everyone knows that you don't wear blue, so this isn't even really a choice. Shoes are shoes, just as long as they're not loafers or cost less than $200. You're a fag if you wear cufflinks. You're poor if you wear a clip-on tie. And you never part your hair in the middle. Ever. So the only real selection left is your name. Your label.

Tommy Hilfiger.

Brook's Brothers.

Perry Ellis. Etc.

At such a young age we become obsessed with stitching and fabric quality, with the color and shade of a jacket's interior, sometimes making conscious wide movements in hallways between periods to show off the elegant emerald or tasteful ashen shades hiding within. We purchase designer tie clips and spend countless hours scouring the intercepted catalogues of our fathers looking for that perfect belt or patterned oxford. We shop watches and wallets. Cologne and aftershave sets. Though most of us have only begun to enter a stage of maturity, we feel we're already years behind and struggling to catch up—if not to our fathers, than at least to the seniors of Penbrooke who stroll about the hallways bawdy and distinguished, as if they take a smug sort of pleasure in knowing something we don't.

At Penbrooke Academy we begin our ascent not into higher learning, but into higher fashion and a more illustrious spectrum of taste, and for those who can't afford to conform to that ideal suffer a most violent association amongst their peers.

I remember a few instances of this, some better than others, but one more than the rest where a kid (a freshman) was nearly killed in the men's restroom for wearing Dickie's brand khakis, something we might not have noticed had he kept his blazer on during class to conceal the label. Details seem to stick out more than the full event: how the blood from his mouth and nose traced those smooth pearl bathroom tiles in ninety-degree angles, turning to vapors when they hit the still waters of the urinals. The blood soaking into the tie creating an off-shade of maroon or brick or maybe even violet, and as the blood-pool spread all I could hear was some future yuppie stomping this kid's face and neck snarling "nigger nigger nigger" even though this particular student was Caucasian Irish Catholic, he was, nonetheless, the son of the academy's head custodian and poorly clothed. This student was not, as they say, "Penbrooke material," and it's the first of many occasions where I see how unaffected I am by the abnormal and cruel.

I take no particular joy in watching, but I neither recoil nor have the slightest compulsion to help this person. More than anything, I'm interested in what happens next. Maybe a hero will save him. Perhaps not. I really can't say for sure because it's fool's logic to begin with. If you want the reality of the situation, this kid, this fake—he's the villain: the snake in the garden being weeded out. Upper-crust Darwinism. And so many weeks later this action is even further reaffirmed by how he answered the investigative questions regarding his assailants. Us.

What were we wearing?

What kind of watches did we have on?

Loafers or dress shoes?

He knew none of it, and if you're not only oblivious to the

details, but also ignorant to how paramount they are, then you obviously don't belong here at the academy. This is much the way we justify it to ourselves as we each make our own individual efforts to forget through our fathers' wet bars and the medicine cabinets of our absent mothers. Their prescriptions become our means of recreation in this world of excess.

Our homes are as exquisite as they are cold and empty, and it's only during the weekends of a full fledge parental jettison do we feel any sort of warmth from others just as neglected and forgotten as we are. The girls of Penbrooke Academy walk into our homes and rooms, and lie in the cold clean beds of our parents, making love to us on 800 thread count sheets. We live vicariously unrecognized for our fathers with debutants young and inexperienced such as we are, but holding on to that very same feeling of living beyond natural years. They struggle to remain chaste while evolving into their womanhood.

Such a fine line we share with these girls. Their walk of life running parallel with ours: the boys of Penbrooke, but in ways that are much more susceptible to shame. I don't think I ever fall in love with them...with any of them, but I indicate it, something much of us are naturally talented at having observed our fathers in their respective lamenting marriages. We're all quite capable of being charming and conveying a genuine interest having seen it portrayed for years. I never feel for them, but I enjoy playing the role knowing that it's behind locked doors and that these emotions will retain their anonymity. It's as they say, "between us," and this understanding affords both parties a certain liberty we don't normally have the luxury of, so we take this freedom and learn from each other. We're young and stupid and not ready for any of it, but our inexperience blanches in the face of determination, never dwelling on our mistakes or inadequacies for more than a moment: the way we bump teeth when we kiss or how you finger her too hard. The way she sucks on you too soft or not soft enough. How the placement of the condom nearly always marks a break in our intimacy. We constantly dream of these moments, but they're reflected clumsy and unsmooth as they transpire in the real, within the quiet rooms of adults where *children break their history of abstinence.*

These are confusing and difficult times we suffer together, and what's worse is we set ourselves up to forget lessons potentially learned with booze and pills and a lack of conscience. We're portraying a version of Lord of the Flies *where we live not on an island of sand and palms, but within mansions and high-end Plaza-side condos of infinite resource. Our war is not with each other, but with the gap that lies between the generations as we come to terms with who we are and the men and women we're expected to become.*

We're afraid and privileged, but most of all, self-destructive without that presence of consequence. We're without boundaries and out of control.

And each of us learn around this age that money does not buy happiness, but merely allows one to remain content should you be able to afford such peace. It's without the rules set forth by our mothers and fathers do we find ourselves in the position of creating our own, and sometimes breaking them. A fair few have, including myself. We go too far to see what will happen, to find out if we really are invincible. With our motives derived from the collegiate classes, we live beyond our years with cocaine and sometimes harder drugs when accessible. With anal sex. With an orgy. Or some combination of the previously mentioned. We experiment. On ourselves. On each other. It becomes a game of escalation yet an ever-changing sameness, and it seems not one of us has the sense to back down until we reach a certain level of enlightenment that we all know isn't coming.

We're powerless.

All of us, and we're too ignorant to realize it.

The years at Penbrooke are the ones that form me, or deform me, if we're examining this in retrospect. I became not a person, but part of a false ideal where happiness isn't based on achievement or progress, and instead, shifted to the material remaining permanent. That first year and the ones that follow are blurry and quick. Not from joy, but abstracted by the nightly gauntlets myself and my peers put ourselves through as cries for help, unheard and ignored.

117

Our boys become cynical and depraved men.

And our girls grow to be calloused through the years of loveless sex and forced maturity. Both groups a result of the other: a vicious cycle of teen angst.

I'm not the product of my environment or my peers.

I'm a product of absence, and even though it kills me and the last of my young ideals to admit this...I just don't think I believe in heroes anymore. Not in this world. This life.

No one has powers.

Nobody is special.

Most of all, me.

SESSION 24
NATURAL

There's a theory that everyone is born with a natural talent. Something they're good at without practice or effort or preparation, and they can't explain how or why, only that they can. Somehow this was bestowed upon them, and the range of what it could be is limited to anything you can imagine.

It could be horseshoes.

It could be open-heart surgery.

Somewhere out there in the world there's a man picking a pool cue for the first time thinking to himself, "This feels right," like the first time you lock eyes with your future wife, a marriage of person and vocation.

Practice makes perfect, but some people are just born that way.

At a hole-in-the-wall bar (on a list assignment), I pick up a dart and come to find that I can put it anywhere I want. The bull's eye. Triple twenty. Anywhere. And I don't know how. I just can.

Remember how talent is a gift, like being born into a wealthy family or having flawless skin. You don't get to choose. It chooses you. The same way people are naturally pre-disposed by genetics to be Asian or thin or born with poor eyesight, well, it's the same thing with this.

Your dream might be to conquer the football field as the next Peyton Manning but unfortunately you're a violin prodigy.

You can train to be an astronaut all you want but you can't help it if your calling is in tap dancing.

Sorry, but this is how it is.

I'm having more and more of these types of moments. Random awakenings of abilities I didn't even know existed until one of my senses went into deep sleep, and honestly, it's starting to scare me a little.

On Sunday afternoons in Nordstrom they have a pianist that plays in the fragrances and cosmetics section so the trophy wives and rich widowers don't have to listen to Muzak renditions of Kenny G while they're getting their faces retuned. After watching this guy play for twenty minutes, I sneak up to his instrument while he's on break and crank out Mozart's piano concerto No. 21 in C Major like I've done it a million times. When I turned around there were about twenty applauding shoppers and one very upset piano player.

I was asked to leave the store but managed to knock out an item in the process, the one that requires me to learn how to play an instrument. It doesn't stop there. For most people it would, but not with me. Most people, normal people, will stop trying new things when they've found their gift. Their talent becomes their life, or a prison, depending on how you look at it. Discovery could very well mean confinement.

Once you find out that you're the next figure skating champion or soccer superstar you're stuck with it. Game over. No more dreams for you.

Think about this the next time you see a musician trying to act or an actor trying to sing.

See: Mariah Carey in *Glitter*.

And: Kevin Costner's country band, Modern West.

I keep going.

I'm in search of mediocrity because every time I solve a Rubik's cube or find out that I can forge signatures, I get a little bit more freaked out.

Refer to the phrase "Too good to be true" if you don't know what I'm talking about. Paradies sure doesn't seem to be familiar with it.

I tell her, "I learned to speak French."

"Good for you," she says, but her tone isn't wholly complimentary, almost as if I told her I learned to tie my shoes or make my bed.

"Listening to an audio tutorial while I was sleeping," I specify, and when she doesn't say anything I'm compelled to ask, "Don't *you* think that's a little weird?"

She asks, "Should I?"

I say yes, but it comes off sounding like a question (as if I'm unsure that I should be inquiring about this more than I am), then Paradies asks me, "Do you want to talk about French or do you want to talk about your condition—and before you answer that, keep in mind that I can't unteach languages nor explain how they were learned in the first place."

Times like these, I feel much in the way I did when all this started. Helpless. Lost. And very much confused. I try to talk to Dana about this but it's more of the same.

In my room, on my bed, she's sitting atop my midsection holding a calculator that voices inputs and answers. Buttons are labeled in Braille. She uses this thing to calculate fifteen percent tips during our lunch and dinner dates. Twenty percent if the service is good. This is merely one of the steps to being a self-sufficient woman. Item #12 on Dana's list.

She says, "Let's try another one," and the computer voice says, "eight-seven-five-six...times...two-six-nine."

"Okay, what's the answer?" she asks. "And no cheating," she adds. "I'll so kick your ass if I find out you're cheating."

"2,355,364," I tell her, and the calculator reads out that value digit by digit when Dana presses the "=" button.

"Ugh, you're such a fucker!" she says, tossing the calculator to my chest. "You have to tell me how you're doing this trick because I hate whipping this thing out in public. The voice is totally creepy."

I say, "It's not a trick."

"Fine—tell me, *then* we'll make out," she says, sounding fatigued. "All this math is getting me kinda hot."

But I can't explain it, and I get the feeling that no one else is going to be able to, either. This is me stuck with my little anti-problem. The way this feels, it's not so much that I'm learning how to do these things from scratch. That would involve a process, trial and error. Varying degrees of success. Mistakes would happen. They *should* happen, but whenever I play a game of pool or round of mini golf I'm perfect, and it never feels new or awkward. Quite the opposite.

It feels like I'm remembering. Picking up where I left off.

You can go ten years not riding a bike and it'll still take you less than a minute to do it again.

You may be a virgin but that doesn't mean you won't know what to do when the time comes. Some things are naturally instilled, either by God or genetics or practice, but none of those seem like the answer. I'm missing something.

And Paradies says, "Did it ever occur to you that maybe you've been able to do these things all along but you were too busy being an ass to notice?" tap-tap-tapping her pen before writing again.

"Ass?"

"Sorry," she says. "Materialistic drug addict bent on promiscuity with self-esteem and identity issues takes too long to say. The question still stands, though."

I think about it, and to think about it, I have to look back. Review the timeline:

At 12 I had my first drink and started smoking.

At 13 I started experimenting with girls, drank and smoked more.

At 14 I got my own credit card, started smoking weed and lost my virginity.

At 15 I took Xanax for the first time, liked it, and started experimenting with pills.

At 16 I got my first car: a BMW. More women, drink, and drugs followed.

At 17 I did pills, drugs, drink, women, and took the SATs hung-over.

At 18 I paid $300 for a fake ID, and things got really out of hand.

Ages 19 through 24 was: shopping, wining & dining, blowing lines in bathrooms, fucking women I'd never call or see again, pills in any color, shape, and dosage, lines racked on smooth tan breasts, day-after pills replacing condoms (procured illegally), speeding tickets, club life, bored elation, magazine ads reflecting into the real, DUIs, sleeping until 5 or 6 in the afternoon, cop bribes, doorman bribes, escort girls, blackouts, trance music, flashing lights, red carpets, name brands labeling people, a 21st birthday that changed nothing, a new Ferrari, a new credit card (higher limit), more tickets, higher bribes, better, faker, more expensive women, women that fucked me without knowing my name or anything about me, more coke, more pills, taking ecstasy for breakfast, Mimosas and vodka tonics at first light, shopping sprees, gourmet dinners, air made of Chanel and Calvin Klein and Donna Karen; a breathable eloquence, one thousand acquaintances, no friends, a different girl every night, an empty house by day, no authority, a perfect life of wealth and complete freedom, and no one to stop it.

So to the doc's question, the one about how I might've been too distracted to realize my potential, I say, "Maybe," because everyone is two people.

This is me staying neutral.

This is me afraid of the truth.

Afraid because I might've just let the last decade of my life mean nothing, and that fact is just sinking in. "A moment of clarity," alcoholics and drug addicts call it.

"Did you ever think that maybe the reason you're so into this list might have something to do with how you've lived your life so far?" Dana asks. "Maybe you're looking for something bigger than watching a few movies and doing a few good deeds."

When you're twenty-four, ten years is a long time.

I could've been writing a book or getting a doctorate. I could've been a marathon runner or a clothing designer. A social worker helping the tired, the hungry, the poor.

She says, "Did you ever think that maybe this list of stuff isn't *just* a list...that maybe these things are designed to get you to start asking questions about yourself and your life."

I could've been painting mountainous Appalachian landscapes and backpacking through Europe. I could've been inventing a faster more efficient computer or finding the cure for ovarian cancer.

Dana speaks into my ear, "When you complete an item—tell me, what do you feel more of...pride and accomplishment or less guilty?"

Out of the million and one things I could've been doing: getting a degree, a job, a wife, a career, making a contribution to the world—I did none of that. I did everything that *didn't* matter. It was the fast track to meaninglessness, and the saddest part is that I don't remember much of how I got here.

"If you ask me," Dana says. "I think you're looking for redemption."

She says this is what most men feel during a midlife crisis with the whole my-entire-existence-has-meant-nothing realization.

"So I guess we should start shopping for a Porsche and a wife half your age," she jokes. "Maybe some Rogaine and Viagra."

I'd give her a look right now but she wouldn't see it.

Hell, I wouldn't even know if I was sending it right.

"This is serious," I say. "Something's happening with me."

And it all has to do with that list, because without it, I wouldn't have realized any of this. You start to ask yourself what happens when greatness *isn't* accomplished.

"What if there was no Martin Luther King?" Dana poses. "Do you think someone else would've stepped up?"

She says, "The difference between a leader and any other person isn't the idea itself. It's the conveyance. You can have the cure for AIDS or a way to stop global warming but it kind of equates to shit if you don't tell anyone about it."

Refer to: The Wright brothers.

And also: Albert Einstein.

Don't forget: Gandhi.

"These people were one in a million," she tells me. "But with the billions of people living in the world today, that's really not all that special. I mean, c'mon...*somebody* was going to invent the light bulb, Thomas Edison just happened to get to it first."

Alexander Fleming revealed penicillin's antibiotic properties in 1928, but there were at least three other guys about to make the same discovery. One way or another, it was going to happen. Fleming just beat them to the punch.

Some things are eventual.

Next time you're firing an automatic weapon or installing the newest operating system on your computer, take a second and think about how it all started with a person saying to himself, "This is good, but I think I can make it better."

Now that we've invented the space shuttle, how do we get it to the moon and back *without* blowing up?

"Greatness means sacrifice," Dana says. "Da Vinci spent most of his life devoted to painting and sculpting...creating things he'd never keep. He gave up his life and now his art will be remembered forever."

Mozart died at 35 years.

His memory lives eternal.

"You're right about one thing...something is changing," Dana says. "You are."

Paradies tells me, "You've taken beatings from men three times your size and laughed. You don't feel pain or sickness or fatigue, the very attributes that define mortality, and now you're picking up languages overnight and learning instruments just by watching other people play them. What do *you* think that means?"

I tell her she's paid to figure that out for me.

"Try this," she says, the writing discontinuing. "Stop asking questions and stop being afraid of this. If you embrace what's happening then maybe you won't need me to explain it for you."

That's the easy part.

It's everyone else I'm worried about.

At Making Sense I'm the minority of the minority: the unheard of and unexplained. The cutters and pokers and bleeders at Circle of Healing do what they do because they know they'll feel it. I did it to see if I could, and by this account it's inspired a fair amount of animosity or jealousy or whatever you want to call it. My welcome is beginning to wear out.

They're competing with the Michael Jordan of disabilities.

I'm the Bill Gates of sensory hindrance and impediment.

Sure, they preach acceptance and understanding, and at first I felt genuinely welcomed, but the only constant in life is that all things change. People tend to hate and fear what they don't understand.

The worst part of picking up sign language is seeing how badly people talk about you when they think you don't know what they're saying. Learn Korean and go get your nails done if you don't know what I'm talking about. See if you can control yourself when a stranger calls you a stupid bitch through her smiling teeth. Try to keep your hand from shaking when she comments on your fat American ass smelling up the joint.

It makes you appreciate those proverbial back-stabbers and two-faced liars. At least they're exercising some subtlety.

It's when I relay my feelings on this to Paradies that she says, "Then don't go to groups anymore."

And it's at this point that I'm like, "Seriously?"

"Well, is it even helping you anymore?" she asks, momentarily refraining from her note-taking. "It sure doesn't sound like it."

At the last Making Sense meeting Carl spoke at length about how they need to start making porn specifically for blind people because DVDs and phone sex are too expensive.

"I shouldn't have to pay $40 for something I'm just going to listen to," he explained, and you'd be amazed at how many people nodded their heads in agreement to this idea. The women, too, but that's when everyone who still had eyes looked over at me and remembered how I can't even get off anymore.

When you're beyond help, you're pointless.

When you don't "act out" your presence is trivial. I'm referring to Circle of Healing, because when I stopped showing up with stained bandages and fresh cuts on my face, I stopped mattering. My godliness began to fade. If you're not gonna hurt yourself then there are plenty of other people putting out cigarettes on their arms and cutting themselves who *do* have something to say.

If it ain't broke, don't fix it.

If you're not hurting yourself, don't show up to group.

This Goth bitch, Carla, she's the type of chick who can't sit still unless she's getting another tattoo or piercing or something that involves a sharp object. She's got this thin silver chain that goes from a nose piercing to one in her ear. So, it's practically the only thing you can look at when she talks. It's like trying to watch Gorbachov deliver a speech without looking at that big red stain on his forehead. You just can't, but moving on.

In group, during open discussion, Carla says, "I identify with the pain, y'know. It's *real*," the silver thread eye-catching like biker Christmas tinsel.

Last week this same bitch comes up to me and asks, "Why do you show up anymore, dude? You know you're never *really* gonna be one of us, right?"

I'm the only one here not wearing mascara or some sort of Wiccan accessory. Fashionably behind the times, I guess you could say.

She spits, "Just fuck off already if you're gonna be a faggot about this."

And she says, "Go back to your country club," turning way from me.

I say, "Hey," and she stops.

And I say, "Hey," and she turns around.

Then I whisper so only she can hear, "My neighbors are gonna be really scared this year at Halloween," and she rolls her little bitch eyes with too much mascara at me.

And I tell her, "Because I'm gonna cut your fuckin' head off and hang it from that chain on your face, you stupid cunt."

Then a smirk. She smirks and tells me, "You shouldn't have said that," but I stop her before she makes the move to complain. This is me saving myself a few thousand in bribes and legal fees.

I show her my recorder and tell her I use it during group, but there's not much of me on there. Hardly anything at all since I haven't been saying much.

"You've been talking a lot lately, though," I reveal. "What was it you said last meeting...that you tried to cut your nipples off with an envelope or something? Was that it?"

She stops smirking.

"And that you squeeze your clit with a hole puncher to make yourself climax? That would sound nice in front of a judge, wouldn't it?"

And her face goes slack.

"Keep fucking with me and I'll end you," I snarl. "Remember, *you're* the freak out there, not me," I tell her motioning to the door. "I'm trying to get better."

"And put some Neosporin on that shit," I say, indicating a sore. "That arm is infected."

Then I put the device back in my pocket and walk to my chair. I don't record meetings, but Carla doesn't know that.

"Yeah, you definitely shouldn't go anymore," Paradies says. "You're lucky that girl was stupid." She scribbles, "Oh, and don't threaten people anymore. For the record I'm supposed to say that *and* ask why you did it."

"I guess..." I start, thinking on it. "I guess I just didn't want to feel powerless. Not to someone like that," I specify. "It felt like I was being ridiculed--"

"--And you thought belittling this girl would make you feel better?" she cuts in.

"Yeah."

"Aidin, you're too smart to get pulled into this kind of crap."

I sigh. "Yeah...I know."

"Seriously," she says. "You're too smart for this."

On the ocean blue chaise, I turn my head to look at her and ask, "Wait...what are you talking about?"

"I think I might have a lead on your newfound capabilities," Paradies announces.

She shifts though some papers, finds the one she wants and shows it to me.

"You remember that test you took last week?" she asks. "Well, I got the results back."

SESSION 25
DR. THORNTON

My first thought when I meet Dr. Thornton is that he looks a lot like what Walt Whitman would if he wasn't worm food already. He's old and bearded with tiny intelligent eyes and a wrinkled forehead from decades of furrowed contemplation. His gait is slow and labored. The clothes he wears are, of course, unfashionable; a walking corduroy ad. No tie. Chest hair plumes billow wiry and thick above the neckline of his button-down. And glasses. Sturdy metal frames embed on the soft tissue of his nose and ears. Blood vessels branch. Crow's feet magnify.

This is about ten days ago.

He smiles and asks, "Dr. Paradies sent you over?"

This is another item from Section 7. All I know is that I'm supposed to be at this place at this time, meeting with this person: Dr. Thornton.

I say, "Yeah, she did. I'm Aidin." I extend my hand.

We shake, the lack of blood shift in his fingertips letting me know he's not squeezing hard. Just another adaptive everyday observation.

"This is my assistant, Miss Caldwell," he says, motioning to the young woman behind him. "She'll be helping me administer today's tests."

And I'm thinking, *tests?*

I don't know anything about any tests.

Then Thornton remarks, "My God, boy, you look like dead foreskin on a cracker." He chuckles, "I suppose it's nerves. No worries, though. No worries," he assures me, leading the way through a short hallway into a gymnasium-sized room. "All we're doing here today is seeing what your capabilities are. Nothing more."

We sit at a table in the center of the room. It's wood laden and gigantic with the kind of acoustics that make whispering seem like screaming. A pin dropping could easily pretend to be a hammered nail. It's that big and quiet.

"I have been informed, I must say, that you are quite the capable young man, Aidin," he says, winking. "But we shall see about that. A fine line between ignorance and intelligence, yes?"

"A wise man realizes he knows nothing," I say.

"Very good," he smiles, adjusting within his seat. "A famous quote by one of the great Asian philosophers, I do believe. Please, if you would, humor me with the source. I'm a bit rusty in this old age."

"Fortune cookie from China Star buffet," I tell him.

Thornton releases a bellowing swell of laughter that echoes throughout the room, "You are a *delight*, young sir! *Simply jocular!*" He peeps over his left shoulder, "Miss Caldwell, please bring our young comedian his test. We can't laugh all day now, can we? Chop-chop! Much to do, as you know."

Miss Caldwell, a young yet plain sort of woman, approaches us hastily bearing a stack of papers and places them on the table in front of me, about ten sheets thick from the look of it.

"The test you're about to take, Aidin, is standard multiple choice/fill in the blank format," Thornton explains. "And Miss Caldwell took the liberty of procuring these pens that come with erasers, so if you make a mistake—fear not, for you only need to buff out you blunder. Technology is a wonderful thing, wouldn't you agree?"

Imagine Walt Whitman impersonating James Lipton as done by Will Ferrell. If you can do that, then you've got Thornton.

I nod in agreement to his comment.

"You will have ninety minutes to complete the test, during which time I will be seated here before you...studying and criticizing your every move," he glares. "After the test, scones will be available to you, but I'm having one now because I didn't have time for breakfast this morning, and Miss Caldwell isn't having any because she is on *a diet.*"

Normally, the idea of a test would be off-putting, but I'm

too busy feeling sorry for this chick to feel nervous.

"Time begins when you open the packet," he says. "Just relax and try not to think about how I'm staring at you with unwavering judgment. You'll do fine."

I open the packet and hear the gunshot-sounding report of the stopwatch starting.

The first question: 24 H in a D

The answer: 24 hours in a day

This is how the rest of the first page reads only it gets increasingly harder.

200 C in a C

52 C in a D

6 S to a H

If you haven't seen anything like this before, take a second to try and figure these out. See how long it takes you just to knock out three of them. Seriously, I want you to do this. Stop reading, go back up and make an honest attempt. Unlike me, you can take all day.

Now imagine doing fifty.

If took you more than three minutes to surmise the following answers of 200 cigarettes in a carton, 52 cards in a deck, and 6 sides to a hexagon, you're never gonna make it. You'll be eating scones before you know it.

If you see 54 S in a R C and the image of a Rubik's cube doesn't immediately jump out and bite you in the ass, then you might be screwed.

26 L in the A

The W P is 7 B.

86,400 S in a D

Letters, world population, seconds.

This is all common knowledge for the most part, just coded. This is a case of having your head in the right place at the right time, but fifty times in a row. It makes me wonder how well I'd be doing right now if this were a few months ago. In the "before."

Seriously, how many people do you think saw the problem 22 S of B in a L and knew they were talking about bread?

I don't think Thornton has seen many. He keeps whispering

things like, "Marvelous," and "Amazing," under his breath as I shoot through this thing.

For every problem there's an answer, and the answers come almost instantaneously. Numbers and letters can represent nearly anything by themselves, but contain only one meaning when paired. I know them all.

Nine numerals in a social security number.

Eight legs on a spider.

Six sides to a die.

Common but coded. Easy for me. So easy it's frightening. Reminiscent of learning a language overnight or mastering a game you've never played before. Knowledge instilled in sleep. Skill acquired without practice.

The next section is patterns.

Such as: M, T, W, ?

And: 4, 8, 16, ?

But that's the easy. See how well you do when you see a particular section of sheet music from a certain composer of the 1700's and have to know that an A flat is the next note.

When you see the series 8, 152, 6640 will you know to add 14 then multiply by 40?

It's sort of a trick question, because I shouldn't yet I do. My contemplation is brief to the point where it borders more on reaction then logistic solution. Results are impulsive, increasing my already heightened anxiety, but Thornton doesn't notice this. Nor Caldwell. She's too busy doing time-keep as the doctor before me examines my person with a sort of child-like interest. A whimsical fascination. I only observe this between page turnings. My eyes will meet his and they'll be shining like marbles frosted in cataracts. He'll nod and smile as if to say, "You're everything I was told you were. Now keep going."

And I do.

Through the canyons of associative wordplay and alphanumeric logic solutions. An algorithm here. A connotation there. Disjointed formulas of pattern and shape beg to be completed with a filled blank or darkened bubble. Just like my list items, they seek a closure only I can deliver them. Peace of mind.

Thornton wants it, too. You can tell by the way he keeps shifting and adjusting. The wood splinters of his chair rub restless and excited. An eager child trapped.

He announces, "Time," over his shoulder when I close the booklet.

Miss Caldwell clicks the watch and my voice echoes throughout the room when I say (when I answer), "12 minutes and 27 seconds," because for some reason I think it's just another question. It's another part of the test as far as I'm concerned. Another knee-jerk reaction of the mind. It can't be helped.

And when Caldwell says in a low horrified whisper, "He's right," you can see Thornton's eyes scan my wrist for a watch, but the space is vacant. He looks over his shoulder to see if there's a clock mirroring the one in the room that's above and behind me, but there isn't.

He asks, "How?" hands shaky. Eyes fixated.

The only answer is the horribly obvious one, the one that's hiding right out in the open spaces of this enormous room. I just can.

He says, "That's impossible."

I change the subject because there's no way I can explain this. That's more Thorton and the doc's job than mine.

I ask, "Can I have my scone now? Apple, if you have it."

"Certainly, my boy," he says grabbing my test with a shaky hand. "Certainly." He yells, "Caldwell! Scones!" jostling her to hustle over to the nearby table. She brings the entire box.

Thornton, however, peruses my test, comparing it to what I can only assume is the answer key on his clipboard. His head swivels back and forth, back and forth like a typewriter, and I don't know what I'm enjoying more, the flavor of the pastry or his reaction. It's sheer delight. Even Caldwell appears to be interested. Her eyes spy the paper with keen intrigue.

"This is...amazing," he says, Caldwell nodding in silent agreement. Both their jaws slack. Eyes wild and excited as they scan the results. After a few minutes Thornton closes the test booklet and hands it to Miss Caldwell. "Process this," he says. "Make it a priority."

The way Thorton is looking at me now reminds me of the groups I'll soon be disbanding from, because as long as I've been me I've never really known myself, and right now I feel like that walking impossibility again. The minority within the minority. An unpredictable variable.

Thornton says, "I'd like to bring you back here for some additional testing...if that would be okay, that is."

"You'll have to ask my doctor," I say.

"Believe me, I plan to," he smiles. "You were exactly what she said you'd be. I see quite a bit of talent, as you'd imagine, but well...nothing quite like you."

And again, the same discomfort. The feeling of being examined and studied and dissected when all you want is to be normal.

"It's funny...hardly ever does anything ever live up to great expectations, and almost never are they exceeded."

And Thorton continues on saying, "I'll speak with Dr. Paradies about getting you back in here again."

He says, "Hopefully, we can get you penciled in within the next couple weeks. I don't think I could wait three months again now that I've seen what you're capable of."

SESSION 26
RESULTS

"234," Paradies reads aloud from the test results sheet. "That's what you scored," she reveals, but I'm rather nonplussed about it. To me, this is yet another item in an ever-lengthening list of things I'm good at without trying. The results come off redundant to me, like defining a word with a thesaurus instead of a dictionary. It's another way of saying the same thing when what I'm really looking for is an explanation.

"Aidin, do you have any idea what that means?" she asks.

And like the cynical asshole that I am, I'm thinking about how I now have a piece of paper to tell me what I already know. This is exactly why doctors hang their certificates and college diplomas behind them, because they're the only people in the world who *don't* need to see it to believe it.

I tell her, "No, I don't know what that means. Do tell," I twirl my finger, my sign language slang for, "I could care less."

"Well, you're a genius," she says, not hiding the pride in her voice. "Certified."

"Okay," I sigh. "And?"

"You scored higher than Einstein," she stresses.

"So?"

"So, this is fairly large accomplishment."

I ask, "Can you make me about 5,000 copies of that?"

"Why?"

"Because I'm going to wallpaper my dad's office with it so he'll shut the hell up about me being an idiot."

Reshuffling papers, Paradies counters, "Actually, I don't think you should tell anyone about this. Not your parents, and not Dana, either."

I ask why.

They are *my* test results, after all.

"Are you *really* asking me that?" she half-smiles.

"Doc, please don't tell me that *you're* evading now," I quip.

"Fine," she says, shuffling and stacking her papers. She sets them down on the table next to her. The legal pad, too. Her fingers adjust her glasses. And suddenly, I don't feel so cocky or smart because she never does this. Paradies never *really* looks at me. Every glare is an examination or dissection of a subject: a patient, never a person. It's almost painful, this eye contact.

"Sit up, if you would," she requests.

It's when I do this that I see Dr. Paradies for the first time in full form, because there's always been something between us. A file or a legal pad or a stack of papers, and she'll be hunched over herself scribbling and making notes to the tune of my admissions. Embarrassingly enough, I know the ceiling pattern of the office better than her face. That's how rarely I look upon her, and even when I do it's only for a moment. Always obscured by something, but not now.

I'm finally able to take in those pale, sharp features. Thin lips. A jaw line that's more of an edge: the handrail to her thin neck. Her eyes settle into me deep and meticulous. They concentrate forcing me to break eye contact and move away, downward to her suit. A matching jacket and skirt. A silk oxford. Very classic. Very expensive. Something my mother would pick out, given her tastes. I can imagine them shopping together, having wine with lunch and swapping stories about their patients, and maybe even about me, but I don't want to think about that now. Or ever.

These sessions are like any trip you've ever taken to Las Vegas.

What happens at #2 Pershing Square stays there, and is between myself and Dr. Paradies. No one else.

"Confidentiality" is doctor's speak for "safety," and safety leads to trust.

She says, "As your doctor, one of my responsibilities is to make sure that you stay out of harm's way...to keep you from hurting yourself, whether it's by way of an accident or on purpose."

See: drugs.

See also: alcohol and pills.

Let's not forget: binge eating, self-mutilation, and fighting.

"I hope you understand by now that when I tell you to do something, it's only because I have your best interests at heart," she explains. "I can't be around all the time to protect you, but I *can* give you the advice you need so you can protect yourself."

She's talking about my baby-proofed house. My nightlights and electric razor and temperature-controlled water faucets. All those items to combat the typical dangers of the common household.

"If you reveal what you are...what you're capable of, it could be bad. You might very well be endangering yourself in a way that can't be fixed," she explains.

I ask her about why she set up the test.

"If you didn't want this brought to light then why did you have me take it in the first place?" Further questioning, "And why did you tell Dr. Thornton I was so smart when I've only been like this for a few weeks? He told me you set this up months ago."

"Aidin, I set up nearly *everything* months ago. The only reason I told Thornton you had potential is because he's old and doesn't like wasting his time. It was pure serendipity that you lived up to it," she adds.

I tell her about how he wants me to come back.

"For additional testing...whatever that means," I relay.

"I know," she says. "The old codger won't stop calling me about it."

I stammer, "Well...I don't know...maybe I should go back," but I make this suggestion rather feebly, twiddling my thumbs.

Paradies sighs and nods her head: the universal gesture for "you're just not getting it, are you?"

"This is what will happen, Aidin. You'll go back there and he'll throw every test he can throw at you. He'll pick you apart and dissect you, and then he'll call in other doctors to do more of the same just so he can show them what he's found."

Everybody is two people.

Paradies says, "This isn't really about what you can do so

much as it is what you can do for *him*. Thornton just wants to go along for the ride. He wants a poster child."

He's an exploiter posing as a guide.

They made an entire movie about finding Bobby Fischer, but what if Bobby Fischer didn't want to be found?

"If you let them, they can and they will stick you in a room for the rest of your natural life so they can poke and prod you. They'll push you until there's nothing left...then they'll push some more, and I haven't even gotten to the part about your condition."

I ask, "What do you mean?"

"What I mean is that when people are presented with something they don't understand, they usually end up caging it until they do." She pauses slightly before offering, "This may be a crude example, but what they'll do to you isn't too far off from those comic books you've been reading."

Paradies is referring to my super-intelligence. My endless stamina and infinite endurance for pain. I don't get hungry or weak or feel the symptoms of illness. Drugs and alcohol don't register with me. Nor temperature. I'm an expert marksman. A master of puzzles and logic problems. Multi-lingual. And without any sort of effort or focus, it seems like I keep sponging new talents and skills. These might not be powers but they're close, and these people will do anything within or outside of their authority to exploit them. To control them, even. With a little combat training and a costume I might have career as a vigilante ahead of me. Or maybe I'm a hero.

"Too bad I don't like spandex," I tell her.

"Don't be a smartass, Aidin. It was just an example," she tells me. Eyes staring me down.

"Sorry," I relent.

"It's fine. You just need to take this seriously if want to have any hope of getting back to normal."

I nod. "Okay, what do you want to do, then?"

Dr. Paradies says she doesn't want me talking to anybody, to think of it like a list item. Silence is Rule #1.

"Seriously, if it gets out there that you're the second coming of Einstein you'll experience legal kidnapping first hand," she says. "So unless you want to work with a bunch of near-sighted virgins at NASA for the rest of your life, I suggest you keep a lid on it."

"What about Thornton?" I ask. "It doesn't sound like he's gonna give up anytime soon."

"But he's the only one, so what do you think that means?"

Just another logic problem.

An algorithm of life.

If I'm the next great mind and only one person is calling about it, then that can mean only one of two things. Either no one else cares, or no one else knows. Making a great discovery is like winning the lottery, you don't tell anyone about it unless you plan on sharing it. Everybody will want a piece of what you have.

Paradies says, "I'll take care of him, but you need to lay low for now."

Rule #2 is I don't draw attention to myself.

"I'm not saying you have to hide in your house all day, just don't go showing off anymore."

It's understandable.

No one likes getting beat at their own game. There are a few dart players and Golden Tee sharks that can attest to that. When you're mopping the floor with a former 9-ball champion and he asks, "How long have you been playing?" whatever you do, *don't* say it's your first time because he's likely to try to beat the snot out of you with his own stick, and graphite doesn't break as easily as the house cues.

It's not that these people so much mind getting beat, it's that I beat them so severely that pisses them off, and I can only use that beginner's luck excuse for so long.

"That's cool," I concur. "Anything else?"

"Just one more thing," she says, picking up her legal pad and paperwork again.

Rule #3 is I continue my list.

"No matter what happens," she adds. "I know I told you not to show off but those items have to be executed to the best of your ability."

I ask about consequences.

The punishment greatness brings.

"Seeing how you deal with adversity is all part of the process, kiddo," she says. "Just make sure you don't get hurt."

SESSION 27
SPEAK

And Dana says, "When I was a little girl...about 7 or 8, I saw a limo in the city stopped along a parkway."

This was back when limousines all looked the same, before the Humvee so-big-God-could-sit-inside-it extended model with that tacky neon undercarriage lighting. Classy over flashy.

"It was the first one I'd ever seen," Dana tells me. "And even at such a young age I didn't need anyone to tell me there was something special about it."

Something important.

A mechanical eloquence.

"I kept finding myself trying to stare through the tinted window," she says. "Perhaps—I don't know...*hoping* that maybe if I saw what was happening within, somehow I'd feel what they were feeling."

Her hand serpentines down my stomach to the tray.

Ashes.

She drags and continues on, saying, "I think we're all doing that in some way or another...trying to stare through the tinted window."

Everyone is two people.

The one thing we want to see most is the one we're not meant to.

"This is no different from a paraplegic trying to walk or Rosa Parks refusing to remove herself from a front row bus seat."

Some laws are meant to be defied.

To quote: "Rules are made to be broken."

"But now the rules have changed," she says, a little despondent. "I'll ride in a limo and won't feel that eloquence or class that I envied from afar as a little girl. I don't even feel completely at ease."

She stomps her cigarette out and places the tray on the nearside table.

Curls into me.

"I can't get comfortable because I know they're out there...the people staring through the tinted window."

The blind defying the blind.

Remember how we're all wearing our worst poker face.

We're all trying to penetrate the impossibly opaque.

"Have you figured out what you're going to do?" Dana asks, those deep dark sunglasses reflecting myself onto me in the late daylight. The frames as pearl as her nude body. She never takes them off.

"I don't know," I shake.

I broke rule #1.

I told Dana.

"Haven't really thought about it," I add.

"*Haven't* or didn't want to?" she cross-examines. "Seriously, Aidin, you really need to figure this out," she huffs, adjusting.

Why do we ride in limos?

To feel better about ourselves or to feel superior to everyone else?

Maybe it's all the same.

"That list won't last forever," she reminds me.

And it's a terribly scary thought, but she's right. It won't. Eventually, I'll have to come up with my own itinerary, and how good could that be? The things I come up with on my own are either some extension of the list or a repeat of what I've already done.

Like sex.

Sex with Dana.

We have sex because she wants to. Wants to help me get off in a way that doesn't involve getting off. And all through it she'll speak things like, "Orgasm with your eyes, not your cock."

She'll say, "Don't feel me come, taste it," riding my chin and tongue.

And, "Listen to me getting off on you."

Fuck-fuck-fucking me for hours and hours.

She'll ride me pale and sweating with Dior sunglasses spitting out dirty speak that's the mind's sexual equivalent of patting your head while rubbing your stomach. It's all very overwhelming and confusing, intense and multi-directional.

In the apex of anti-romantic settings:

Brightly lit.

Dead silent.

No scented candles.

She wants to make sure that I'm seeing, hearing, tasting, and smelling every bit of the experience I can't feel. Every detail.

She removes the tinted window: the darkness and mood music.

"What we need to do is apply what you're learning in here out in the real world," she tells me. "But being as smart as you are, you'd think you'd be able to figure this out on your own."

This is that sad classic tale of the man in the wheelchair who could cure everyone around him but his own person.

This is every celebrity who went off the deep end because they couldn't handle the weight of fame.

"If you don't figure out what you want for yourself," Dana says. "You'll be crushed by the wanting of others."

This is why God never shows his face.

This is why we didn't get that second coming of Christ.

No one wants to come back to a bunch of mooches with their hands out.

"Y'know, you're kinda stuck with this life you're living. What do you want from it?" she asks.

I tell her I want to be happy.

"I just want to be normal," I say.

She snickers, "Dude, that's kind of like, the default answer, isn't it? That'd be like asking me if I'd like to see again."

Or asking me if I'd like to feel again.

"This may sound like a gay parental thing to say, but you seriously can do whatever you want," Dana smiles into my ear.

"Even your butt?" I joke.

She tells me I'm evading again in a very Paradies-like tone

and my chest bounces in laughter.

Dana's right, though.

I am evading.

There's a major difference between your parents giving you the same old you-have-so-much-potential speech and having proof of said potential by way of a 234 IQ.

"I'm gonna need you to come up with a cure for cancer over the weekend," Paradies said in our last session. "Just e-mail it to me with detailed instructions on how to recreate it myself when you get it," and I just sort of looked at her unsure until she finally revealed, "It was just a joke. I don't have to be serious *all* the time."

Obligation might not be a factor yet but it's in the mail. Seriously, it's only a matter of time before people start asking for formulas and cures like gifts from a shopping mall Santa.

"Yeah, I definitely wouldn't tell anyone," Dana says, her hand grazing the surface of my stomach. "Anyone *else*, I mean," she corrects. "You'll disappear like Hoffa and shit."

They'll lock me away in a little room and it will be problems and formulas and cures for the rest of my life. Algorithms and proofs. Solutions.

"The irony about this is that if you come up with the cure for AIDS, you'll totally have a bunch of chicks who had AIDS wanting to fuck your brains out as thanks," she examines.

I can always count on Dana for perfect social commentary.

"Oh, and gay men, too," she adds. "You'd get more ass than Elton John and Queen combined, and that Pedro guy from *The Real World* would probably be first in line...y'know, if he wasn't already dead from AIDS."

Michael J. Fox has dibs on Parkinson's.

Sally Field has Osteoporosis.

"What will you do?" Dana asks.

I'll try to see through the tinted window.

I'll glare into the impossibly opaque and wonder what's on the other side for me, and just like everyone else, I'll never really know.

Until Paradies tells me, I'll never know.

And neither will Dr. Thornton.
He's gone now.
Dead.

SESSION 28
DETECTIVE STEPHEN FINCH

I'm watching *Trainspotting* while building a model aircraft carrier when this insinuating little twerp—this sorry excuse for a cop, Detective Stephen Finch comes to my door. On my stoop, this guy is your basic *Law & Order* rip-off in a trench coat without the leading man presence, and what he wants to do is ask me a few questions regarding the untimely death of one Dr. Thomas Thornton.

Mr. IQ test. Mr. I'll-keep-calling-until-you-pick-up.

Finch asks, "Do you know anything about what happened?"

But I'm more concerned about the glue drying to my fingers, rubbing them together, shrugging, "Why the fuck would I kill him? He gave me scones," and it's still not coming off. The glue.

Finch says after clearing his throat, "We pulled his phone records. He was calling your doctor a good four or five times a day regarding you. Doesn't that strike you as a bit odd?" he asks, eyebrows rising. Examining.

Leave it to a cop to accuse and question in the same sentence.

"Not really," I admit.

"Not really?" he crosses.

I shrug, "I don't know what to tell you."

I did it.

I did it.

I did it.

That's what he wants to hear.

A nice fat confession will see this asshole celebrating in some shit-hole bar with a handle of bourbon or whiskey or whatever this dried-up faggot drinks.

"Can I get you some water or coffee?" I offer.

"No, I'm fine, thanks," he smiles that shit-eating grin of his. "Aidin, do you think you could tell me you were on the night in question?"

Actually, I could.

So could Paradies.

And Frank.

"At a bar," I tell him. "I don't recall the exact name, though. Sorry."

I have a tendency to put things on my to-do list out of my mind once I do them. I'm still normal in that respect.

"Doin' a little drinking, then?" the detective smiles congenially. "I understand. Does a nightclub called Vox on the Plaza sound familiar?"

And I'm thinking, *eat shit.*

"Yeah, I believe that was it," I gander.

He scribbles.

Nods.

I ask, "How did he die?"

Could it perhaps have been from a chemical compound that was cut into his black tea that slowly ate away at his esophagus and stomach lining?

Maybe it was a liquid bio-toxin applied to the inner surface of his refrigerator door handle that soaked into his fingertips every time he went to make a turkey sandwich or Caesar salad.

Finch says, "We're actually not really sure yet."

Check his central air unit. There could be a poisonous anomaly hooked into it, which acts as a fatal pathogen.

That's how I would've done it.

"The autopsy report is inconclusive thus far," he tells me. "But there are signs of struggle so we have to look into it."

Detective Stephen Finch, you just don't get it, do you? Only a moron would leave the sufficient evidence to get caught, and I'm definitely not one of those. Thornton could attest to that, if he were available.

"At what time did you arrive at the bar?" he asks.

10:00. Sharp.

"And departure?"

147

"Close...so—what?" I think aloud. "Like 2:30, I guess."

"And your driver, Frank, took you home?"

I nod. He's obviously already spoken with Dr. Paradies regarding the subject. Maybe my parents.

"Well, Aidin, you seem like a nice young man," he says, folding up his notepad. "I'm really sorry to have to come bother you with this on a weekend, but well...it's all in the job."

"Oh, no problem," I say.

Finch informs, "I'll give you a ring if I need anything, but chances are you'll never see me again. This guy probably just reached the end of his line."

And so will you if you don't get the fuck off of my porch.

"Yeah," I ponder aloud. "Shit happens."

He nods.

Exits.

SESSION 29
THE DANA SYNOPTIC

Dana Lafon was born on September 7th, to Michael and Brooke, a businessman and real estate agent in the upper-class suburbs of Leawood, KS.

About Michael, she says, "He keeps his cocaine stash in a balled up pair of argyle socks from Banana Republic...the same ones I bought him as a Christmas gift."

Sound familiar?

Stop me if you heard this one.

Regarding Brooke, she observes, "The funny thing about my mom is that I used to see her everywhere...on billboards and bench ads and those tacky movie theater advertisements that play before the film starts, and now...well...not so much."

This is why we connect so well.

Because there's more than one way to *not* see your parents.

"Dr. P. says my mom feels responsible for what happened to me, which I guess is why she's become so overbearing," she relays. "It's seriously annoying, though, sometimes."

In doctor's speak it's called the "too little too late" factor.

Rapists usually experience this when some ball-busting Nazi skinhead is making their asshole a personal playground for the first of many times.

Remember how we're only really sorry when karma comes full circle to bite us in the ass, or in this case, sodomize it.

"At least her heart is in the right place," Dana concedes.

The difference between being born blind and going blind is how many times you have to learn the million simple little everyday things in life. Just like me, for Dana, everything became a challenge, the biggest one being going from denial to acceptance.

Everyone is two people.

A before and after.

And before Dana was a Tri Delt at the University of Kansas, majoring in physical therapy. In the spring she would tan on the front lawn of the house while listening to Mix 93.3 at full volume and watching boys run by. Shirts off. Sweat pouring. Skin: tan and smooth and alluring. And when the leaves turned and fell away in the fall she switched to the UV beds at Endless Summer, the salon on 22nd and Louisiana Street. Dana had a membership. So all year, in any given season, she was tan. And blonde. In those days she was tan and blonde and drove a Gold Lexus. She even bought shoes to match the paintjob. Then a belt she found at Express. Dana did stuff like that. She collected handbags and sunglasses: by Dior and Kate Spade and Coach and Prada. By Dolce & Gabbana and Louis Vuitton. By Liz Claiborne. All on her dad's AmEx and Visa Platinum cards. Her parents rarely called or visited. She faked sick on Dad's Day because she knew he couldn't make it. Stomach flu, she told the other girls. And to feel better about things she shopped more than usual and had some cheesecake. And pizza. Dana and her roommates began having period pizza night once their menstrual cycles finally synched up, swapping stories about all the whores and skanks in the house, none of which ever included them. Even when they did openly admit to being fucked by a guy and never called again (which was rare; the admission, not the act), they were never a skank or a whore. Ever. It was "just a night of fun." Details often changed or were embellished, like the time Dana fucked the school's starting point guard when all she really did was blow him. And did his laundry. But not in that order. His words (while pulling himself out of his track pants), "I guess I owe you this much," haunting her entire week until she finally drank them away and blacked it out. He watched the movie *Hoosiers* while she did it and called her Diana when she left. And it was raining that night. Pouring. So when Dana came home and her mascara was bleeding charcoal down her cheeks, no one knew she had been crying. A small part of her wanted them to know that, though. To be acknowledged. For the comfort. It was a bad night for her. But still, according to Dana, she'd say of him, "He was cool right up until the point he starting talking, the fuckin' jock idiot," causing her friends to laugh and giggle loud and long enough to mask the memory she was recreating every time she told it. There was definitely a difference between what happened and what *really* happened.

Dana was never as important as she felt.

She was never as pretty as she was told.

She was never as composed as she pretended.

Remember how if all Barbies are created equal than none of them are really special. An elite little socialite Dana was, yes, but she was merely one of many. She had opinions, but regarding only the most trivial and irrelevant of subjects. She had friends, but they called her a whore and a skank every time she turned her back (especially when it came to that basketball player thing). She had money, but so did everybody else. Collectively, she fit right into the scene. That Greek sub-group of the all-American college girl. She'd go to The Wheel and The Hawk and Brother's with about six or seven of her sisters. About four or five nights a week it was Quentin's, Louise's Downtown, and Last Call. Fatso's and Henry's upstairs. But never house parties because those were for people who couldn't get into the real bars. That was the off-brand Wal-Mart version of nightlife. The lowest quality of partying. That was what house parties were, except if said house was a frat house, then it was okay. It was fine because those guys had standards. Invite only. DJ. Open bar. That's the only kind of house party worth going to as far as Dana and her group was concerned, and they were invited to about as many as they could handle.

Rush parties.

Costume balls.

And date nights.

Without fail, these guys were always as good-looking as they were hungry to get inside her pants. Up her skirt. No matter the event, Dana had that knowledge in the forefront of her brain, that *every* guy, no matter how sweet or genuine or harmless he seemed, wanted nothing more than to fuck her, and would act in any fashion, portray any degree of gentleman-like behavior, to achieve that.

Because everyone is two people.

This is who I am and this who you *think* I am.

They were good-looking, charming young men seeking higher education. They were sexually crazed pricks that bought their friends and inebriated their women to the point of making a bad decision.

They were brothers.

They were brothelites.

And Dana was that little anti-Cinderella who'd end up leaving a bra or her underwear behind because she didn't want to wake the man she was trying to escape from in the morning. Wake up too late in a fraternity sleeping dorm and it's the walk of shame for you, and Dana wouldn't be subjected to such of thing. What no one ever told her though, is that even if no one's watching--even if you're walking alone and barefoot on a vacant morning campus, you still feel it. You feel it more, even. Through the most severe and heavy of hangovers, you still feel it. And that's how it went for a while. Dana's sisters were her friends and her friends were kept as close as enemies could be.

She went to class and studied and read (but only when she had to).

She blew the occasional line (but it never became a problem).

She hooked-up more than what she let on (as everyone did).

She drank and smoked (but only socially).

She lived well (or so she thought).

But that was Dana before. Before the shift into the now. And the transition began on spring break. In Cabo. She was staying in Cabo for the week with four of her sisters from the house. The trip was what she thought it would be: drinking, sand and beaches, boys: tanned and bronze, coconut cocktails and shots, swimsuits, sunglasses, boys from northern schools: ashen and pale, hotel swimming pools, bar lounges, all-you-can-drink specials running on and on for days so long you lost track, $1 Coronas, $2 shooters, electro pulsing from the outer bars to the dry sky above, gentle wind and cool water, more drinking, a little coke here and there, the northern school boys looking tanner, more attractive, a little more desirable, a walk down the beach never unabridged by catcalls and whistles and drink offers. The cheap merchandise peddling of street vendors. Then, right in the middle of it all, it became different. Something changed. About Dana. She woke up one morning hung-over, nude and tan in her hotel suite. She woke up and things were a little fuzzy. Blurry. And the next day it was a little worse. The sun shone a little harsher to her, but she made no mention of it. Not immediately. Not until the day of departure when everything looked watercolors. It was only when Dana was seeing Cabo like a Monet rendition did she speak up. She said she needed to see a doctor but her friends, her sisters, just kept telling her to wait. Just hold on until we get back, they said. And, don't ruin this for us. Just hold your ponies. So she did. She waited silently and without further complaint. Through the last moments of the trip and the plane delay and the flight. The three-hour layover in Dallas and the final approach home, she waited. And waited.

But when Dana finally got home it was too late.

It was too late because then became now.

And now was a terribly scary place.

"That feeling of having a hair trapped between your contact lens and your eye," Dana sets up. "Yeah—totally so much worse than that."

Imagine staring at the sun until your tear ducts exhaust and dry up.

Picture someone practicing the cursive alphabet on your pupil with a thumbtack.

In doctor's speak this is known as "relative imagery."

"But there's a major difference between knowing and pretending to know," Dana says. "I mean, yeah, I bet it would suck if I were black and someone called me a nigger, but unless there's a race and history changing machine out there I don't know about, then I'll never really understand it, will I?"

In short, empathy isn't experience.

This is how it feels and this is how you *think* it feels.

"But those fuckin' Tri Delts wouldn't even give me that,"

Dana snickers. "Let's just say that comforting the resident blind girl didn't exactly make their list of priorities."

After she got back to the states and had received the official diagnosis that a foreign bacteria had infiltrated its way into her corneal regions and essentially eaten them away, Dana underwent surgery. Then rehab. Then another surgery. More rehab. Then one more time under the knife.

"Not one of those cunts came to visit me," she says, a tear slipping down her cheek from behind a Dior lens. "I did get a text, though."

Her mother read to her: *Can you see yet?*

"I dropped out of the house...out of school," she speaks. "Had my mom pick up my stuff and set up my old room at home."

Enter: Dr. Paradies.

Say hello to little Miss I-can-fix-anybody.

"At first I thought my mom was pawning me off...y'know, because she didn't want to deal with it," Dana recalls. "But then I realized this was the first situation that she couldn't schmooze or smile through."

Can you see yet?

Everyone is two people.

"The first time in my entire life I saw my mom cry I couldn't even observe it," she says. "Which is probably what made it so hard for me."

Your ideal moment will never live up to how you imagined it. Same rule applies for the bad.

And when you can't see, your imagination runs wild.

Remember this when you're picturing your perfect wedding or sex with a celebrity, because odds are, it's going to be nowhere near as good as you thought.

There's no such thing as a perfect life.

Just perfect moments.

"It was when she broke that I knew she cared—like, *really* cared...and I also knew how terrified she was for me."

Which is why Dr. Paradies came in.

With her doctor's speak and precautionary tactics. Her

advice. The constant scribbling on her legal pad and tapping of her pen. Dana's mom picked up the pieces but Dr. Paradies was the one that put them together.

And with the list we arrive at the now.

Item #114: Learn Braille.

Item #31: Set each contact in your cell phone to a distinctive ring.

Item #271: Get a massage.

"That list seriously became my life," Dana admits. "Not *quite* like you, but close."

Lose your friends and your social life, your job and your ability to do anything independently, and let's see how well you take it. Look me in the eye and tell me your priorities are the same as they used to be.

Ticking off on her fingers, she goes, "I gained ten pounds, stopped tanning, and went back to my natural hair color for a few years. So, I guess you could say I stopped giving a shit."

Looks don't mean much when you can't see them.

And right on cue I tell her, "I think you're pretty the way you are."

She says, "Wish I could say the same for you," with a grin.

And that's everything about Dana.

She knows me and I know her. We share a doctor and have our lists, though mine is decisively longer and closer to complete than hers. She helps me. Helps me see the bright side that she can't. Makes me appreciate what's left. What's important. And I help her. With simple stuff. Like leg shaving and finding certain CDs or checking her e-mail. I helped her make a MySpace page even though she probably won't use it that often. We have dinner and wine often. Lunch occasionally. Dana likes to go on walks. On the Plaza. Through the park and the zoo. She likes the sounds and the safety of me being next to her. I enjoy the company: her offbeat comments about life, about relationships, politics and society. And after spending time with her, being with her, recognizing that I need her as much as she needs me, I know could never go back. And so does she. "That life's behind us," she said. As people like us know, there's a before and after. A now and then. And there's no way we can go back to that life: the drugs and the scene and the surfaces of the unimportant and superficial. We're moving beyond that together. We progress as people. Evolve. She's become my world.

That's life for me: my list and my girl.

The things I do and the person I love.

And one of those is going to be taken from me.

SESSION 30
SECTION 7

It's colder now.

We're in early November when decent weather is hit or miss, and the morning dew on grass and cars and windows is no longer liquid and soft, but rather, a thin skin of frost. The sky is, more or less, consistently overcast and I have to pay "particularly close attention" to the weather forecasts and garb of civilians passing to ensure I'm appropriately dressed for the day. I have to observe the details.

My steaming breath.

My reddened hands.

The tells of cold that speak when you can't feel them. You have to pay attention. You have to listen to the wind blowing in hard gale to recognize its burn crisping your ears to a seared red. The cold has a smell. A taste. A personality all its own, and I'm familiarizing.

"I'd like to keep you from getting sick again, if I can," Paradies says, scribbling away as per usual. Adding, "And I don't want to hear anything from you about how this isn't important because it *is*. You need to learn to take care of yourself because I'm not going to be around forever."

Paradies baby-proofed my house.

Now she's doing the same to me.

I wave her off from my usual spot on the chaise lounge, saying, "Whatever," sucking on a sugar-free mint because this isn't really a concern.

The common cold isn't so common anymore.

I never cough or sneeze.

There's no fever.

Nothing.

Coughing and sneezing are reactions to uncomfortable

sensations, and sensation is a non-factor in my world. The truth here is that I didn't even notice something was wrong until my sense of smell started to cut out one afternoon. Not all the way, but it was noticeably dulled. Then, shortly after, I started to taste salt on my lips from the mucus river running down my face that, apparently, no one felt comfortable pointing out to me. Even though I had been openly in public with Dana in restaurants and parks and sidewalks, no one was courteous enough to give me sign.

"Could be worse," Paradies offers. "She could've kissed you on the mouth."

"How do you know she didn't?" I ask.

"I don't think I'm breaking any sort of doctor-patient confidentiality when I tell you that's *definitely* something she would've mentioned," the doc smirks.

And it's tempting to pry for further information about Dana, how she feels about me, etc., but I stifle myself.

Paradies wouldn't tell me, and some things are best left unsaid.

Besides, I've got bigger issues on my mind.

Namely, Section 7 of the list.

How it goes:

I'll show up at my specified location at the predetermined time, usually in the extended Lincoln town car but occasionally by cab or bus or on foot—sometimes with an item: a manila envelope or a prepaid cell phone or $10,000 in unmarked bills. Sometimes I'm carrying a 9mm weapon tightly nestled in a leather holster concealed by a designer jacket or coat by Prada or Guess or Banana Republic and I'm mentioning this because appearances are everything. I'm always looking for a man in the camel hair coat or a blonde-haired semi-attractive waitress wearing a red Kabala ribbon around her wrist. A specific gender and height. Hair and eye and skin color. There's always an article or accessory to tip me off, and they always have a question. A nonsensical query.

They'll say, "What does the 'H' in Jesus H. Christ stand for?"

And I'll give the predetermined answer I'm supposed to give, a response that makes even less sense than the question itself, because that's how code works.

Remember that when you're setting up your after-school tree house hangout or united coalition of anarchists base of operations. It's all about security.

Safety. And safety leads to trust.

The guy wearing Gucci sunglasses will ask me, "What does the 'H' in Jesus H. Christ stand for?" and I'll give him the password.

The answer.

I'll say, "Unicorn," and neither of us smile or snicker or grin because it's not funny.

It's a security measure.

Then they'll nod to me.

The universal gesture for, "Yes, that's correct," and we'll make the exchange.

I'll give up whatever I'm supposed to hand over: a bubble envelope holding a data disc or a hollowed-out statuette of the Virgin Mary casing microchips or a tin of Altoids containing a folded sheet of binary code, and I'll get something in return.

Sometimes money.

Sometimes an address.

I never know because I'm not supposed to. It's always changing, this section. The people I meet but never see again. They're in and out of my life, looking for me the way I look for them, and once they get what they've come for, they're gone. Vanished.

This is what Section 7 has become.

It's orders and directions and addresses.

Numbers and coded questions.

If a stunning blonde wearing Curve perfume approaches you at the secondary bar of the Empire Room and asks if you'd like your cock sucked, make sure to answer, "Children should be seen, not heard," because that's the only correct answer there is for this. That's how this works, and what happens after that is she'll pull you to her by the lapels of the Dolce & Gabbana jacket you were instructed to wear, her mouth open and dry and emotionless, sliding an envelope into your pants while she takes the one from your inner-breast pocket for herself, deep-kissing you until the exchange is complete. And what's inside could be anything.

A phone number.

A memory stick.

I never know.

So now I'm asking, "How is this part of my therapy?" real indignant and bitchy and scared. "This feels a little wrong is all," I state (possibly for the first time in my entire life), wondering what Detective Stephen Finch would have to say, if what I'm doing would be referred to as "suspicious behavior."

And Paradies sort of grins and scribbles, "Wrong is a sight better than nothing."

See the phrase: "Beggars can't be choosers."

She says, "Right now you're learning more about yourself than you ever have."

And, "You may not see it just yet, but by the time we get to the end of this thing, believe me, you will. We only have a little ways to go."

Just a bit further.

"But I want to know what I'm doing," I plead to her, sitting upright and staring her down. "Can't you at least tell me that? Give me *something*."

Paradies sighs.

She momentarily discontinues her scribbling and tells me, "You're doing exactly what you're supposed to be doing." Paradies says. "That's all."

I sigh, frustrated, probing further, "Yeah, but what's the point?" my fingernails probably digging into palm. My teeth maybe gritted. I'm not sure.

"It's best if we don't discuss it just now," she tells me, the scribbling resuming.

Another way of saying: what you don't know can't hurt you.

And like the ungrateful little shit that I am, I cross my arms and lean back into the chaise lounge pouting, "Well, maybe I'll just stop then," but I'm so full of shit.

I won't stop.

I can't.

And she knows it.

Paradies knows.

Because everyone wants to feel complete. Nobody ever puts together a 1,000-piece jigsaw puzzle and stops when there's only three pieces left.

Nobody takes an online personality quiz only to bail out on the last question.

We're all living a life where our means justify the ends.

And Paradies knows this about me.

She says, "You won't quit, Aidin," a hint of a smirk rising above the horizon line of the legal pad she continues to scribble in. "You and I both know you won't stop, so let's not delude ourselves here."

But I push it a little bit further. Even though I know she's right, have already accepted it as fact, I keep pushing. I'm always fighting the battle I can't win—that I'm not meant to no matter how many times I try.

The Washington Generals vs. the Harlem Globetrotters.

Every Civil War reenactment the South has lost.

My therapy sessions with Dr. Paradies.

Repetitive losing battles.

We keep fighting.

I'm still pressing when I ask, "But what if I do? What if I just quit right now? All of this," more angry now than rational.

And Paradies tilts her legal pad down so quickly it slaps against her leg. She lowers it hard and points at me, "Then the next time a detective comes to your house you might not get out of it so easily! That's what happens!"

A metaphorical chill runs down my spine when she tells me more composed, "I made you, and believe me when I say it would take a minimal effort on my part to unmake you."

She says, "It's time to take some responsibility, Aidin."

And we both know she's right.

We *both* know, because everyone is two people.
Everyone.

Session 31
Shape

Some of these items are ongoing. Continuous.

"Positive lifestyle changes," Paradies calls them.

They're currently crossed off on the list but they never really end. Ever. Not until I decide to stop doing them, and I can tell you right now, that's never gonna happen because this is just like the jigsaw puzzle and coloring book. The Rubik's cube and my Lincoln Log cabin.

I see results.

And results are addictive.

I'm just your run-of-the-mill success junkie.

Mid-way through the list: after Section 1 but way before Section 7, I started some routines, things I could do in between therapy and groups and my items, and now that the list has wound down and I no longer attend Making Sense or Circle of Healing, I'm finding my devotion to these activities has markedly increased.

"We need to heal your existence," Paradies informed me, and she actually used *that* word.

The word "heal."

"Because if you continue your current lifestyle in the condition you're in," she said, "You *will* destroy yourself...and you've already come close to doing that once."

Her throwback example.

Let's not even think about it right now.

Tapping on the particular section of the list, she told me, "These will protect you." Then, finger sliding down, she said, "And these will arm you."

And the first part is exactly what you'd think, a list of precautionary measures.

Quit smoking.

Hire a nutritionist.

Consume no drugs.

Drink little or no alcohol.

Start and adhere to a diet.

Incur no harm upon yourself.

Refrain from unprotected sex.

Avoid excessively sharp objects.

Sleep at least eight hours every night.

A list that basically contradicts everything I was at the end of the "before" and the beginning of the "after," and there was no question as to how I could do any of these things, but rather, how long.

"Go back to your old ways and you fail," Paradies said.

That's doctor's speak for "relapse."

See also: "retrograde" and "backslide."

Those were the other words she could've used.

Just like knowing that "sexy panda cutie slut muffin" translates to a cheerleader orgy, I'm also fluent in doctor's speak. I'm a walking thesaurus of clinical terms now, but only one of them bothers me these days.

It used to be "feel."

Now it's "fail."

I'm afraid of failure.

But I'm more afraid of conclusions.

And this is why this particular section of the list is getting so much of my attention.

Now let's go back. Go back to when I was eating ten meals a day and forty pounds overweight. Remember my restaurant tourism days and think about how I could've eaten myself into an early grave had Paradies not jumped in with her list and stopped me, giving me that "healthy alternative."

The "sound option."

Look back on that and think about how I was so disgusted with myself that I had the Herford House and Bo Ling's and The Cheesecake Factory cater to my home so I didn't have to be seen gorging myself in public.

Remember that and look at me now.

My nutritionist Samantha has me stripped down to my navy blue Gap boxers saying, "I can't believe this," pinching me with stainless steel physician tongs while I'm trying to surmise if this would normally hurt or tickle, remaining undecided.

She asks, "It's only been a month, right?" the tongs moving to my love handle (what's left of it, anyway).

Samantha is referring to my last examination.

I nod yes.

"This is really impressive, Aidin," she comments genuinely. "What have you been doing?"

The old me, the egomaniacal womanizer that was my former self—he would brag at this point. He would assess the situation and start formulating a plan as to how to turn this compliment into more. He would invite her out that evening and bed her that night. Then fire her the next day since it would obviously be too weird to see her anymore. That's what the old me would do.

The "before" version.

But I'm different now.

Evolved and changed.

So instead I modestly grin and say, "Y'know...working out, eating right. Nothing special," but that's complete bullshit.

I've traded in my cheddar-shrouded Kobe beef patty for the rice-oat Semolina burger. The firebrick oven meat trio flatbread has become the eggplant and olive vegan pizza. I am high-fiber. Low fat. An organic fruits and vegetables convert, but that's just the diet portion.

I'm so regimented and in shape I could join the marines. The police or some elite Special Forces unit.

My abs are cubed and sharp. Building blocks. Obliques are like Roman armor. Every corner and aspect of my body is perfect, naturally sunned and toned and hardened from hours of shirtless running. The shoulders ripple. Thighs tense. I'm sculpted. A perfect specimen. A tank. An army of one.

"Your body fat is at five percent," Samantha tells me with a look of concern. I ask what's wrong, and she says, "Well nothing, I guess. It's just that it's down eleven percent from what you were back in July."

And this is November.

Just before Paradies decided to freak out on me.

A couple days previous.

"I've been working out a little more than usual," I explain, to which Samantha gives a sort of accusatory lift of the eyebrow, as if I'm not telling her the whole story.

"Okay, *a lot* more," I admit.

Samantha grabs her clipboard and starts noting results not unlike Paradies, telling me, "Just be sure you don't overdo it. You don't want to burn out."

Samantha doesn't know about my condition.

Neither does my trainer.

Scott.

My personal trainer's name is Scott and I've been going to him since early July (right around the time I first went to Samantha), and what I told Scott was two things.

1) I want to get into the best shape of my life.

2) I have coordination and balance problems.

That way when I dropped something or tripped over my own two feet I didn't have to explain myself. Having no coordination sounds a hell of a lot better than not being able to feel your feet when they hit the ground or not realizing your right arm is pushing harder than your left on the bench press. It took care of a lot of questions.

Except one.

I never get tired.

Scott noticed this on the first time I came in overweight and dumpy-looking in my designer sweats and styled hair. You could tell he wanted to find out how much of a puss I was.

To size me up.

To see what he was working with.

He said, "I'm going to hold your feet down and I want you to start doing sit-ups."

"How many?" I asked.

He said, "Do as many as you possibly can until you physically feel you can't do anymore."

A max out. These are used to determine a client's personal baseline of physical activity.

And I shrugged and said, "Okay," carefully lying down, legs bent at the knees. My feet held down by his weight. I cross my arms in front of my chest and sit up.

I do one.

Then twenty-five.

Then seventy-six.

Then one hundred and forty-eight.

I do three hundred and two.

Then four hundred and fifty.

Then five hundred and nine.

I never get tired and he never tells me to stop.

So I do five hundred and eighty-eight.

Then six hundred and seventy-three.

Then eight hundred and thirty-seven.

And when I reach a thousand nothing happens.

So I keep going to one thousand two hundred and eighty-nine.

One thousand four hundred and ninety-nine.

Fifteen hundred. Fifteen hundred and one.

Sweat pours and my face would appear burnt red to me if I could see it. My eyes are blurry and bloodshot from all the hair product and salted juices leaking into them. The suit is soaked. The floor beneath me has pooled. Damp and slick on the rubber gym tarp. A wet slapping noise happens every time I lay my back down to the floor. My shoes squeak when they slide. I'm drenched. And everyone's watching. At around five hundred or so they started glaring. I've just hit two thousand but the only people that would know that are Scott and myself since neither of us is counting aloud.

He tells me to stop.

The gym applauds.

He smiles, and when he does this I get the feeling he doesn't do it often, but he smiles at me and says, "Nice job, kid."

Adding, "I'm not even gonna ask how you just did that."

And he says, "I'm looking forward to seeing what you're

capable of," which registers a certain sort of déjà vu within me, but he buys me a protein smoothie and the feeling quickly dissipates.

Slowly I transform.

Evolve.

I start out going to see Scott a couple times a week.

Mondays and Thursdays.

Needless to say, this is a trial and error process.

Everything is process. Like running. I could no longer think of running as a fluid motion anymore because that had landed me facedown on the tarp too many times already. You have to crawl before you walk and jog before you run.

That's what we did.

And no matter how many times I fell or dropped something, a barbell or a weight or a medicine ball, I got up and kept trying. That's what mattered to Scott, that no matter how badly I scraped myself up or how many fresh bruises I had at the end of the day, I always kept going.

He said, "Falling isn't failure. Not getting back up is."

He said, "You can't run because you're approaching it wrong."

"We need to break this up into steps," he told me.

Because when you tell someone to build a rocket ship it seems impossible. Beyond comprehension. But when you break it down into a million easy little steps it becomes something else. Something capable. Viable.

This was just another logic problem.

And logic problems are nothing when you're a genius.

Scott kept giving me tips like, "Listen to your footsteps."

And, "Always keep your chin slightly in front of your pelvis."

And, "Use your eyes and ears as much as your feet."

Training with Scott was a lot like fucking Dana: that sensory substitution to do the things that were no longer simple anymore.

Every Monday and Thursday I learned a little more.

Then I started going on Sundays, too.

Then Wednesdays.

Always, we were doing new things while improving on the old, and if the big numb got in the way, we worked around it.

Benching more than a couple hundred pounds was dangerous because of the balance issue, so we took the sit-up approach.

Repeat.

Repeat.

Repeat.

I can't bench 250 pounds but I can do the bar 250 times.

"You have a natural endurance about you, and endurance leads to strength," Scott told me, and just like Paradies, he was right.

I learned to run.

Then I learned to sprint.

It's November and I'm in the best shape of my life. I'm in perfect health. My body is lean and toned and hard, and when I go to the gym, I can feel them watching me. They watch me run around the indoor track, shirt off and glistening, and I can feel the eyes follow. Mouths moving. Whispering. I hear them in fragments at certain points of the track.

They'll say, "...his fourth mile and he's still..."

And, "...in fifteen second quarters..."

And, "...unbelievable..."

It's when I'm running like this—so fast my legs and the faces of spectators blur, that I realize that there would be no way I could do this if it weren't for the numb. I'd be feeling pain right now, out of breath and sore and tired, but I'm incapable of that, and for the first time ever I'm thankful.

It's that feeling of gratitude that makes me think a crazy thought; something I never imagined could cross my mind. Ever. Not in a million years.

Running at top speed on my twelfth lap, I grin through the sweat and think, "This isn't so bad."

I think maybe I could get used to this.

Maybe I don't want this ride to end.

My therapy, however, is questionable.

SESSION 32
ITEM #80

In the future, our youth of America won't know anything about Hercules, Zeus, or Hades. Outdated are the names Poseidon and Aphrodite. The Earth goddess, Gaia.

Greek mythology and all its lore will be lost on these kids, replaced with figures such as Spider-Man, Green Lantern, and Captain America. Daredevil and Batman, guys running around in capes and underwear, knocking the crap out of some cat burglar or purse snatcher and hanging their unconscious bodies from a telephone pole.

These are our idols.

Our modern heroes.

And Item #80 is my study of them, reading Superman, The Flash, and various other titles where the relative trends and patterns remain the same.

Woman in trouble. Save her.

World in trouble. Save it.

Nuclear war. Stop it.

The protagonist, or hero, is presented with a problem, but most of the time it's not even *their* problem. You begin to ask yourself: exactly what kind of person jumps between two rival gangs knowing full well they'll be caught in the crossfire? Who actively goes *looking* for trouble?

In doctor's speak, this is known as, "conflict-seeking behavior."

Sometimes referred to as: "the hero complex."

But for all their heroics, these characters are inherently simple and predictable. Read enough comic books and graphic novels and you'll see the patterns. This is just another logic problem. Everyone is two people.

When Superman isn't flying over the skyscrapers of

Metropolis, he is mild-mannered Clark Kent, reporter for the Daily Planet.

When Spider-Man isn't swinging through the concrete canyons of Manhattan, he is the awkward dork known as Peter Parker.

In the comic book universe, the citizen persona is known as the "secret identity," and therein exists the problem. One of these identities is living a lie, sometimes to the point where their friends and family members are put in immediate danger based on what they *don't* know. The hero is naïve in this way, because eventually—sooner or later, the face behind the mask is exposed, but it's usually the people around them that suffer first.

These are the consequences that happen when you only devote yourself halfway. It's what happens when you think you can alternate between normal and super. Show me a hero and I'll show you a girlfriend with a gun to her head or a relative being thrown off a building. For every mask there's a man behind it scared shitless because he has to choose between his wife or diffusing a bomb on the Brooklyn Bridge.

They call this particular kind of climax "the impossible choice."

The same way these guys idealistically believe they can be two things at once, they're looking for that loophole as to how a rigged-to-explode subway train can be taken care of while delivering their rent check on time.

How can you take your chemistry final *and* foil the robbery currently in progress at the First National Bank of Tribeca?

Our modern heroes, despite their daily sacrifices, are trying to have their cake and eat it, too. They're double booking, so they'll never be completely heroic or a fully functioning person. Always fragmented. Always making the impossible choice.

This is why characters such as the Joker and Dr. Octopus are so dangerous, because for every part-time hero there is a full-time nemesis. The true villain has no costume, no personal life or job they need to report to. Most importantly, they have no rules.

Unlike the hero, they are completely and totally free.

Never forget how dangerous freedom can be.

SESSION 33
THE CATALYST

It's November 11th (a Friday), and I'm waking up before my alarm goes off because I have a lot on my mind right now and much to do if I want to have any hope of clearing my head of it, but this—my current disposition reminds me of the past (the before) because it used to be that if I was ever distraught about something, I could pop a Xanax or masturbate or drink a couple vodka tonics and I'd be fine. I could go to Hush for bottle service or pick up a couple strippers at Temptations or Whispers or some other flesh joint of an equally obscure name. It was just that easy. All these immediate solutions that were at my disposal turned ineffective when I became what I am now. When I became numb.

And it wasn't so long ago that if I woke up this way I could work on my list.

I could climb a tree.

Fly a kite or go to a movie.

I could build a birdhouse or a feeder.

All these little activities were available to me, and for a time, things were good, but the list has wound down and progress can't be undone. Nowadays, when I flip though the booklet I get frustrated. Seeing all that red ink and those checked boxes, the dates and initials sealing these items into finality. It's a glass half-empty/half-full mixture of emotions for me.

Sometimes I feel pride.

But mostly I feel regret.

And I know what you're thinking because Paradies thought of it, too.

At the first signs of distress regarding this she posed to me, "You know you can do these more than once, don't you?"

I sort of nod sullenly from the chaise lounge, hoping she

wouldn't suggest that, but not so deep down, I knew she would.

But you can't recycle an experience.

Think about all the things you've done twice: riding a roller coaster or doing H, a threesome with two Swedish models, eating filet mignon window-side at Skies with a $240 bottle of red inches away, listening to the new Radiohead CD you've been waiting three months for. Think about these things. Think about them and how there's only one first time for anything but the sequels can number infinitely. The first time you watched *The Sixth Sense*. The view of the Paris skyline from the Eiffel Tower at sunset. Your first visit from the Tooth Fairy.

Constantly, we're trying to relive and recreate these moments and experiences in the exact way we felt them the first time only to stopped short in a taunting state of nostalgia. We're cloning memories of the real in our most desperate of dreams.

The exquisite thrill of a woman's touch.

Or the perfect drug we love too much.

That used to be me.

And what I was once so devoted to I feel I've potentially abused in my haste to get through it. I devoured these experiences so quickly that the time was never taken to savor them. Now it's down to this:

Five items remain:

Three are from Section 7.

One is an appointment.

The last I can't control.

The three from Section 7 will be what they have been, I expect. I'll show up at a certain place at a certain time. The clothes will be wardrobe, predetermined and chosen not by me. I'll receive an item (an envelope, a package, or a briefcase) and will exchange it for something else with a person I've never met and will never see again. It will be smooth and quick and vague just like the last fifteen or fifty times I've done it, and after it's over we'll never speak of it again.

If I try to talk about it with Paradies, I'll be deterred.

Anyone else, and they won't have the heart to care.

Speaking to Dana a couple weeks ago I say, "I don't know

if I want to do this anymore."

Her response: "Got anything better to do?"

She said, "There's a reason why she's the doctor and you're the patient. Maybe you should stop asking so many questions and finish what you started."

And on the outside I'm nodding my head and saying, yeah, you're probably right, trying to be understanding and empathetic to the cause. I try to examine this from an outsider's point of view and recognize how far our therapy has taken us, but inside, just below the surface of things, I'm thinking, what if I started something I shouldn't have?

What if I'm not supposed to finish?

Just because someone is a doctor doesn't mean you can automatically trust them.

See also: cops, politicians, and judges.

Don't you dare forget: Catholic priests.

As a society, we're brought up to believe that these people are there to guide and protect and serve us. They're our icons and leaders of the world, our forefathers of today. The virtuous.

I had complete faith in Paradies.

Had.

Until last session.

Now there's one word of doctor's speak that keeps revolving in the back of my mind, a word that can kill your career if you're in the position that Dr. Paradies is in.

They call it "malpractice."

Like taking the lord's name in vain in a church, it's something you just don't say unless you're absolutely sure, and I'm not quite there yet.

Not yet, but I will be soon.

Tonight, actually.

So until then, it's business as usual.

I eat a light breakfast: cinnamon oatmeal with green apple slices. Ocean Spray grape juice to drink. Both of my parents, of course, are already gone. I watch Fox 4 News at nine while listening to The Republic Tigers album on my iPod. Frank sends me a text from the circle drive outside. It says: *Ready when you are.* I grab my gym bag and head out the door. In the car I drink a half a bottle of Evian while watching *The Sopranos* (season 2) with the sound off, subtitles on, skipping the therapy scenes and wondering if I was being threatened or warned.

...the next time a detective comes to your house you might not get out of it so easily!

And before I can think, *get out of what?* I realize the scenery has stopped moving and we're at the gym. It's about 9:30 in the morning, so I tell Frank to give me a couple hours, sliding him a $50 and mentioning that Le Peep does a really good breakfast. Three blocks down, two over, and he's smiling. Smiling like I'm not the spoiled brat that I once was and easily still could be. We go our separate ways.

Inside the gym, I'm immediately recognized by Jill who works at the front counter; a girl that I fear has "flirting with clients" listed in her job description, though now I'm sure she might actually feel something genuine for me. "Feel," in the obtuse, meaning that she's seen me arrive in the extended Lincoln town car nearly every day wearing designer clothing. Today it's T-shirt and jeans (both from Armani Exchange) and my black Prada loafers with Burberry sunglasses. She's seen the American Express card and the wad of 100's I carry (usually a couple grand). Basically, she's seen the surface, the one defining facet of my ever-lacking personality before the numb (which, of course, she doesn't know about).

In all honesty though, if you really want to know why I think this girl views me as more than a client, why she might just have some sincere intentions of attraction towards me that aren't monetarily related, then I'd have to say it was the transformation.

I'm not talking about the exterior because there are plenty of people that come in here looking like I do now. Muscle and tone is fairly common. This is about the process. Watching what a person goes through to become what they are.

Seeing a caterpillar and a butterfly are fairly mundane.

Watching one evolve into the other is something else.

I came in 212 pounds and pudgy.

Today I'm 188 and ripped.

Aesthetically perfect.

A sculpture made right before her very eyes, and it's the fact that Jill has witnessed this transformation first-hand that I've been able to captivate her.

I must admit, when I look back on it, when I review everything I've done to arrive at this point, I can see why she'd feel this way.

And again, I have that thought.

...this isn't so bad...

Thinking, *I could live with this.*

Jill with her perfect blonde hair and magazine ad smile, she says, "Hey cutie, how are you?" because she's nineteen or so and doesn't know anything about being subtle, but I play it cool and tell her I'm doing good, attempting to walk by. Unsuccessfully.

She presses, half-whining, "Come here and talk to me-e-e-e. You're *so* business all the time."

The old me echoes, *you could've banged this girl weeks ago.*

I say, "A little later. I gotta run," pacing on, because my current persona doesn't see any point in teasing this girl.

She says okay with a little faux pouty face (or is it real?) and I walk through the main gym and into the locker room to change.

Ten minutes later I'm on the track wearing Adidas running shoes (the ones with the air bubble cushioning) and black Nike track shorts. Sprinting the third lap of my eighth mile I'm coated in a layer of sweat. I'm sprinting and those same spectators are out with their stopwatches again. They're clicking and marking and watching and whispering in sound-bytes. Fractional commentary. There's about five of them at different parts of the track. Guys at least twice my age with adolescent expressions of glee. They're always here. Watching me. Studying. But despite what you'd think, they never speak to me.

I finish my ten-mile run.

Move downstairs.

To the weights.

Jill comes over while I'm on one of the machines and hands

me a bottled Evian water. She smiles hopefully, telling me, "Thought you could use it," and though I can't feel thirst, I know that I'm probably parched, so I receive it and take three large gulps, thanking her afterwards.

Making obvious conversation, she asks, "How was your run?"

I give a little nod. Satisfied. Remarking, "It was good."

"Yeah, you looked good out there," she tells my chest, my abs and obliques, but she quickly catches herself and adds, "Y'know, good like, you look like you're ready for whatever you're training for."

I'm not training, though (am I?).

"No, this is just for, y'know...me," I disclose a little anti-climatically. I don't even believe it myself when I say it, it comes off sounding so phony.

"Well, it certainly looks like you're training for something," Jill observes.

It does, doesn't it?

...maybe I started something I shouldn't have...

"Those scouts on the track seemed to be impressed," she tells me. "They show up to watch *you*," she smiles encouragingly.

I conspicuously check over my shoulder.

They're nowhere to be seen.

But I feel them.

Suddenly, I'm thinking about switching gyms but in nearly the same moment I nix the idea for a couple reasons. The first is that I like this gym and don't want to bother finding and joining another one. The other reason is that no one has bothered me, so why should I care if they watch. I should feel good about it. I should, but I don't. Not in the least.

Questioning harmless strangers in doctor's speak is known as "paranoia."

What I do next starts a domino effect because I need to find out.

For my own sanity, I have to know what will happen.

And Jill, she's standing here in front of me: young and pretty and available—more than available. An aggressor. A hunter. She's poised before me waiting for my word, for a sign that I might be interested. I say to her, "Look...Jill, I think you're a really nice girl," and instantly her face slackens. The smile hides and her eyes turn vacant. Her lips purse ready for rejection. She's prepared for it. Willing to take it, but I have to know.

I conclude, "So if it's okay with you, I'd like to take you out for lunch."

Guilt cascades.

And when you can't feel thirst or fatigue or muscular exhaustion, when the sensations that would normally be announcing their presence remain absent, the guilt is all you can feel.

But Jill is smiling at me, telling me ever so eagerly, "Let me just change real quick and get my stuff, okay?" to which I nod gravely because I know it's not too late to turn back now. I know this, but I won't.

I take a shower. A quick rinse. Put on my civilian clothes and stuff my running shoes and shorts in the gym bag. I send a text to Frank to let him know that I'm ready and spray myself down with some Kenneth Cole Black. My mouth tastes stale and everything smells like stink layered upon soap layered upon sweat carried on steam; an odor orgy.

Jill is waiting for me when I come out from the locker room, as is the car. It's parked just beyond the front doors, and we exit. Together. But only one of us will come back here because I have to be sure. I have a theory. A suspicion.

And when she disappears I'll know.

I'll know I was right.

SESSION 34
SACRIFICE

You know that feeling you get in the pit of your stomach when you're in the presence of someone you've wronged? The one where you feel nauseous like you're about to get sick but you never do? I should be feeling that right now.

I *yearn* for that feeling.

Anyone who can do this much damage to a person and still find it within themselves to enjoy their lamb served with garlic-mashed potatoes and chives has something seriously wrong with them. If you can still stomach your baby carrots douched in butter and Italian oil—no bones about it, you're an asshole and you should be ashamed of yourself.

"How's the lamb?" Jill asks.

"Phenomenal!" I exclaim. "Here, try some of this," I offer, cutting her off a piece and sliding it onto her plate with my silverware, and quite smoothly, I might add.

See me doing this same knife-and-fork motion four months ago and I would've been flicking meat right at her chest.

"That's how long it took me to get the hang of utensils again," I reveal nostalgically.

Jill finishes chewing and smiles, "Well, for my sake, I'm glad you got the hang of it again," she tells me, motioning to herself, or more accurately, the new top I just got her from Arden B.

This is just like old times.

Sort of.

The difference is that I'm only *pretty sure* I'll never see this girl again. Not definitely. Other than that minor detail, it's exactly how it used to be.

Almost.

After leaving the gym, Jill and I rode in the extended Lincoln town car to The Plaza for some light shopping. I bought her a skirt with a matching pair of heels from Guess. A couple tops from Arden B. Two bottles of perfume: Armani Mania and Delicious by DKNY. Three pairs of underwear and the new Gel-bra from Victoria's Secret (all of which I was present for during the fitting). Realistically, I probably could've had her in the car before we even hit any of the stores, but I'm saving that part for later.

It has to be the last thing that happens.

Right now we're at Brio, and I'm looking particularly sharp in my new suit that I just picked up from Banana Republic, ash gray with a crisp white oxford underneath. A black belt. A pink diagonally patterned tie that's so tasteful, so expensive, that I could sense Jill's pulse skipping behind me as I knotted it a double-Windsor within the dressing room. I could see her tan slender thighs quivering as I slipped on $48 black cotton socks, her underwear moistening when I stepped into a $225 pair of black leather shoes, but this was only after I initiated the whole affair by taking off all my clothes in front of her—every piece until I was nude and rigid, stepping into my new boxers. I was standing there in pastel pink boxers spraying my chest and abs and arms with cologne. I was standing there perfectly tan and defined, and Jill put her hand on my rippled shoulder and slid in down my back. She slid her hand down my back and moved it along my waist. Then down. Into my boxers, and she whispered to me, "This skirt hikes up y'know." With her lips so close to my ear—so close she was practically inside it, she told me, "I can be quiet if you can."

She said, "I bet you could feel *me*," and I looked down to see her mashing my hand into her pelvis, ready to undress herself upon my word, but I had to wait.

I have to.

Until the very end.

And I say to her coolly, "Just hold on for me a little bit," turning and kissing her softly on the mouth. Teasing her. Procrastinating this passion that would normally be so overwhelming if I could still feel it, but with the numb, you can overcome practically anything. Including this.

At Brio, Jill has slipped one of her feet in between my legs, caressing my balls with her toes as a tell her, "I speak 14 different languages but have only used three of them so far."

Her toes roll around my cock like owl talons on a piece of coiled parchment, jacking it slowly as I continue, "And I have an IQ of 234 even though I had all my grades bought for me in high school and never went to college because I knew I wouldn't pass any of the qualifying exams."

And Jill, with her perfect hair and teeth and complexion, she leans towards me until the spaces above her collarbones become a pair of smooth basins and admits, "Did I mention how hot it got me watching you out there...watching you run."

She smoothes one lip over the other. Wetting it. She says, "It got me thinkin' about what else you can do."

Remember: unlimited endurance and stamina.

Refer back to: sport-fucking marathon threesomes.

A mischievous little grin crosses Jill's face as she poses, "Do you think we could skip dessert?"

I tell her we can, wondering which picture of Jill they'll use for her missing persons milk carton ad. If they still do that. If I'm right, because I've told her so much. I've told her everything about everything, about Paradies and my list. Section 7.

Remember that old saying about knowing too much for your own good.

That's how much danger I've put this girl in. I've crossed the secret identity line of safety that most heroes go to great lengths to protect.

In the car, on the way to my place, Jill is straddling me with her skirt hiked-up and kissing my neck and face. She's kissing me, breathing hard, "Say something in French to me. I wanna hear some."

And in French I tell her, <"I think I've been exchanging contraband with anti-governmental syndicates.">

"Italian!" she says hotly. "Say something sexy to me in Italian, baby."

And right on cue I say, <"I'm fairly certain I'm being used as the primary operative in a plot to overthrow certain political factions.">

And Jill exclaims, "Oh FUCK!! That's so fucking hot! That's so hot," breathing on me all lips and tongues and sweat. She pleads, "Portuguese! I want you to tell me how bad you want me in Portuguese. Tell me tell me tell me."

<"I'm gonna use you as bait tonight because I think my therapist is having me followed,"> I speak to her faux turned-on. <"And I'm gonna fake the orgasm when I fuck you.">

"Oh my God! Oh my God. I can't wait to have you, baby. I can't wait," she pants, mouth smeared and wet. "Do you want me, too? Do you? Tell me you can't wait to have me Chinese."

<"If you end up dead, I'm sorry.">

Jill gives me a look. Then laughs. "Okay, *not* so much on the Chinese, but I still totally wanna fuck your brains out."

In Spanish I warn her, <"And that will probably be the last thing you ever do.">

"What does that mean, baby?"

I look over through the tinted window at the house. "It means we're here."

When we walk inside the TV is still on in the living room from when I was watching it this morning, but instead of pacing over to it and turning it off with the remote, I decide to show off a little more because Jill has to see. She knows, but she has to see, too, because seeing is believing, and seeing too much is the only way this is going to work, so I take the deck of playing cards sitting on foyer table next to the Rubik's cube and remove one. The two of hearts. I have it between the index and middle finger of my right hand, displaying it to her.

Looking from the card to my face, she asks playfully, "You gonna show me a magic trick?" to which I fling my arm hard towards the direction of the TV twenty-five feet away, snapping my wrist at the end of the motion and releasing the card. My arm blurs with speed and the card splits the air so quickly that you can't even see it move, only the result of what it does when it hits its intended target. The TV. The card punches the TV's face so hard that it dog-ears one of the corners, making the first of two pops. Then the second pop happens. Successive but different. It's the sound of the TV turning off because that card was meant for one particular spot: the Power button.

And Jill's like, "Holy shit! How did you do that?" all gasp-y and wide-eyed. "Seriously," she presses. "I know you don't have a second remote on you. I watched you put that suit on," she reasons.

I place the rest of the deck back on the foyer table and grab the unsolved Rubik's cube sitting next to it, ready for my next "trick."

Jill asks, "You're not gonna tell me, are you?"

Already pacing towards the stairs, I say, "Let's go up to my room," to which Jill catches up and sidles me.

She looks down at the cube and inquires, "What's that for?"

And already working it out, twisting and rotating sides and cells, I speak absent-mindedly, "What most people don't know about the Rubik's cube is that there are exactly three ways of solving it."

Going up the stairs with Jill watching intently, so much so that she stumbles and has to catch herself on the handrail, I say, "The first two are done by algorithmic methods, but even with those handy, you'd still have to be proficient enough in mathematics to understand and use them," I tell Jill, to which she just sort of nods in acceptance, watching my hands as we both ascend.

"The third method, though," I continue, "Is as easy as remembering how to get home from a friend's house." I say, "This is the retracing-your-steps-when-you've-lost-your-keys method of solving it."

My hands twist and turn.

Jill steps and watches.

"There are no algorithms involved," I tell her. "No math"

Nearly at the top of the stairs, which lead to my room, I reveal to Jill, "I unsolved this cube in a series of 174 specific moves."

And now on the top floor, I hand it over to her (solved) and proceed towards the bar, speaking unbraggingly over my shoulder as I pace, "As long as I remember every move, all I have to do is reverse the order."

I smirk, "Pretty simple, huh?"

Looking at the thing like it's cursed, she tosses the cube onto my bed and says, "I'm just trying to figure out why you're still trying to impress me," posing a statement in the form of a question. She walks to the bar, "I mean, I think I made it obvious in Banana Republic when I basically said you could fuck me in the dressing room that we were past the whole you-need-to-captivate-me stage."

And for serious, like a cold bucket of ammonia it hits me. How right she is. It's like I'm purposely trying to sabotage myself here.

I find myself asking, what would Batman *not* do?

And I'm running out of time here. I never thought I'd say this, but if I want to have any chance of screwing this up I'm gonna have to be a lot more fascinating than this. Turning off a TV with a projectile playing card and speaking fourteen different languages just isn't gonna cut it. Solving that Rubik's cube should've been a red flag on a par with a *Star Wars* obsession.

For Christ sakes, what does a guy have to do to *not* get laid around here?

"I get the feeling you're trying to tease me," Jill flirts. She moves around to the other side of the bar where I am, where I'm standing scared, regretful, and deeply guilty. "Shouldn't we be in that bed by now?" she asks with a soft motion of the head towards the center of the room.

Her perfect little fingers start to undress herself.

She undresses in front of me, and what she says next gives me chills because I feel like I've been hearing this more and more all the time. I hear it, and then something bad happens.

She says nude and tan and so very desirable to me, "You don't know how long I've wanted this," with one of her hands pulling the tie away and off of my neck.

I try to speak, to interject somehow, someway, but Jill's voice stops me cold when she tells me, "I'm so looking forward to seeing what you're capable of."

Not a word can be formulated I'm so frozen.

And she says, "You've got so much potential."

SESSION 35
SABOTAGE

I'm not going to think about you, Dana.
I have to keep telling myself that.
Over and over like a mantra.
I won't think about her.
Not yet, anyway.
Until it's over.
This.

Stop me if you've heard this one: "I can't believe you haven't come yet."

Is this déjà vu or have I travelled far enough to go full circle?

And Jill says, "God, you really go, don't you?"

Her ass-cheeks red. Glazed in sweat.

This is just oh so familiar, isn't it?

My life is either on repeat or I'm solving this problem the same way I solved that Rubik's cube: the retrace method.

If you recall what I said about secondhand experiences than you can probably guess how I feel right now.

She screams, "I want you to get off, honey," and inside I'm groaning and wondering just how many times I've been here, and how many times will I visit this place again.

And I'm not going to think about you Dana.

Because believe it or not, this is the right thing for me. For us.

In doctor's speak it's called "serving the greater good." Remember that phrase the next time you admit your junkie brother into the local rehab clinic for what's going to be the worst twenty-four hours of his life. As much as it's going to hurt to tell him "I can't see you again until you're better," in the long run, this is the right choice.

Even the crusaders of God murdered countless members of the opposition in the name of their lord and savior. Forget about that whole "Thou shalt not kill" thing. Every rule has an exception.

That's why I'm not going to think about Dana.

Because what I'm doing to Jill is a loophole.

See also: area code rule.

If having sex with someone not your girlfriend is a definitive part of your plan to find out if you're involved in some sort of grand conspiracy, then by all means, cheat away.

I've been pummeling this girl for north of three hours now.

For three hours I've been faking the "before" version of me.

We're all stuck in this taunting state of false nostalgia.

Here with my pharmaceutically-induced hard-on pumping like porn on fast-forward, I'm remembering all those other girls that I spent so much time and money and effort on, girls not unlike this one, realizing that the ends never justified the means. Because that's all I was really looking for. Ends. The bottom of a bottle. The end of a line. The consummation of meeting these girls.

But they were never really girls. They were brand names and pay grades. They had automobile and lodging requirements. Stipulations and terms and conditions. You could never be *just* you. It was all about what you owned and had access to. Where you could get them in and take them for dinner.

What you drove.

Your credit limit.

I never said "I'm buying you" just like they never said, "I'm purchasable," but let's face it, this is how prostitution works in the upper classes. This is just like my Section 7 items and all those junk e-mails I receive on the daily. Just like doctor's speak. Everything is coded. Nothing means what it sounds like anymore.

If a girl comes up to you at Ice Bar asking, "Does your limo have a sunroof?" then you know she wants to be on top.

"Headboard or posts?" means she wants you to tie her up, or in some rare cases, tie *you* up and rip you off.

Regardless, maybe this is why foreigners have such a hard time learning the English language, because even when we're using perfect grammar and pronunciation, what we say only makes sense about half the time.

Refer to: it's raining cats and dogs.

And: biscuit mama cum gag flower shutter flatware anus.

And: I love you more than anything, Dana.

See? Not one goddamn bit of sense.

Then Jill screams, "I'm gonna come again! I'm gonna come!" and I just sorta roll my eyes from behind her because it was barely exciting the first time. She screams and comes and collapses. Her midsection expands and deflates. Expands. She's panting, body pulsing and saturated, and deflating again. Like a giant lung. My cock slips out of her when she rolls over, laying in the fetal position, and she's saying, "I'm sorry."

Over and over, panting, "I'm sorry, I'm sorry, I'm sorry."

And I'm thinking, "It's not you, it's me."

I say, "Don't worry about it."

Jill speaks, "I'm just—I'm so fucking tired. I'm so tired."

She says, "I've never been fucked that hard."

"I'm so tired," she repeats again.

She fades. Passes out.

Understandably.

Already her breathing is stabilizing as she phases into an exhausted sleep. Beads of sweat rolling off her body. Her vagina engorged. Irritated shades of purple and red. Gaping like an open dog mouth.

She snores.

She sleeps.

That saying, the one people say about how they hate it when they're right—it's all I can think about right now looking at Jill for what might very well be the last time, because if it is, I'm really going to hate myself tomorrow. The guilt I'm currently feeling will only be the tip of the iceberg. A prelude.

But I follow through.

I keep breaking the rules.

And this is about when I black out.

Everything fades and I think...
...maybe I started something I shouldn't have.
And tomorrow I'll find out I was right.

SESSION 36
THE NOTE

In the morning, I wake up in my bedroom to no alarm in the Banana Republic suit I bought yesterday. Alone. Jill's nowhere to be seen (of course), and possibly not safe, a future milk carton model smiling next to nutritional facts, but I recall last night only slightly clearer than the rest of Section 7. Something about numbers and a disc I was supposed to give someone. A girl in Versace glasses asking, "Why do the good die young?" and I think I told her something about Janis Joplin not being able to sing or Reaganomics, but it's way foggy and there's soft blood under my fingernails. Key marks on the walls. There was an exchange made that might have been launch codes or the combination to some kid's locker...maybe a PIN number, but I can't be sure since leaving here (this room), is the last and only event I can semi-accurately recall, and everything stinks of heavy sweat and ash so I spend most of the morning sorting the wreckage that is my living space. Looking for clues of what might of happened. Thinking...

...maybe I started something I shouldn't have...

...as the breaking sun heats the stink of the room. I try not to think about Dana and what I still don't know. And my Blackberry has been deleted.

Not just the texts.

Contacts, appointments, and directions.

What to wear and where to go. Gone.

And so is my list. It's nowhere to be found.

"Panic," might be pushing it, but that's the approximation of what this feels like, as if I've lost the only thing I could ever count on.

I'm a blind without his seeing-eye dog.

A cutter without a razor.

I've never worn a worse poker face.

This is me going cold turkey and considering the alternatives, a grocery list or anything that states "some assembly required." Something that will guide my actions and allow me that sweet taste of success I was saturated in last summer and fall when the list was fresh and endless, and granted, I didn't have much of it left, but I wanted to finish.

For once in my life, I wanted to feel accomplished.

But now I'm that 1,000-piece puzzle that's been halted at three short of perfect. I'm disjointed. And when all I want to do is go back to Paradies and tell her that she was right all along, that I should have just done what I was told and been grateful for her help—that's when I come upon it.

A little yellow note.

From a legal pad.

Just like the ones I've seen those blush red white-knuckled fingers burn through every session. It's folded in half, laying on top of my night-stand, and scribbled atop it reads: *Aidin*

I'm kneeling on the floor hoping—praying, actually, that this is from Paradies and not some idiotic request or comment from one my parents. It's either from my mom or my doctor based on the handwriting (professionally girl-ish), and slowly I begin to unfold it, silently willing it to be from the latter. My eyes focus onto the paper, reading:

Your therapy has been indefinitely suspended until further notice. No return contact is needed from you regarding this.

And I read this, then reread it several times swelling with rejection. With failure. It's the first time I've ever been dumped. By anyone. And that's probably why this tastes so bitter, because you always remember your first.

I've never looked past the tinted window this far, and now that I have, I'd do anything to go back. To get that second chance to do it right. It's when I notice the post-script at the bottom of the page that I go from dejected to indignant.

Like when a girl says she wants to see other people.

Then you find out she had someone all along.

Giving you advice she's already taking.

It feels just that way.

First, Paradies has the nerve to reel me in with all of her bullshit: her portion control and scheduling. That fucking list. She gets me hooked on this system only to leave me flat. When I need her the most. When she knows what kind of person I am.

She's disposed of me, and with a goddamn note. A meeting would've been nice, but I would've taken anything. A phone call. An IM. A text.

But I get a note.

And she doesn't even sign it.

Instead, she has the audacity to give me a final piece of advice.

In her post-script. She writes:

P.S. - Try not to overreact.

That's exactly what I'll do.

SESSION 37
FULL CIRCLE

It's December now, and the winter is fickle and indecisive going from 48 and humid to -3 and snowy and back to tolerable again. Sleeted icy mornings and slushy afternoons. The cars in traffic melt and pollute everything white and pure down to lead snow cones, and I'll turn on the radio sometimes and listen to the traffic updates competing with the weather reports who pit themselves up against the point break waves of crime, thinking about how this is just another group therapy session where everyone thinks they have it worse off than the next guy.

It'll go 15-car pile-up on I-35 to an impending ice storm warning to something about an armed and dangerous so-and-so on the loose.

Gas prices are back over $4.00 per gallon and Sprint is having another corporate holocaust of an estimated 5,000 people.

And the Chiefs won't make the playoffs. Again.

Just stay tuned. There's a lot more where that came from.

When there's an 11-car traffic orgy clogging up the downtown triangle with a flu epidemic in tow, the fear practically sells itself. You start to hope the commercials will never end, but not me.

I'm special, remember?

Death would have to tap me on the shoulder twice, and I could definitely use the company because everyone's left me.

And I'm not just talking about Paradies, either.

In a convenient turn of events, Dana has gone back to Cabo to "face her origins" as the doc put it to her. A geographical confrontation. This is just like when your best friend dies scaling Everest or K2 so you have to climb it for him. In dedication. Almost out of revenge, but not really. This trip was part of Dana's

Section 7.

She knew she had to pack at least two weeks worth of clothes, and she knew she was flying somewhere.

That was it.

So now Dana is in Cabo facing her past while I'm in the present up to my ears in oil wars and the crippled economy and another wreck on I-70. She's on a sandy beach with her Dior sunglasses while this cold front moves into the city, and the overpopulation of vagrants chokes the Plaza shopping district something sado-masochistic.

She's away from me, and that's bad enough news.

Plus, my list is gone and I might be responsible for a missing/dead girl.

I don't need to hear anymore about Senate representatives ordering call girls or the average college tuition rising 21% nationwide. The wreck on highway 40 doesn't concern me one bit.

I'm alone with nothing to do, so it's only a matter of time before I do something stupid. Before I overreact.

And mom says in an e-mail: *We can get you another doctor. Just buy yourself some puzzles or trade stocks to keep yourself busy. Think about enrolling in school. Your father would like that.*

And Dana tells me in the airport terminal, "I'm sure she has her reasons, babe," but I'm too pouty and pissed off to listen. I want her to say that Paradies was wrong but I know it's not Dana's style to pander.

"She didn't leave you," I mumble. Emphasis on that last word. On "you."

"I didn't botch a mission on purpose, though," she counters. "You should've just done what you were told," is the last thing she says before jettisoning off to Mexico for however long. It wasn't one of our best good-byes, but I think about what she said, regardless. Dana has that kind of effect on me.

Maybe I should've finished what I started.

Just follows orders. Do as your told.

Hindsight is 20/20.

I go full circle.

Frank drops me off at Hush: that ever-changing sameness. The Barbie colony. But now the queue before the black velvet rope is doused in furs and parkas and overcoats. By designers that I'm not even going to bother naming. Mouths are either steaming heat or exhausting Marlboro fumes. I can't tell. And when the doorman lets me though, he's smirking, making a comment about how he's never seen me fly through here solo, but this is me facing my origins. This was the last place I was before everything changed. Before I met Paradies. And Dana. I'm escorted into the club by some hostess I had another life ago, and I can't tell if she's trying to make small talk or be snide when she says, "Never thought you'd show your face back in here," because it's heavy with a certain tone of finality (like I was dead or something), but she seats me and I begin perusing the drink menu, realizing this is maybe the first time I've been in total control of this decision, the ordering process. No influence. It's almost as if I can't choose because there's too much choice, but the waitress comes over (new girl; very cute) and explains how you can never go wrong with champagne, so that's what I end up getting, and the space seems so much brighter than before. The lights. They're teal and orange and rose and emerald, shifting and widening on a predetermined pattern, but I'm not wearing sunglasses by Versace or Bulgari or Prada because I know I don't need them. I want to see everything: the girls (both underage and barely legal) dancing and flirting, making those bodily promises. Showing just enough. Just a sample. A whisper of Victoria's Secret or some pale section of skin untanned and soft. They gloat. When they dance and move. In Barbie talk they're saying, "There's plenty more where that came from." And there are labels everywhere. Booze and coke and pills. All around. There's no soul out there, but I'm looking. Searching. Because I want to find out what I thought was so paramount about this place. This life. I don't want to believe I made a false investment of myself, and it's not long after the champagne is delivered that I start to acquire some watchers, girls with no table and only their own money to spend. Dateless, single girls on the hunt. I make eye contact with more than a few of them taking their time with cosmopolitans and appletinis and

Long Island ice teas. They're paying $15 to $20 per drink with a light tip until they can find someone to pay that for them, and now I'm looking like a viable candidate for that. With my bottle of champagne. My Voss water and chocolate-covered strawberries. The suede leather seating. I'm on that greener grass they've heard so much about. Better pastures. But I restrain myself, exercising patience. I pour myself half a glass of champagne. Louis Roederer Cristal from 2002. And I slide myself back into the tan suede, crossing one leg over the other, holding the flute as tenderly as I can. Sipping. Enjoying the character and charm of the drink for the first time since the "before," watching the room watching me. More women (and some men) glaring without subtlety. They're talking. Conspiring to invade. I can't hear what they're saying, but after so many sessions at Making Sense, I don't have to. As long as I can see their lips move, I know exactly what they're discussing.

Let's just say that along with lock picking, computer hacking, and sleight of hand, being able to read lips is another one of my semi-useful talents. It's grouped right in there with code breaking, forgery, and symbology. Card counting and marksmanship. So many abilities, so little opportunity to apply them.

Until now.

At Hush.

I'm scanning the room, focusing on anyone who glances at me for more than a couple seconds. Reading them with sensory substitution just like I've been taught. By Dana and Dr. Paradies. Hearing with my eyes, not with my ears. I see their conversations in visible whispers.

They say:

"...we know him don't we? Did you fuck him? Maybe *I* fucked him? ...on coke or something, because that would be so-o-o-o like me, y'know? And this was months ago when I got raped here, and I think it was him. But we should go over there later—not right now, but definitely later. Before he runs out of Cristal. But I thought he was sweet up until he blew smoke in my face. He's definitely looking more fit. That's for sure. So, let's finish these and say hi. He's got the coolest house and car, so *yeah*, I'd put up with his shit. Sure. I want to go, too, bitch, but I don't want to look desperate. So maybe we should move in soon because those skanks over there are eyeing him, too. I'm about ninety-percent sure I fucked him. Sixty percent sure he gave me the clap. And I think he filmed it, but I was so fucked up I didn't give a shit. He's too fucking shallow for me. Eighty percent sure I'd do it again...and I bet he's got some blow on him. He always does...and when that girl went home with him she never came back..."

And I'll catch them saying these things between minimal sips of Cristal and playing with my new iPhone. There's about fifteen or so in my line of vision. A few standing around high tables. By the faux ivory pillars. The outskirts of the dance floor and bar. I'll watch them speak until they look at me, at which point I move onto the next pair or group, making mental notes of which ones have bad intentions. The exploiters.

It's at the end of the first glass that a couple girls approach me: both of them blonde and thin and tan. Just your typical cover model type. So glamorous and un-special. Marvelously mundane. And I shoot a quick glance beyond them to the others rolling their eyes and scoffing, catching the words "bitches" and "skanks" and "whores" from about eight different mouths.

The first one says, "You look like you could use some company," smiling and positioning herself to sit next to me. Next to my bottle. Not unlike a stripper, but she stops short when I tell her flatly that I don't have any coke. That I don't even do it anymore.

"That's why you came over, right?"

We're all wearing our worst poker face.

"Why don't you find someone else to use?"

And the both of them storm off cursing and bitching. You don't need to be a lip reader to know this. The pair of them are being rather audible about it, calling me "prick" and "asshole" as I refill my flute and wait for my next contestants, deciding that maybe I'll try to be a little more accommodating from here on out since it's the only way I'll get the answers I need.

So I begin to invite women over to my table, and they all talk about the surface-level things you talk about in a place like this. Like Hush. They're either aspiring models or actresses on their way out west or east to New York or LA because nothing happens in between ("Unless it's Vegas, but that's the *only* exception."), and Kansas City is just a way station. They try not to look completely crestfallen when I tell them I'm not holding anything (coke or X or prescription painkillers) on my person nor back at my place. That I discontinued that scene. Some of them are competent. Most of them not. There's a couple secretaries and interior designers. Lots of shop girls, one of them is that Asian blonde girl. It's difficult to tell because of her eye shape, but she doesn't look too happy to see me. Maybe embarrassed. Or maybe angry since I basically kicked her out of the house half-naked the last time I saw her. Last summer. The morning the big numb swept in. So I'm certain this cold shoulder is more than intentional, but I yell at her in Japanese, "<Hey, I'm sorry for what I did. Let me make it up to you.>" And she walks over, either perplexed or impressed, confirming, "<You speak Japanese now?>" to which I respond, "<Do you work at BeBe?>" and she smiles, taking a seat next to me. I pour her some champagne and the others—the Barbie shop girls and secretaries, they all begin to eavesdrop on a conversation they can't understand, but I read their lips in the meantime; they comment about how "that girl" or "that gook" is being rude, a few of them too impressed that I speak the language to care. Asian blonde, or Tiffany, only sticks around for a few minutes before telling me she appreciated the sentiment but she has to leave. Off to her own table. It gets later. Past 1:00 A.M. We're on the second bottle of Cristal and I'm getting steadily frustrated: by the conversations, the surfaces and plastic, the obsession to find someone who's got coke, or even some pills—something. Anything. There's about twelve of these girls who will sit down with me in rotation. Some who get a fresh flute of champagne before disappearing back into the crowd of silhouettes, usually to talk to other men less engaged or more fun. They're pulling out their cells trying to find a decent after-hours session, asking me what's going on, if I have a place and where at. They want to know what kind of booze or drugs I have, but they never say it that bluntly. Just like my Section 7, this place uses code, too, be it ever so simple. Word for word, they inquire, "Do you have anything?" because that's what they'll take. Anything. As long as they don't have to pay for it. And some of them are so wasted or pilled-out it's annoying. Pathetic. Girls half-passed out, half-conscious looking balled-up, crumpled, and beyond incoherent. Looking easy, and everything stinks of booze and smoke and desperation. It's dripping with emptiness, and the longer I stay, the more it sinks in, that answer I've been searching for.

There's no soul in here.

So I walk.

I get up and walk out, and I don't pay the tab, which I know is well north of $2,000 because I never plan on coming back. That, and this place has already taken enough from me. These women and this scene, I decide to give them no more of myself, stepping into what I can only imagine is a frigid night based on how thick my breath comes pouring out. In plumes. The red faces and purple lips of those still waiting beyond the black velvet rope. They're shivering and sober, but just as desperate as the people inside. My feet begin their well-rehearsed pace through the poorly shoveled snow towards the limo idling curbside amongst white and yellow cabs driven by illegals. It's humming silently in park when Frank gets out to open my door for me, asking how my night went but I can only manage a shaky tilting of the hand: sign language slang for "Could've been better," and I can tell he's taken aback by this.

It is, after all, the first time I've gone to Hush and not only left early, but also left alone. I'm alone, and that fact continues to soak deeper and deeper as I think about how everyone that mattered to me has just up and disappeared. And the rest are either dead or kidnapped or unaccounted for. Banishment without leaving home.

Residential solitary.

We're traveling along Ward Parkway at a steady 30 miles per hour with season 2 of *Lost* in the DVD player. Sound off.

Subtitles on. People walking outside hunched over and rigid. They look right at me and see nothing but tinted window, and the track lighting glowing a pale yellow. So gentle and calming that I don't even think about where I've been or who's left me behind until I focus in on the HD screen displaying the beach in smooth choreographed pans. That sand and ocean. Opposites touching forever and ever and yet totally unaware of each other. It reminds me of Dana and how she's all I have to look forward to now. Her face and those Dior glasses. She never takes them off. Her own personal tinted window.

I've never looked past it. Not once.

And it makes me wonder what else I've missed.

What else will look different the second time around?

SESSION 38
RETRACE

Backtrack.

Retrace your steps.

This is just like any Rubik's Cube you've ever reverse-engineered back to normal. Another complex algorithm or logic problem. A proof.

Everything is based on an equation.

Even me, the unsolvable.

It's when I start going backwards that I find out just how much this *doesn't* add up.

And Jamie—remember Jamie? Little miss sperm bank. She's staring at me from the front desk with the same glazed-over look she gave me all those months ago. Those old misunderstandings still coming to light as she recalls, "Aren't you that religious homo that came in here a while back to donate?"

Questions like these, there's no right answer.

Agree to disagree, that's all I can do.

"I'm sorry," she dismisses me, marking something on a clipboard. "We still don't carry any gay material...unless you want to borrow the *Men's Fitness* from the waiting room," Jamie suggests.

"It's over there," she points to the space behind me.

I don't even bother turning around.

It's during this second encounter I realize that Jamie is like a cold, you just have to wait until she's run her course.

"And for the love of God, *try* to give that back in the condition you found it," she requests, as if this isn't the first time she's dealt with a male misfire. "*Some* people want to read that thing."

"For the millionth time," I press. "I'm-not-gay."

"Ri-i-ight," she rolls her eyes. "I'm gonna take this from the guy who took two fingers up the rectum."

My anal casserole.

The prostate potluck.

We'll come back to that.

To see how well the formula *doesn't* work, you need to see the big picture. Just pay attention. By the time this is over, you'll be more lost than you ever have. Pinky promise. Cross my heart and all that other shit.

We're back at Making Sense.

At Circle of Healing.

Same time. Same place.

Different people.

Different groups.

It's the weekly Thursday congregation of Alcoholics Aware, and the head moderator is asking me why I'm here, prodding me with those deep soul-searching questions that remind me of some hippy-dippy new age bullshit.

"Have you lost your way?" he poses. "Or maybe you're just now finding it, hmm?"

If he's talking about in the room or here on Earth, I'm not sure.

But I don't feel like role-playing today, so I just blurt out what I want to know, the part about what happened to the group that *used* to meet here. All my blinds and deafs and mutes competing in that never-ending sport of sensory absence.

"That's the one I'm looking for," I tell him, sounding a little too desperate.

But this guy laughs at me like he's never heard anything so funny. Sides in stitches.

"I think you might be the butt of someone's joke," he manages to say between howls, his eyes welling to tears, and I look about the room to the other group members in the meantime, searching. The sober ones are obviously familiar with what he's talking about. With their crooked grins. Their bemused expressions.

"Seriously! You people need to read those descriptions

better," he shakes his head, intoxicated with his own wisdom. Drunk with this little amount of power he has over me.

"Wait..." I plead, hoping he'll be civil about this. Humane.

"What descriptions?" I ask.

And Circle of Healing isn't much different.

Same place and time.

Different group.

Soul Purpose, this one's called. A Christian-based assemblage from what I can tell, so I try to get my answers quick. As painlessly as possible.

Again...no pun intended.

And again, I think I missed something the first time around.

I ask about the group about Circle of Healing, but instead of laughter I get something else.

I get recoil.

Hesitation.

And questions like, "You're not really one of *them*, are you?"

And, "Don't *you people* meet somewhere else now?"

But the really important stuff is coming out of the mouths of the people I *can't* hear. The whisperers and secret spreaders. I can only read so much at once as they gossip amongst each other.

Always in hushed tones.

They say, "He doesn't even look like one them."

And, "We don't want a repeat of last time."

And, "Oh God, we're screwed."

Then, out of nowhere, this middle-age housewife type in denim and plaid jumps in front of me yelling, "Take *this* you Christ-hating fuck!" dousing me in some sort of orange liquid that stinks so bad I sneeze. It stains the front of my shirt. My pants and jacket. A deep rusty orange. I'm drenched in it. She empties the entire container of the stuff on me, but I don't know what it is until the few people adjacent to me start to react. A different kind of recoil.

Just like those alcoholics, they start to well up and tear.

But for a completely different set of reasons.

It's spreads virally, and I ask the lady as her group starts to moan and writhe, "Did you just fucking mace me?"

The room wilts and the canister slips from her frightened hand as she begins to whimper, "oh-god-oh-god-oh-god."

"Lady," I calmly state. "This shit doesn't work on someone like me."

Eyes reddening and gasping, she's clutching her chest, bumbling, "Oooh-God! God, help me help me help..."

I tell her, "I'm special," forcing an evil smile.

She screams, "AGGGGGGHHHhhhhh!!! *Satan!!* Satan is here!!" pissing herself as she claws her own face in agony. The stain in her crotch deepens and seeps through the denim, stinking slightly less than the airborne chemicals. A man falls out of his folding chair, cracking his head on the floor, and the mace is everywhere now, choking the air so much these people try to breathe through their shirts. Their hankies and coat sleeves. I can literally only imagine how much pain they're in right now, exiting the room with a calm smile of triumph.

Grinning, but not happy.

And more confused than ever.

Until I pay a visit to the police station.

I walk into this place—and wouldn't you know it, I see a picture of myself fastened to the pushpin wall. Black and white and blurry, but I know it's me. I'm frowning and wearing designer sunglasses, hovering over the words: "Last seen with" just before my name. My age and physical description. The "missing" portion is covered. I'm sure I know who it is, but I don't want to confirm it.

It's easier if I don't see.

And the guy working the front desk is your basic example of what fifteen years of cold coffee and vending machine lunches of Nutter Butters and Fritos will do to you. His name is Earl, but I'm not here to see him or his crate of powdered donut holes.

"I'm looking for Detective Stephen Finch," I tell him. "He came to my house a while ago to ask me some questions."

"Don't see how that's possible," he responds just before inhaling a donut hole, chewing slowly. Without shame.

"*Why* is that not possible?" I ask, sensing another dead end.

"'Cause he's dead," he tells me, swallowing, a small beat passing as he clears his throat. "Been dead for a while."

And I can't even think straight anymore.

Because as long as I've known me I've never been myself, and the same might be true for everyone I've met along the way.

...maybe I started something I shouldn't have...

"Anything *else* I can help you with Sixth Sense?" he goads, popping another one of those donut holes. A chocolate one this time.

"Yeah," I say, a bright idea occurring (and maybe a smile). "Dr. Thomas Thornton...do you have anything on him?"

Now let's go back to the sperm bank.

Back to Jamie and how the ends don't meet.

"I want to see Dr. Trask," I'm ordering, my patience officially spent. "When can you get her up here?"

"About a quarter after never," Jamie quips. "She went bye-bye a lo-o-o-o-ong time ago." Adding in an afterthought, "And I don't even know why you want to see *her*, anyway. Aren't you like, into guys or something?" she squints at me.

"No," I yell. "I just want to know what the fuck you people did with my jizz."

"*Ejaculate!*" she hisses, smacking her hand down on the counter. "I told you before we don't use those words around here!"

"Fine! What did you do with it?" I beg. "That's all I want to know. Just tell me that and I promise I'll leave and never come back," and this seems to lower her defenses slightly. Just enough to make her civil.

"Duh, asshole," she mocks, twirling her index finger about her temple. "We send it off to a fertility clinic."

Amped that I'm finally making headway, I follow up with, "Which clinic? Do you have an address or phone number you can give me?"

"Of course, I do," Jamie admits, rolling her eyes at the absurdity of the question. "But why should I tell you?" she teases, but this is the last straw for me. It's the third strike so I switch to brass tacks: the kind that's never failed. Ever.

I pull out a lighter.

My chrome Zippo.

"I'll show you why," I challenge, igniting the fire and burning the tips of two fingers on my left hand, which go from red to brown to black. In seconds, it does this. Tendrils of smoke spiraling once the flames reach the fingernails, bubbling it to yellow and coal. I never react as Jamie's eyes shift from me to the flames and back again. I never wince or feel any sort of remorse that I'm doing the thing I said I wouldn't do anymore. This little parlor trick. And the stink becomes unbearable, much like the point I'm making, so I stop.

A moment of rare silence passes before Jamie regains control of her gaped mouth, asking me horrified and so genuine it's sad, "You want to boil your own sperm?"

It just doesn't add up.

And Earl at the police station is asking me, "Why do you want to know about this—what did you say his name was?" he searches. "Dr. Thornton?" he checks with me while typing, powdered sugar dust over half the keys, a CSI unit's wet dream in case this guy decides to keel over right here and now.

"I think he might be in trouble," I admit, trying not to sound overly concerned, as if I know more than I really do. "I just, y'know...wanted to check and see if he's okay."

"He should be," Earl concludes, his eyes moving from the monitor and back to me. "Looks like he's in protective custody."

"He is?" I ask, taken aback by this bit of information. "Where at?"

"C'mon, kid, gimme some credit," Earl snickers, powder lining the corners of his mouth. He says, "For all I know *you* could be the guy trying to kill him."

He's right. I could be.

Because everyone is two people.

Nothing is the same the second time around.

The more I go through this, the more I see it: a tinted window.

It's when I finally manage to convey my situation to Jamie that it starts to dawn on her that my sample might be tainted.

Somewhere, someone might have a miniature me growing inside of them, ready to burst bloody and silent into to the world.

"Now you see why I need to take care of this?" I reason.

Call it: damage control.

Or: cleaning up your own mess.

So Jamie retrieves my file from one of the numerous steel cabinets, mumbling, "You totally owe me, dude," as she flips through it, her fingers lazily making their way towards the back page. She stops on this one and begins writing down the address. Contact info and the name of the presiding doctor. In blue ink on a pale yellow Post-It.

Jamie peels it away whispering, "You didn't get this from me," as she hands it over, but I know this can't be right when I read it.

It can't be.

Yet, when I view it again the words remain unchanged.

Everything continues to not add up.

The note reads: Dr. Paradies

The address is: #2 Pershing Square.

SESSION 39
III

Most stories, including mine, consist of three parts or acts.

The first act is called "the set-up."

This is where you're introduced to the main character; the central protagonist, and receive a basic layout of their person. You get a name. A description. And sometimes a past.

You find out their likes and dislikes.

What they do and how they live.

Their dreams, and on some occasions, their secrets.

You're given just enough information to relate to this person, but not everything.

And just when you think that their life is more or less as normal as your own, that's when they encounter a problem, which leads us into the second act.

They call this, "the confrontation."

It's the necessary conflict that gives rise to a character dilemma, thus, compromising their walk of life.

It can be a slain wife or the loss of employment.

A car accident or the inheritance of a cursed heirloom.

Or, it could be something like my situation.

Regardless, the central character is dealt a particular problem, and as you (the reader) survey this person's every move, you're expecting it to be solved, which brings us to our final act.

Called "the resolution."

Normally consisting of a climax or series of climaxes, this is where you're given new revealing information, typically as an extension of clues or hints mentioned only in passing throughout the story's progression. Usually, these hints are deliberately small to increase their odds of being viewed in a trivial and meaningless nature when it's just the opposite. These allusions always sneak

in something unimportant until just the right moment.
And now you're looking for the trick.
But you won't find it.
Because just like me, you're not supposed to know.
Not until you're told.

SESSION 40
#2 PERSHING SQUARE

The worst-case scenario, I'm thinking, is that if I get caught breaking in here, I'll finally have the chance to try out some of the abilities that have been rusting in my proverbial shed all these weeks.

My marksmanship and hand-to-hand combat. Weapons training: with knives and small projectiles. With "common items" such as playing cards and ballpoint pens and letter openers. Stealth and evasion tactics.

I'm seriously dying to get caught.

Craving a confrontation.

This isn't really any different from Winona Rider shoplifting in some upscale department store or Russell Crowe beating the shit out a guy with a telephone in front of a room full of spectators.

They both knew full well what was coming next.

In doctor's speak, they call that "a death wish."

An "overreaction," Paradies would say.

But I don't think so.

More than anything lately, I'm just feeling underutilized. Deprived of challenge. Of accomplishment. Restless and frustrated, like I don't know what to do with myself, to put it in familiar terms. So, I do something stupid. Something against my better judgment.

But let's not forget that this lady might or might not have my sperm in a mini fridge somewhere.

She has my legacy and statistics.

My test results and list of talents.

A big fat file of me, so it really doesn't make much sense that she would specifically tell me to steal it. Unless it's a trap. A set-up.

Nevertheless, the handwritten note said: *Break into my office tonight. Get your file. I'm sorry I haven't been in contact, but please trust me. I'm giving this note to your mom to pass along, so I hope it finds you well. Don't get caught and don't try to contact me. They're watching. –Dr. Paradies*

I wake up to this on my nightstand, and for the next few hours a debate ensues. A decision has to be made as to whether or not to trust this person again, if the risks are worth the reward. I'm either about to get all the answers I've been wanting or caught red-handed, but I figure that this could be my redemption for not following orders. Despite what could very well be my undoing, I'm compelled to comply, to do what I'm told like it's another item. Nothing more.

So, it's a small wonder that the lock on the office door is a standard single deadbolt. Odd, because she knows I can pick this thing in a heartbeat. She knows this because she told me to learn it. To master it, along with everything else on that list.

Foreign languages and chemistry.

Japanese fighter kite assembly.

Sudoku puzzles.

Etc. Etc.

On my knees in a dark hallway, I'm working the steel pick and tension wrench just as I was taught how. Just as I was taught with anything, that sensory substitution so instilled within me by Dana and Paradies that it's second nature by now. I do this with my ears, not with my hands, listening for that distinctive series of clicks as I drag the upper tool along the pins cased in the lock's shear line.

Upon entry, the office is darker than I originally anticipated, but I wait until after I've closed the door behind me before pulling out my flashlight and moving past the imported chaise lounge. Past the chair Paradies occupied in our sessions and a candy dish brimming with sugar-free starlight mints.

I move silently beyond those things to her desk, opening a drawer and beginning my search for either supporting or conflicting evidence of what I've been told. At Alcoholics Aware and Soul Purpose. The police station.

I don't know which truth I hope for more.

It's a lose-lose situation at this point.

Fucked either way, that old saying.

The first drawer holds almost nothing of interest. A few blank legal pads and a rubber-bound stack of prescriptions. Clickable pens in blue and black and red. Some blank data discs (by Memorex). Spare staples. White out and liquid latex. Loose paperclips.

I double-check to make sure I haven't overlooked anything, fastening the pad of blank prescriptions in one of my jacket compartments with full the intention of using it later. For Colace. I almost snicker at the idea that a half a year ago this would've meant so much more to me, being able to write myself false remedy for whatever I wanted. Those counterfeit cures:

Xanax and Adderall and Concerta and Percocet.

Gigantic sticks of Oxycontin and MDMA.

Concentrated medical marijuana.

I would've immersed myself in these escapes, but not anymore.

Despite the fact that I'm breaking and entering and robbing my former doctor's office, I'm a fairly responsible guy. That's what I keep telling myself to justify this. Along with that *other* word. The one you don't say unless you're certain. Unless you have proof.

In clinical blasphemy it's called, "malpractice."

But it might be worse than that, even.

That's why I have to check this out.

...and maybe I started something I shouldn't have...

The second drawer is far more interesting. Roughly the same size, but different contents. Files. Thick forest green sheathes folded over paperwork. Tabbed with names. Of patients. Looking down the row there's approximately fifty or so, and my initial instinct is to find mine, my fingers already dancing over the tops with the flashlight beaming upon them, moving it halfway down the space once I notice it's alphabetically arranged.

It goes Jacobs, Ethan.

To Jones, Katherine.

And I'm moving closer to me. To my secrets. The answers. Fingers tabbing through fervently because as long as I know me I've never been myself, and now I'm finally going to find out who I am, and more importantly, what I'm meant to do.

It goes Keller, Ashley.

To Kent, William.

But I stop on a dime when I see the next name.

At Lafon, Dana. I just can't help myself.

In relationship terms, this is known as "an invasion of privacy."

And suddenly, I don't feel like that responsible guy anymore. Not with this breach of trust. Of love (if you could call it that). Remorse reveals itself as slick ovals of sweat from my fingertips and palms. Light tremors and oblivion to everything outside of this office. Tunnel vision. Nothing matters when everything is about to fall apart.

I lay Dana's file down on top of the others, using the row as a makeshift podium of support as I begin to peruse. The first few pages are medical records. Results of tests and exams regarding her condition, the first bomb dropping when I see the name Dr. Trask at the bottom of all of these.

I keep going until I get to the hardcopy of her list, promising myself that I'm going to keep this infraction down to a minimum so as to avoid being a *complete* prick, but my tendency to read rather than skim progressively increases. The temptation proves to be too much.

It's laid out just as mine. In sections. In categories and subcategories. All of the items numbered with that little box next to it, waiting for its mark. A void craving to be filled. Everything detailed. Nothing left to question. Not unless it's supposed to be, of course.

Item #1 is almost exactly like mine.

It reads: Pick a comfortable and quiet place in public that you can occupy for at least one hour, and have a friend or family member dictate word-for-word as much of the list as they can for you. During this time, you should have a digital recorder activated so this information may be chronicled and, thus, accessible to you at anytime.

And I'm thinking, *As much as they can?*

Mumbling, "What the fuck does that mean?"

But the list—Dana's list is far too engrossing to dwell on this particular question. It's only after you've seen a person's contents that you can say you truly know them. Or don't know them.

Item #5: Make a full mental layout of your household using standard paces as measurement.

Item #12: Have handrails and carpeting put into all stairwells.

Item #20: Move all loose electrical cords to the edge of their rooms.

This is all just another form of baby proofing.

Another version of safety, and safety leads to trust.

There's another section on music.

On movies and educational enhancement.

Books on tape. Electronics that speak.

A million little changes. An army of adaptation.

Item #53: Learn trigonometry.

Item #68: Play Jenga.

Do everything that Paradies says because she'll never steer you wrong. She'll never give up or abandon you. Not unless you're me.

I enthusiastically read through Dana's list, occasionally seeing an item here and there that I assisted her with; setting up a MySpace page and attending an art gallery. Navigating different parts of the city: the art district and the Plaza and Westport. Walks through the dog park. Visits to the zoo.

Page by page, I take all of this in until the last part is reached. Dana's Section 7, and at first it looks like a bunch of blank sheets, but something's off about them. The paper is noticeably thicker. A higher quality and different shade of white. Even with only a flashlight, I can still only feel these bumpy shadows with my eyes.

It's all in Braille.

The one language I was never meant to speak.

Sighing with a heavy heart, I fold everything up and slide Dana's file back in its place, right behind William Kent and whatever his problem is. I retrieve my file, which appears to be much thicker than the others, and I lay it down on the row as I did with Dana's, opening it slowly.

It's a legal pad.

A stack of legal pads.

At least ten or so of them.

The ones that Paradies used.

Every time in each session.

She would use these.

Scribbling forever.

And ever.

Those blush red fingers. Those white knuckles.

They would be constantly noting and documenting. Always moving. It got to the point where I barely noticed anymore, but that didn't mean I didn't want to know. What she was writing. On days that I was angry or crying. Days that I made progress. The day she yelled at me. Threatened me. I never believed she told me everything.

And when I read these words, it feels like I know even less:

forgive me, forgive me,

forgive me, forgive me, forgive me, forgive me, forgive me,
forgive me, forgive me, forgive me, forgive me, forgive me,
forgive me, forgive me, forgive me, forgive me, forgive me,
forgive me, forgive me, forgive me, forgive me, forgive me,
forgive me, forgive me, forgive me, forgive me, forgive me,
forgive me, forgive me, forgive me, forgive me, forgive me,
forgive me, forgive me, forgive me, forgive me, forgive me,
forgive me, forgive me, forgive me, forgive me, forgive me,
forgive me, forgive me, forgive me, forgive me, forgive me,
forgive me, forgive me, forgive me, forgive me, forgive me,
forgive me, forgive me, forgive me, forgive me, forgive me,
forgive me, forgive me, forgive me, forgive me, forgive me,
forgive me, forgive me, forgive me, forgive me, forgive me,
forgive me, forgive me, forgive me, forgive me, forgive me,
forgive me, forgive me, forgive me, forgive me, forgive me,
forgive me, forgive me, forgive me, forgive me, forgive me,
forgive me, forgive me, forgive me, forgive me, forgive me,
forgive me, forgive me, forgive me, forgive me, forgive me,
forgive me, forgive me, forgive me, forgive me, forgive me,
forgive me, forgive me, forgive me, forgive me, forgive me,
forgive me, forgive me, forgive me, forgive me, forgive me,
forgive me, forgive me, forgive me, forgive me, forgive me,
forgive me, forgive me, forgive me, forgive me, forgive me,
forgive me, forgive me, forgive me, forgive me, forgive me,
forgive me, forgive me, forgive me, forgive me, forgive me,
forgive me, forgive me, forgive me, forgive me, forgive me,
forgive me, forgive me, forgive me, forgive me, forgive me,
forgive me, forgive me, forgive me, forgive me, forgive me,
forgive me, forgive me, forgive me, forgive me, forgive me,
forgive me, forgive me, forgive me, forgive me, forgive me,
forgive me, forgive me, forgive me, forgive me, forgive me,
forgive me, forgive me, forgive me, forgive me, forgive me,
forgive me, forgive me, forgive me, forgive me, forgive me,

forgive me, forgive me...

It's goes on forever. Every single solitary page is covered in this. This mantra. This plea.

I'm so wrapped up in this, the potential meaning of it, that I don't even hear Paradies open the door and turn on the light until it's too late.

She looks old. Tired.

The hair is slightly unkept with random cowlicks and flyaway strands. Her body rests lazily against the doorframe in lavender silk pajamas with pearl buttons.

"Found your file, I see," she examines, moving away from the door and placing herself heavily on the chaise lounge. My chaise lounge. She doesn't look surprised at all. "You can stop reading that anytime now," she suggests, rubbing sleep from her eyes before fixing a soft gaze on me. "It gets a little monotonous after a while."

"What is this?" I ask, gripping one of the legal pads. Shaking it at her.

Paradies crosses one leg over the other, tiredly propping herself on a knee with her chin resting in her palm, sighing again.

Weakly. And sad. She tells me, "It was the one thing I could never say to you."

And I'm looking at her—angrily, I'd like to think, asking her what it means.

"And why the hell are you here in your pajamas?" I shoot out as an afterthought, to which Paradies snickers.

"God, I really fucked you up, kiddo," she speaks solemnly, and on pure reaction I whole-heartedly agree with her on this, but she starts shaking her head.

Looking down at the floor, nibbling on one of her fingernails, she's shaking her head in short motions telling me, "No, you don't understand."

She says, "It's so much worse than you think."

I tell her snidely, "Well, I already know everything, so you can stick that apology up your ass."

"No, Aidin, you *really* don't," Paradies tells me, shaking her head again. Boney fingers circling temples. She says, "If you did, you would remember how you got here tonight. If you knew everything, you would know why you never see me except in this room."

Recall how I never seem to be anywhere or doing anything before a session.

I've never seen Paradies enter or leave this place, and I've never seen her outside of it, either.

We're both living in a world based on limitation.

She asks, "Doesn't it seem a little odd...these things you do? And doesn't it seem strange that you keep forgetting what you did? Who you met?"

Because sometimes I'll do what I'm told and wake up the next day not caring what happened. I'll arise ready to do the next thing, the next item. Always moving forward. Never looking back.

"Isn't there a person that seems to have vanished into thin air...someone you've been close to for years?" she asks with one eyebrow slightly cocked above the other. "I'll give you a hint," Paradies teases. "Check your driver's license."

And as my hands move to my pocket containing my wallet

she speaks, "Sometimes we only see what we want to see, Aidin."

I unfold the leather and she continues on, saying, "Sometimes though, we can only see what we're told."

And I pull out the driver's license, reading it line-by-line. Studying it. Every word and number. There are at least two major mistakes on here.

The address reads: #2 Pershing Square, and now I'm shaking my head because I know this can't be right, looking to the woman on the chaise lounge for answers. Desperate. And lost.

We're both wearing our worst poker face.

This is who I am, and this is who you *think* I am.

She says, "Face it, kiddo...you've always been Aidin Paradies."

SESSION 41
AIDIN: AGE 24

I think I had a future once.

I used to believe in heroes.

It's been easy to forget those ideals over the years, and my daily actions only facilitate the progress of erasure. I'm a prime example of a bad situation becoming worse. A self-exacerbation. If I was ever a good person, if there was ever any hope of me following in the footsteps of my father or those awe-inspiring predictions of my mother—then I've completely lost my way since.

There are no more boundaries left to cross.

I've found neither enlightenment nor purpose.

What I do know for sure though, is that in the most abstract of ways, time-travel exists. When I wake up in a different month, or a different season for that matter, I can confirm that theory. Years have passed...years that seemed like days, and I can barely recall any memory from the supposed "time of my life" known as Penbrooke Academy. It slipped right through my fingers as I let myself unravel.

In the present, I'm just as untested. My parents have remained (for the most part) a constant absence in my young adulthood as they had in my adolescence. There are those rare occasions, however, where I receive a few ill-timed words of "motivation" from my father that almost literally go in one ear and out the other...mostly due to the Xanax. I hear him but am incapable of listening.

The major inconsistency of Aidin Paradies has to be that I'm in a completely weakened state yet seemingly invincible. I'm free to a near-absolute degree, and the methods in which I endorse this are limited to nothing: how I can break any law, be it local, state, or federal. I can rape. I can kill.

It was at Penbrooke that I started to test the boundaries. We all did in a sense, but our weekends of self-destruction and debauchery slowly generalized into weekdays, beginning a brand new descent where the many that had blazed the trail before became fewer and fewer by the month. Sunday became not the day of rest and recovery, but an opportunity for that last hurrah before our lives were bound behind the elegant walls of Penbrooke for another infinite five-day stretch that some of us simply could not endure.

We break up the week on Wednesday.

We prematurely resume on Thursday.

And it's only a matter of time before we return the respect our parents showed us in their absence that we become absent in the very life they set before us, sometimes skipping periods or a whole day for that matter, never fearing consequence, but never expecting any, either. The faculty shows more of a concern then they do, sometimes asking publicly at the beginning of period, "Why weren't you in attendance yesterday, Mr. Paradies?" and I'll have to quickly conjure a lie because most days I don't remember. Most days I'm physically present but missing in absolutely every other regard, planning my next endeavor while recovering from the last one, eating myself alive. My priorities are simply that misguided and I see not a trace of boundary as my reputation at Penbrooke continues to grow, and therefore, reinforces my behaviors.

I become something of a playboy to the girls of Penbrooke, using those young unspoiled freshman as my training wheels and quickly working my way beyond them to more experienced lovers. I find in them women, not girls, who are just as uncontested as I am. They are past that experimental stage in life where they consume and lust for the simple advancement in theoretical years. Their curiosity is nonexistent along with their inhibitions and morals, neither party indicating the romance or love we used to in our final moments of innocence. We trade pleasure for pleasure. Pills or liquor or coke or heroin—anything that can be bagged and served, I give for a temporary sense of connection and the progression of my own reputation. I begin purchasing as opposed to coercing my objects of affection, never having the same one more than a few times. Their memory never getting a chance to implant itself as we erase the present in the present, constantly in blackout or delirium. We're the walking dead running full speed at a wall of disaster that isn't there.

Years pass this way.

I become a sophomore.

A junior and then a senior.

I don't know exactly how this comes to pass, but every year in early August I receive the same forms from Penbrooke Academy: the dress code, rules and regulations, and my class itinerary. Until commencement. In what were supposed to be known as "the best years of my life," I find no true sense of self or evidence of personal growth. I retain hardly any memory as my adolescence shifts into adulthood, and the boundaries are just as absent as they were before.

As my age progresses, so do my measures of exploration for that ever-elusive limit. For the next six years I push this envelope, never reaching a state of enlightenment, and with deep intuition that I'll die in my attempts to find it. The search for myself, my soul, could very well mean the end of me, and the danger of this game I play spikes in its magnitude without Penbrooke walls containing it, without teachers attempting to umpire the errors so obviously being made and rules shattered. Lost are those last whispers of structure and regiment to the past while my walk towards the future is dark and uncertain, the path of a villain. A rogue.

It's when all things I hold to be germane fully permeate with the unsafe and damaging do I catch that first glimpse of what's meant for me, a sort of preview of destiny as I continue these misadventures in different locales like L.A. or New York or Vegas, Miami and Newport Beach, all things in solitude...how I walk the beaches and city streets, my various table services amongst countless establishments, I'm always alone. Even with company, I don't feel accompanied, and the joy I once took in substance and sex has since deformed to a motion, something mechanical and so well rehearsed the meaning has been lost. Not in translation, but in repetition, and so I escalate.

Unlike my years at Penbrooke Academy where my concern for the rules kept me slightly obedient, the rebellion I exude now can only be termed as foolishly obtuse, as if I'm now actively searching for my own penance, a self-revenge where I am my own worst enemy and greatest supporter to the cause. My bad behaviors become exaggerated to a point where I'm not just a young man of wealth and taste abusing his freedoms and resources, but something more criminal given the intent of my actions and broken morality. The aspect that I come to find most intriguing regarding myself is how I'm perceived by others, the way I'm viewed to be this normal, collected person when nothing could be further from the truth. It's this realization in particular that gives me my first paramount shred of insight: that when people believe you to be one of the innocent, it's that much easier to manipulate them.

The best villains are always the ones the people side with.

Their assumption is your cover, and in this case, an identity.

Aidin Paradies could be anybody, take any form. After all, parents always tell their sons that nothing is impossible...that they have so much potential.

I just wish I knew what my calling was.

SESSION 42
DIRECTION

"You were going to kill yourself," Paradies says to me, looking off into the distance through the window behind me, absent and present at the same time. "But I want you to know that your father and I had a long talk about this...our decision."

She says: you failed us, but we failed you, too. Probably because we weren't around enough to get the point across that we expected great things from you, a life you could call your own and we could be proud of...and for *years* we kept telling ourselves that when you got a little older you'd straighten yourself out...but...that didn't quite happen. You were so—I don't know...unmotivated, I guess is the word I'm looking for. You didn't want to work or go to school or do *anything* to contribute or better yourself, and it made us really sad, honey. We thought it was our fault...but we weren't ready to believe you were beyond help. Y'see, deep down, we knew that you could change if you really *needed* to. Your father and I...we believed it, but we also knew you'd never accept any of *our* help. So, we bent the rules a little.

Your father, she says. I know you don't know much about what he does, nor do you probably care, but believe me when I say, he's a brilliant man. Right now he's doing everything in his power to make this country a better place, and you, Aidin (she looks at me with pride, or perhaps fear)...you're the proof of how that will work.

Now think outside the box.

Beyond this office.

Imagine soldiers that never get tired. They never miss. Soldiers that never get hungry or cold. They can get shot and keep going. For miles and miles, they can run and not feel a single cramp or sore muscle. They can learn languages overnight. Speak what the opposition speaks. And they'd all be geniuses. That was the best part about it. That miracle side effect. Not only are these men practically invulnerable, but brilliant. Soldiers that can be scientists and engineers and statisticians. Surgeons and chemists. Soldiers that can hack the enemy network once they've infiltrated their base. Finally, a person you can't torture no matter what do to them. They can laugh it off, but chances are, that'd never happen in the first place. These men do exactly what they're told, and being captured isn't part of that.

Go here. Destroy this.

Invade them. Take over that.

"This wasn't exactly our plan for you."

Odd, though...how much you and you're father are alike. Those "addictive personalities," she says, throwing up air-quotes. I guess the apple didn't fall far from the tree, in that regard. He has his work, and you have...well, all the stuff you were doing back then.

Drugs and drink.

Pills and women.

That magazine life of an ever-changing sameness.

All we wanted to do was clean you up...to put you in a position where if you couldn't *feel* these things, you'd forget about them and move on.

"What *exactly* did you do to me?" I cut in. "I want to know. *All* of it."

"You were injected...and you were so doped up you didn't even feel it," Paradies, my mother, reveals in a rather vague fashion. "I don't know all the details," she sighs.

The blood on my sheets from that morning. It was mine but I never bothered checking it out.

"You don't know *anything*?" I try again.

"I know what you know, and I know that you're the first."

A guinea pig.

Patient zero.

"You'd have to ask your father about the rest," she adds.

"So what did *you* do?" I ask, moving to where Paradies

usually sits. The therapist's chair. "Why am I not able to see some things and not others?"

She sighs.

Thinks about it.

And for a moment she stares at me, as if she's weighing the pros and cons of what she's about to say (or not say), and this lasts for maybe ten seconds. Ten minutes. I can't track time right now, but eventually give her away, as if to say she's ready to come clean.

She says, "I will tell you, if you really want to know--"

"--I *do*," I cut in eagerly.

"Wait," she halts me, holding up a finger. "I'll tell you, but you have to know that when I do, you're going to have to make a choice."

She explains, "And I won't be able to make it for you...it's how this works."

"Now do you still want to know? Or would you rather forget?"

"I can do either one," she tells me.

Because as long as I've know me I've never been myself.

Not in my whole life, and now I think I'm ready.

"No," I answer. "I want you to tell me."

"Tell me everything."

SESSION 43
DR. PARADIES

"Believe it or not," mom says, "I've tried this on you a bunch of times."

Adding, "It's the reason why your father and I decided to take such extreme action with you."

The people that come to see Dr. Paradies, my mother, they all know what they want. Everyone is trying to make the worst of themselves disappear. Not me, though. That's why it never worked.

"Some people just want to stop smoking," she explains. "Or drinking."

"They want to make some bad habit go away without all the meetings and step programs and temptation."

Even with ten years sobriety under your belt, a relapse is always one sip away.

"They want to get it right the first time," Dr. Paradies says.

"Without failure."

That's why she gets paid the big bucks, because not only can she make your addiction a non-memory, she can also make sure you never go back to it.

"Second-hand smoke to one of my patients is like dog shit vapor."

"The fat ones looking to get thin again," she smirks. "I make it so they can't even see a McDonald's or a Burger King."

Whores walk out of here virgins.

The introverted become charming.

I think you get the point.

"And you wouldn't believe how many men come here asking me to make their wives look like Angelina Jolie or some porn star."

227

"I'm booked solid on those."

For the low price of $10,000 you too could be married to Jenna Jameson.

In a mere hour you could drive home to Nikki Benz or Scarlett Johansson.

You can have Eva Longoria, Lady Gaga, or some Romanian model whose name you can't even pronounce.

Granted, $10,000 may seem like a lot, but just think about how much all this would cost if you were getting it done a la carte. When you consider how much a tummy tuck, face-lift, and boob job cost, what Dr. Paradies does is a bargain.

"My clients are picturing these women when they're with their wives, anyway," Paradies reasons. "All I'm doing is taking the mental effort out of it."

Putting image back in imagination.

That's what my mother does for these people.

"As long as they really truly want it," she says. "I can make them see it."

Not me, though.

I'm different, remember?

Special.

"I had to wait until the right moment with you," she explains to me.

"The first time you went to the ER," she says. "That was when you finally gave in."

Cut up and bleeding to death, covered in blood and my own vomit with about ten different substances floating through my system, numb and so close to death—it's moments like these where you swallow what's left of your pride for the sake of mortality.

It was when I finally could be helped.

"Right there in the hospital bed, you asked for it," mom tells me.

I made you remember that night only in passing...made it so that when you saw me, you only saw a doctor; someone who would help you and that you could trust. You would retain your free will, but when we spoke, you'd listen. You'd follow directions and entertain reason. Don't make me soulless, you said to me. Help, not control...that was the fine line we were riding. So, I set the parameters. Made it so you wouldn't see or hear certain things. Your name. Our relationship. This office. You would walk right by it and not even know it was there...not unless it was time to for an appointment. That's what made it hard for me, I think...one minute we'd be talking like mother and son in the living room, and the next minute you didn't even recognize me. Session time would hit and (bam!), you'd walk up to the second floor thinking you were in an office building, not caring how you got there or what you were just doing, only that you were there...and I think that's why I felt so remorseful a lot of the time. You were the first one that didn't go away once you were under...made it so I could barely look at you during those sessions, even though I knew it was for the best. Tough love, and all that...then came the list...our gift to you. It was like watching my son grow up all over again. The toys...making the house safe again...protecting you. I felt like more of a mother than I had in a long time, she smiles, her eyes tearing. I got to know my son again in those months, watching you fly kites in the park and learning to run. I would sit at my desk for hours waiting for your e-mails of what you had accomplished that day...but as I'm sure you already know, the fun couldn't last forever. Your father and his people needed to test you...to push you to see what you could do. They were always watching.

Dr. Thornton and Trask; both under your father.

Your trainer and your nutritionist, too.

The men at the track.

Your driver.

All of these people played their little part. Their job: don't ask too many questions and keep a watchful eye. Don't approach the subject (the specimen). Not unless you're supposed to. Such as detective Stephen Finch and his questions: to find out what you know or don't know. Or like Jill. She was our gym contact, but you got deliberately sloppy and told her everything. You became tactless and willingly put yourself out there...in danger.

"That's why your room got raided," Paradies concludes.

"And that's why those 'missing' signs were planted. Believe it or not, it was all for the best...but sometimes a few deceptions need to happen for the greater good."

In government speak, they call these, "cover-ups."

See also: conspiracy, anti-trust, and Aidin Paradies.

"You are so very important now," mom says. "A lot of extreme measures had to be taken in order to keep you under control."

Like the groups: Making Sense and Circle of Healing.

"What were those about?" I ask, because at this point, everything is questionable.

She says, "Psychology, Aidin."

You put a person in a situation where they're admired for their condition, another where they're pitied for it, and a third where they're supposed to be coping with it. One subject in three highly contrasting scenarios. This is also done with viruses to see how they respond to boiling, freezing, and neutral temperatures. Basic science.

"Data is compiled and compared," Paradies says. "We're able to study the psychological element of this without you knowing about it."

When you can't feel, it's hard to know when you're getting strings pulled. Dana was right when she said that when you're desperate for help, you'll trust almost anyone. I was too trusting. All of those group members and women I was assigned to date—for all my reservations and attempts to conceal the condition, it never occurred to me what *they* might be hiding.

Because everyone is two people.

This is who I am, and this is who you *think* I am.

But I don't care about that, any of them. Except the one.

"What about Dana?" I ask, closing my eyes. My breath stopping. Waiting for it. The answer I know is coming.

"She was hand-picked," Paradies says.

And my heart sinks. It plummets in just the way Paradies and Dana taught me how to feel this: with my ears, not with my chest.

I'm destroyed but Paradies continues on:

She was the girl you needed but couldn't buy. Your counterpoint. Your better half. A girl that would challenge you...make you think...and smile, but most importantly, need you as much as you needed her. You wouldn't just wad her up and throw her away, and you'd finally find love in someone.

She stops talking here.

Stops because I'm crying.

For the first time in a while.

She offers, "If it's any consolation, she thought very highly of you."

"It really isn't," I respond, face pinched. Stifling myself. "So this is why you told me to break in here? To throw all this shit at me?"

Paradies says, "I never told you to break in here," but she doesn't sound mad, defensive, or even confused about the accusation. If anything, she's intrigued. So I show her the note. Rub the proof in her face so I don't feel completely clueless or stupid, and she looks it over. For a few minutes my mother, Dr. Paradies, sits on the blue chaise lounge with fingers draped thoughtfully on her dry lips. Contemplating.

It's just another logic problem.

Just another liar's algorithm.

"You received this when?" she asks.

"This morning. And before you start," I throw out in warning, "I don't want any more of your tricky shrink bullshit."

"No, actually, I'm pretty sure you did this," she smirks. "In fact, I'd be willing to wager you don't remember anything about last night, do you?"

I don't answer.

When you're right, you're right.

Her theory: you were upset and distraught...there were blank spots, and that was my fault, of course, but I believe that some part of you was catching on to the fact that you preferred to follow orders...to take directions, whether it was from me or your peers or a magazine—that was always sort of a constant with you. And then that was taken away along with Dana, so you went looking for answers. Unavailable ones. I made it so you couldn't come here unless you were supposed to…but you, Aidin…you were trained in so much. You know how to solve logic problems and pick locks, and you also know how to forge handwriting, including mine. You can't just write yourself items and missions, though. You had to trick yourself somehow into believing it came from me, so you took a page out of your old playbook…something you were quite familiar with, but not necessarily firsthand.

Flunitrazepam.

Also known as: roofie or "the date rape drug."

Take it, and the next twenty to thirty minutes never happened.

"Quite brilliant, actually," Paradies concedes. "Sick…but brilliant."

She's not lying. Something tells me that analyzing the envelope it came in would reveal nothing but my own spit. One set of fingerprints.

You can only fool yourself for so long, that old saying.

"Well, kiddo, I know it's been a rough night for you, but we have one more thing to talk about," Paradies pushes through.

"What?" I ask, attempting to collect myself. "More lies?"

"Quite the opposite," she says. "We need to discuss your future."

And this is the choice everything was leading up to.

The fork in the road. My life-changing decision.

Paradies says, "Now that you know who you are, it's time for you to decide who you want to be."

SESSION 44
ENVELOPES

My mother reaches into a side table pulling out two packages; envelopes (one red and one a pale yellow), saying to me, "If you were anybody else you'd only be seeing one of these," holding one package per hand as if she's about to present them to me.

"I just don't think I could live with myself if I didn't give you a choice."

Because everyone is two people.

A doctor and a patient.

A mother and a son.

In government terms this is called, "a conflict of interests."

She says, "It's completely up to you, honey."

There's no wrong answer.

Not this time.

Motioning to the yellow envelope, she tells me, "I put this together as soon as I realized you were figuring this out."

An escape clause.

Exit plan.

Everything you need is in here. Start-up cash. Fake passport. A new name. Airline credit. You can get on any flight you want...just fly away and disappear. To Paris. To Italy or Japan or whatever is departing right then, and if you don't already know the language, you'll pick it up in no time. You'll blend right in and no one will find you. Oh, they'll look, I'm sure...but they'll be looking for Aidin Paradies, and he won't exist anymore. They'll be chasing a ghost. A phantom. And you'll keep moving from place to place...from Amsterdam to Spain to Indonesia, using each of your talents as you go. It sounds cliché, Aidin, but you *really* can be whatever you want to be. A doctor or a lawyer or a scientist...and if they ask for paperwork, you can forge it...and if they start to get wise, you can disappear again. Reinvent yourself. Keep moving and lay low. Trust no one. Find a place to stay that takes cash and doesn't ask questions...get a job at a coffee house or a record store, part-time. Make just enough to get by and never settle because that's how people running away get found. Stay in the shadows and forget about Aidin Paradies. You've done it before and I know you can do it again. The world is a big place, son, and with a man of your talents wondering about, it'd be like trying to find a needle in a haystack.

And who knows...maybe after a while they'll stop looking. They'll cut their losses and give up...because you can only chase a ghost for so long, and maybe then you could relax a bit...stop living out of suitcase. Stop running and looking over your shoulder everywhere you go. After ten or fifteen years, you'd be old news to them...the one that got away, they'd call you. It'd fade like heartbreak.

Then your life could begin again. You could get an apartment with some furniture and a job at a lab...start working on a cure for yourself, if you hadn't figured it that out already. Make some friends...maybe meet a girl who loves you in just the right way. Someone who you can spend your new life with. Start a family. Have some kids. You could be the root of your own family tree watching it grow and extend as the years pass by...becoming a father...then a grandfather, and if you make it this far, Aidin...if you can survive this long, one day it won't matter anymore.

You'll have outlived anyone who was sent to find you.

And your father and I will be gone along with our only son.

Because you'll have your own family and your own name, but maybe...just maybe you'll tell them the truth like I'm telling you now.

You'll gather your family around you and tell them a story of a young man named Aidin Paradies who woke up one day and couldn't feel. He was neither hero nor villain, but had great power...power he didn't even fully understand. Power he didn't want or ask for, just like in those comic books I had you read. It would be the story they'd tell for generations to come, always with the same ending...that your family was so close to never happening had it not been for the choice you made on this day. A choice between two envelopes.

"But you've been looking at this other envelope almost the entire time, haven't you?" she asks, motioning to the red one. "And I bet you already know what's in it."

Because there's only one thing that could make me stay around. After all the lies and deception and betrayal, there'd only be one appropriate way for them to say they're sorry: to give me back the thing they took away.

"Another list," I whisper.

"Correct," she nods.

"You'd be working with your father...with the government—not officially, mind you, but you'd be compensated. Handsomely, I might add...to the point where your wealth might one day rival your father's. And what's in here," she gently shakes the envelope, "I'm not sure exactly. I had nothing to do with this one. But I can tell you this...you'll be challenged far beyond what you could ever imagine...finally put those talents to use. You really do have so much potential, Aidin, and they'll find out just how much you're capable of. Remember though, it's a lifelong commitment. You'd never be free and you'd never be alone. They'd make all your choices for you and the tests would never end."

"So, Aidin?" my mother speaks, giving a flick of the head. "Which one will it be?" she asks, holding both envelopes. Ready to pass over only the one.

"What do you want to do for the rest of your life?"

EPILOGUE
SIX MONTHS LATER

Remember what I said before about how this wasn't my fault.

How everyone wants to see through that tinted window, but no one ever tells you what it's like to live behind it.

I'm a permanent resident.

And as the days move on I'm Aidin Paradies less and less, but it's not hard to miss someone who was never really there to begin with. Some people are just born soulless.

Ghosts that walk.

And breathe.

We can appear and vanish at will.

I'm in Berlin, Germany in a cafe wearing dark designer sunglasses smoking Parliaments. Shaved head. Leather jacket and jeans.

I'm at the Tokyo Hyatt overlooking Shibuya Crossing wearing a white robe and drinking a glass of Dewers scotch. It's overcast, but I'm in silhouette.

Everyone is two people, but I'm not just anyone.

I'm special, remember?

And if you don't, just ask them, the people I'm working for.

They'll tell you I'm doing a bang-up job.

Item #34: Invent a non-traceable anabolic steroid.

Item #12: Find a cure for ovarian cancer.

For the country's prosperity. You don't have to be a genius to know that those long-awaited cures really boost the economy.

It's just like eating a really good piece of cheesecake or onion bisque. First you get a taste, and then you want to know how to make it.

This world was built on trade secrets.

The borrowing of ideas.

I know this now.

Item #31: Invent a more efficient fossil fuel.

Item #106: Bomb Vatican City.

I'm in Italy wearing a three-quarter length coat and Aviator sunglasses scouting out the Leaning Tower of Pisa, how to make it look like another 9/11 before jet setting off to Ontario to check out this new strain of influenza.

It's exactly like my mother said.

No choice. For the rest of my life.

Anyone who knows me and my addictive personality saw that coming, and I'm sure mom did, too. For all I know that other envelope had nothing but newspaper in it. Another test, but my choice was my own, and I guess I'm satisfied. Not happy. I just didn't feel like hiding out and running from hostel to hotel for the next twenty years.

I wasn't ready to be my own boss.

And sometimes I see Dana.

Between the assassinations and plane trips and cures for whatever, she'll slip in there from time to time. For dinner. Or a film.

She'll say, "I still have feelings for you, Aidin," but I'll immediately shush her because when in Rome, I'm not Aidin Paradies.

Same goes for Moscow, St. Petersburg, and Omaha, Nebraska.

And sometimes Dana and I will fuck. For the simple mortality of it. I'll look at myself in the mirror at night...reflecting on what I've done that day...and the words come to me:

"There's no soul in there."

So Dana and I will sleep together in a Vietnamese hotel or Euro spa and I'll try to feel just a little bit human again, sampling those Earthly delights.

I'll come back to Kansas City sometimes to visit mom, entertaining the idea of bombing Hush with a truckload of C-4 or melting all the exits to blank with sulfuric acid, trapping those Barbies forever away.

But I never do.

Never will, either. Not unless they tell me to.

When you're as busy as I am, you don't have much time to contemplate a rebellion. There are too many places to go and people to see.

Too many assignments. I say too many but there could never be enough. They come up with more everyday, thankfully.

Item #4,906: Gather intelligence on the Iraqi terrorist cell in Baghdad and report back to base.

Item #17: Learn to operate a Sherman tank.

I'm in my father's lab when the one-year mark of the big numb hits, both of us in white lab coats with identical name plates that read: Dr. A. Paradies

His name is Adam.

And he says, "Wanna see what we did with your sperm?" but it's been so long that I almost don't remember what he's talking about.

My new "before" era ends at the two envelopes, and I rarely think anything of it except in passing, especially my missing DNA.

"Let's take a walk," my dad suggests, exiting the lab and leading me to another room in different department. We cross the facility making small talk along the way about other projects we're not involved in together.

My trips and my list. Missions.

He's just a little bit jealous of "the action" he's missing out on.

"This is pretty neat though, too," he smiles, leading me into one of the rooms in the Research & Development wing. We approach a small fiberglass basin.

And I stand over it nonplussed for a moment before mentioning, "It's a baby."

"It's your son," my dad says.

"Is it..." I start to ask, but can't finish. It's the first time I've been caught off-guard in while.

"Yeah," my dad says. "Watch." He takes a little needle off the side table and pokes it a few times in the arm, the blood beads swelling large enough to the point where they can no longer maintain shape, pooling over and around its elbow. It bleeds onto the sterile white tarp unmoving and still.

It bleeds but it doesn't cry.

I was prepared for that.

Like father, like son.

"Wanna know something *really* creepy?" my dad asks, swabbing the wound with gauze and alcohol; cleaning it.

And I'm thinking, *creepier than this?*

And, *there's no soul in there.*

But when I don't answer my dad whispers, "It understands us."

He says, "Sometimes I think," but he stops himself, trailing off and sighing heavily.

...maybe you started something you shouldn't have...

And I offer, "It's never too late to change your mind," but he smirks and laughs desperately at this. The impossibility of it. I knew he'd feel this way.

"There's no going back," he says.

"Not for either one of us."

My father pats me on the back and I feel this with my ears, not with my shoulder as per usual. He smiles encouragingly and says, "Trust me son, one day people will know your story."

"Everyone is looking forward to seeing what you're capable of," I hear, staring at the child (my son) and fading away.

Losing myself in its eyes so much like mine.

My father says for the first time in my life, "I'm very proud of you."

There's no soul in here.

Never was.

I try to lose myself in my work, hoping the through the pure and simple immersion of myself in these things I can drown out my ever-increasing rue. My guilt. The items keep coming and I keep doing them.

I invent a filtration system that can purify any body of standing water, no matter how high the bacteria levels. My solution to the water shortage crisis estimated to hit in the next twenty years. America's bartering chip for fossil fuels and crude oil and the spread of Democracy when they can charge $20 per bottle.

I bomb a Sprint/Nextel outsourcing facility in metropolitan India to bring jobs back to America. The customer service has never been better and the insurance pay-off was in the millions.

I kill a CEO of a major corporation with a sniper rifle from 300 yards out. His death will cut the national debt by an estimated two billion. Don't ask me how.

"For the greater good," I'm told.

For prosperity. And our nation.

Remember what I said about right and wrong sometimes being the same thing.

Remember: the crucifixion of Jesus Christ.

And: Aidin Paradies.

Depending on what side of the line you are, I could either be patriot or terrorist. Hero or villain. Read up on the Boston Tea Party if that doesn't make sense to you. Every hero has a dark side but not every villain has a conscience.

"This is sort of like when Spider-Man got the black costume," Dana says from the bed in our hotel, nude and smoking. "Or when Nixon became president."

"What are you saying?" I ask, distant, reading a text from the Pentagon about tomorrow's assignment. They want me to reduce a mosque to rubble.

"Don't let it go to your head," she breathes.

Then another outsourcing facility. This time in China.

"Don't lose your way," she whispers.

...and maybe I started something I shouldn't have.

"Don't forget yourself," and I see a tear breach one of Dana's cheeks when she says this. Past her Dior lens, it slides down, but I remain unmoved. And numb.

Item #324 - Torture terrorist suspect Uded al Bariste's wife and two children in front of him until he gives you the location of his missile silos. Start with the wife and go from there. Don't hesitate to rape her or the children if you don't make immediate headway. Good luck and Godspeed.

Item #4,002 - Develop a new STD.

240

"To promote abstinence," they say.

When you consider the overpopulation problem, this isn't really a bad idea. Not everyone agrees.

The Merchant of Death, they call me.

Captain anti-America.

Because no one knows about Aidin Paradies. Not unless they need to or have the appropriate clearance. This is just like all those conditional pet names and occupational slang terms you have for your kinky sex habits. Your occupation and drugs of choice.

Governments have them, too.

See: Agent.

See also: super soldier.

I've been called both.

And so it goes for the next however many years: I travel (under different names), always on business (even when I see Dana), sleeping for the flight's duration and dreaming in cycles of my "before" periods in swells of sweet nostalgic memory that linger not long enough. I'm fluent in twenty-seven languages now. Proficient in thirty-one forms of combat. The ender of 2,892 lives spanning forty-six different countries; by bombs and poison gas and political influence. By gunpoint and strangulation. My bank accounts add up to over thirty-four million but I never pay for anything. Not even tax. And my cell phone is packed with explosives just in case I need to use it on someone. On another like myself because I'm considered a terrorist nearly everywhere I go. Private enemy #1. The corporate avenger. I've bombed so many outsourcing facilities the CEOs and vice-presidents sweat at the very idea of traveling abroad for vacation, fearing their first step on foreign soil might be a land mine. Or that their plane might get delayed in the Atlantic Ocean due to incoming missile fire. Or "engine failure." And they'd be right. Because it's not enough to say America is the greatest country in the world. Actions speak louder than words and I'm taking action everyday. By catching up to Asian technology. With medical advances. And eliminating the threats. The competition. Any entity that could compromise us. Our advancement. And Dana says, "What happened? I don't even fucking know you anymore," because she thinks I'm the one that killed those eighteen priests in Vatican City. Those 252 AIDS infected in Africa. And others I don't care to recall. She blames me but all I can say is it's classified before hanging up and moving on to the next thing. The next item. Build a concussion bomb. Improve night vision cameras. Figure out this global warming problem. It never stops. I never stop. Like father, like son. I spend Christmas sabotaging a research facility in West Germany. Hack the Russian nuclear defense system on my birthday. I know I said I didn't want to be hopping from hostel to hotel for the next twenty years, but that's exactly what I'm doing now. On the run. In hiding. Not from the U.S. but from *every other* country you can possibly imagine, and one afternoon I ask my father if he's still proud of me—if the story is worth knowing, but he doesn't answer. Can't even look at me because everyone wants a happy ending. Even if it's not realistic, it's still the expected maxim. The standard. And it's only a matter of time before someone puts it together, this logic problem: that there's a man globetrotting the planet, going from country to country bombing buildings and assassinating public figures. Stealing information and bringing it back to the States. It's inevitable. The reaction. World War III.

That's the reason I keep going.

Because when this is over I'll be just like Jesus Christ and Malcolm X and Napoleon Bonaparte and Hitler. I'll be Genghis Khan and Benedict Arnold. The anti-Christ. A Typhoid Mary that brought destruction and disease and death in every country he ever touched, even his own. Because I could be devout. I could be the villain. Remembered forever and ever, amen.

A tale of club fashion vogue and a socialite rogue.

They'll say, "He had so much potential."

And, "This was all his fault."

As nukes criss-cross the oceans and seas of the world, people will look on and remember how this was my greatest and most horrible act, that I was the catalyst and so out of touch I stopped being human. Stopped living in that traditional sense. So they'll put me on an airplane, flight 8160, and they'll order me to crash it. Fake your death, they tell me. Get off the grid.

"The ocean is simply too big to find all the bodies," I'm told, and this is how it starts. When I'm deemed as one of the "unfound" or "unrecovered," just know that I'm still out there. No paper trail. No identity. And no heroes to stop me. The death of one man and the origin of another.

But in their memory I'll live eternal.

The one who brought the fall.

A walking apocalypse.

A legend.

Also from
OTHERWORLD PUBLICATIONS

Otherworld Publications
Let's Form The Future Together

TRANSUBSTANTUATE by Richard Thomas

"They say Jimmy made it out. But the postcards we get, well, they don't seem...real."

When an experiment with population control works too well, and the planet is decimated, seven broken people are united by a supernatural bond in a modern day Eden. Most on the island are fully aware of this prison disguised as an oasis. Unfortunately, Jimmy is on the mainland, desperate to get back, in a post-apocalyptic stand-off, fighting for his survival and that of his unborn child. Back on the island, Jacob stares at the ocean through his telescope and plots his escape, reluctant to aid the cause. Marcy tries to hide from her past sexual escapades that may be her saving grace. X sits in his compound, a quiet, massive presence, trapped in his body by ancient whispers and yet free in spirit to visit other places and times. Roland, the angry, bitter son of Marcy is determined to leave, and sets out on his own. Watching over it all is Assigned, the ghost in the machine. And coming for them, to exact revenge, and finish the job that the virus started, is Gordon. He just landed on the island and he has help.

Transubstantiate is a neo-noir thriller, filled with uncertainty at every portal, and jungles infiltrated with The Darkness. Vivid settings, lyrical language, and a slow reveal of plot, motivation, past crimes and future hope collide in a showdown that keeps you guessing until the final haunting words.

Transubstantiate: to change from one substance into another.

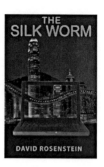

The Silk Worm by David Rosenstein

CIA agent, Richard Gibson, is sent to Hong Kong where he is to meet with a known informant to assess the possibility that a major assault of cyber terrorism, the next terrorism, is about to be unleashed on the free world by brilliant Chinese graduate student, Lee Yong, in an attempt to remove the evil influence of western values imposed upon his country by the capitalist countries of the world.

Richard assembles a team of America's top computer experts to try and thwart the attack. Within days of Richard's team starting to work out possible scenarios, the first attack of the Silk Worm hits an airport control tower in northern Taiwan, which results in the crash of two airliners and the death of over three hundred and fifty passengers. The American Ambassador in China is instructed by the President of the United States to lobby the Chinese government in an attempt to allow this team to setup shop in Hong Kong to lead and work with Chinese agents in an effort to kill the attacking computer program and capture its creator. Richard and his group of field agents hit the streets of Hong Kong with telemetry coordinates in hand to search for the physical locations of the ones responsible for the attack and soon discover that they are the ones being hunted.

The Oracle: The Succession War by Richard Wayne Waterman

What price would you be willing to pay for an instrument of absolute power? Would you be willing to betray your friends and family, to even kill your own father? Or would you be willing to commit even more heinous acts of mass murder, including genocide?

Guided by the spirit of a dark and powerful villain, the demented Count Belicki, various vibrantly articulated characters discover that they must sacrifice something they treasure more than life itself in order to acquire the transcendent power of the mysterious Oracle. Driven by an insatiable ambition, these individuals seek unlimited power, for if they are strong enough to bend the Oracle to their own will; it is capable of translating mere thoughts into stark reality.

But these mere humans are not the only ones who seek to control the Oracle. For the battle for omnipotence also occurs within the Oracle itself.

Remember by Laura Griffith

After a freak car accident, Professor Robert Madigan begins to suffer impairment of his short-term memory. Suddenly, moments that have just occurred are impossible for him to recall. His family and friends struggle to help him, but, as time goes by, it starts to appear to be more than a temporary condition. His job, his marriage, and his life begin to suffer, but nothing he tries to do works.

On his way home from work one evening, Robert finds himself standing over a battered, dead body. His hands are covered in blood. He has no recollection of what transpired before that very moment. The police arrive on the scene and take the professor in for questioning as their lead suspect.

As the police investigate the murder and sort out the details, Robert and his family begin to question the professor's lost memory. Had he been under enough stress to snap? Or did he witness a crime that he cannot remember the details of? And if he were a witness, what would a murderer do to keep his only witness quiet?

To uncover the truth, Robert must work with the detectives to piece together what happened that evening, no matter what the cost. But will he remember anything, and will it be too late?

LaVergne, TN USA
31 January 2011
214736LV00002B/11/P